THE AGES ♂ OF DESIRE

PHILIP GRAHAM

Contents

LEARNING TO BE A MAN

'No.' I shout for what is probably the fifth but feels like the twentieth time. 'No.' I repeat as Ellen tries to push a heaped teaspoonful of shepherd's pie with onions in it between my firmly clamped lips. And again, when she pulls the spoon back and I am able to speak, 'No, no, no.' You would think she would get the message. 'No' isn't just a word. It's a statement, a statement that has a lot of feeling attached. Especially when you're talking to someone who is trying to jam into your mouth a great wodge of shepherd's pie with onion in it.

This sort of trouble with Ellen pretty well always starts early in the morning when I wake up, usually at about 5.30. 'Course, I want a cuddle and a bit of company, so I cry for a bit waiting for either Ellen or Rob to come in to my room. I always think of my mother as Ellen because that is what Rob and everybody else call her though I have to call her 'Mum' to her face. She seems to think that being my Mum gives her the right to treat me just as she likes. Sometimes when she is trying to get me to do something I really, really, don't want to do, she says 'Just do what I say. I'm your mother, for God's sake'. So, I call her Ellen to myself to remind myself that I have just as much right to do things my way as she has.

Anyway, when I been crying for about ten minutes, I decide to get out of bed and go to Ellen and Rob's room. This isn't as easy as you might think. It involves dropping to the floor without falling over, remembering to take my mussy with me. I can usually manage this but once or twice I have fallen and hurt my knee. This only makes me cry more which is why it would be much more better if Ellen or Rob came to get me and take me into their bed straightaway.

I then have to push open my door and walk along the corridor to their room. There is no problem with this though I have to be careful not to knock into the chest of drawers in the corridor or fall over any shoes they may have left lying there before they've gone to bed. When I reach their door, there may be a problem with the knob. Usually I can just push the door open, but sometimes, and I don't understand why, the door is shut. They know very well I can't manage to turn the knob. I'm just not strong enough, though I'm getting there.

If the door is shut, then I just bang on it until they open up. This doesn't usually take much time. Then comes what I think of as the best bit of the day. I have to be helped up into the bed, which I do on Ellen's side. Then I get into my favourite place between Ellen and Rob and snuggle into Ellen's side. They both turn over so that they are facing away from me, but, although I prefer their fronts this doesn't trouble me. I just put my arms round Ellen's back and lie there very still, thinking of things. What I mainly think of is Amy and Charlie, especially Charlie and the games I'm going to play with her and what else I'm going to do when I go round next door.

After about fifteen minutes I get a bit restless. The next thing I do is stroke Ellen's back. Although I know she goes to bed wearing her night dress, for some reason in the morning she's not wearing it. I've discovered she quite likes me stroking her back. Sometimes she makes good noises like 'Mm' or even 'Mmmmmm' to show she likes it. She has the most lovely back, smooth and soft like the special silk cushions on the sofa in the living room Ellen and Rob are so proud of. When I get up to her neck it's a bit bony and the best bit is right in the middle of her back. When I've stroked her back and neck I start to go down to her bottom and then her legs. To do this I have to move around a lot as obviously I'm not big enough to stroke her legs without shuffling down the bed and moving round quite a bit.

It's at this point Ellen gets cross. She starts to say things like

'For fuck's sake, Tom, it's only six o clock. Just lie quiet there until half past six, can't you? You're a big boy now, nearly four. You've got to learn.'

I don't say anything back. I lie still for a minute or two but then I get tempted by her legs again. Ellen says:

'Rob, you take him. I need another half hour.'

So, he turns over and puts me on the other side of him, away from her. Then he turns over towards Ellen leaving me on the edge of the bed. I'm frightened I might fall off, so I put my body against his back though I don't put my arms round him as I know he doesn't like it. His body is soft too, but it's more hairy so it feels furry like Amy's cat. He has a lot more hair on the front side of him, which I start stroking after a few more minutes.

Rob wears trunks all the time he is in bed. While Ellen's night dress is nearly always a dark colour, grey, mauve or even black, Rob's trunks are more bright. He seems to like orange and yellow stripes or even whirly patterns in red and blue. A few times when I've got bored stroking the top front of him, I've started to move my hands down to his trunks so that I can feel what the hair feels like lower down. I know he's got a lot of hair lower down because sometimes I see him without any clothes on at all. I've wanted to touch his hair lower down round his widdle to see if it feels any different from higher up. The two or three times I've moved in this direction he has taken my hand and pulled it firmly upwards. The last time he did this he really helded my hand so that it hurt. I won't be trying that again.

At half past six Ellen gets up, goes to the bathroom, and I hear the shower. I stay in bed with Rob. I wish it were Rob getting up first but there you go. If I get up Ellen doesn't take much notice of me and it's warmer in bed, so I stay there. Ellen doesn't hang round. She dresses and half an hour later she's off to the hospital. Sometimes I get out of bed and look out of the window to see her cycling down the road and away. Rob doesn't move and I get back into bed with him. It doesn't seem to matter when he gets up but sometime between eight and half past he rolls over in my direction.

'Well, young man', he says, though why he calls me 'young man' when he treats me as even more of a baby than Ellen I don't know.

'Well, young man, it's time we got going.'

He washes, shaves and showers before coming back into the bedroom where I'm still in the warm bed. He just says 'Up' and I have to get up. While he is getting dressed, I'm supposed to go into the bathroom, have a pee and wash my hands. I always do have a pee but usually don't do the handwashing business. Then we go into my room where Ellen has made a little pile of the clothes I'm to wear that day. I put my shirt and trousers on, but I need help with my socks and shoes. He does this without saying a word. I just say 'ow' if he's too rough when he puts my socks on, which he often is.

Then we go downstairs where Ellen has laid out the breakfast things for both of us. He puts his earphones on and takes no notice of me while he gets on with his drinking and eating. I pour myself some orange juice and then put flakes into a bowl. He doesn't even look at me, so I eat them and then go up to play with my cars in my room until he has finished his breakfast and is ready to take me to Amy and Charlie next door. He always leaves all the dirty breakfast things on the table when he's finished so Ellen tidies them up when she gets back from work in the late afternoon before she gives me my supper.

After breakfast, Rob is on his mobile for a bit. He does a lot of laughing on the phone. This is the only time I hear Rob laughing as he never laughs when he is with Ellen. Then he comes into my room to tell me when it's time to go next door. I really like playing in Charlie's room. She's got more things to play with than I have, especially a lot of Lego.

The other thing about Charlie that is good is that she always gives me what I want even if she really wants it herself. So, if I am looking for more yellow Lego bricks and she's got them, she just hands them over. It doesn't seem to matter how often I change my mind about what I want, she'll still carry on giving in to me. I've tried to make her cross by asking for things I know she really wants but she still just gives them to me. When I knock down a tall tower that she's built, she just walks away. Then she starts doing something else or maybe builds another tower. This is not at all what the boys in the nursery are like. I suppose it's because she's a girl. I'm really glad I'm not a girl.

After about an hour Amy takes me and Charlie to the nursery. That's where I go to school. Next year, I'll go to proper school and be in Reception. As soon as we get into the play area I let go of Amy's hand to join the other boys. I really don't want them to see me with Charlie. We play chasing games outside until it's time to go into the room. There are about six of us boys and I'm the fastester and the strongester though sometimes Richard or Mustafa cheats and catches me. In the room, we have story time and making things time and break time for drinks and lunch and snacks over and over again until it's time to go home.

Then Amy comes to collect us and we go back to her place until Ellen comes to pick me up, take me home and give me supper. She's been away the whole day and then she expects me just to eat my supper up so that she can do her stuff upstairs though she does read to me before I go to sleep. Of course, I want her to stay with me having my supper for as long as possible so we always have a fight over whatever it is she's got for me. I always want her to carry me upstairs but she says I'm too heavy now. It's difficult going up the stairs, each step is so narrow, I fall down quite a lot. The steps in Amy's house is a lot easier. Anyway, if I've got my two teddies and my mussy with me, once I'm in my bed and Ellen has read me two stories I pretend to go to sleep straightaway. Actually, I lie awake and listen to Rob and Ellen talking. Nearly all the time, it's listening to Rob and Ellen having an argument.

They shout at each other about everything. It's often money – why doesn't Rob either spend less or earn more of it? Sometimes it's about Rob not telling Ellen where he's been when he's out late in the evening. From time to time it's about Gerry, Ellen's younger brother. This comes up when Ellen wants to ask Gerry round for Sunday lunch.

'He hasn't been round for ages', she says in her firm, no nonsense voice.

'I'm not having that little squirt in the house', he says, equally firmly. 'When he pays us back for what he owes us, then we'll start talking'. Then he gets into his stride.

'Just because Tom thinks he's the bees' knees ...' I feel quite pleased he brings me into it. And he's right, I do think Gerry is great.

But Ellen doesn't give up. 'When you start paying the bills, you can tell me what to do about Gerry'.

'He'll never grow up and get a proper job if you keep him going. Why should he bother? It just goes on smokes and weed, anyway'.

Ellen stays silent.

'He's never going to earn his living as an actor. Who's going to employ a five-foot five funny-looking gargoyle like him..'

It isn't like her but Ellen begins to plead. 'Look, I promised my Mum ......'

'Your Mum and Gerry were like a couple of limpets. They couldn't find any rocks to stick onto, so they stuck onto each other'.

Ellen continues to plead 'He's all on his own and I'm sorry for him. Why can't you be?'

'Of course, he can't manage on his own. But he can't manage any better when he's with somebody. He tried with Gill and it didn't work out. In fact, Gill was just as bad as he was. Just doubled the number of people on our payroll'.

When I've listened to this for about an hour I fall asleep and stay asleep until about half past five the next morning.

One morning I go into Ellen and Rob's room at my usual time. The door is open a bit which is unusual. I push it and see straightaway that Rob is not there. Once or twice Ellen has not been there as she's gone off for the night for a meeting. When that has happened, Ellen has always told me the night before that she won't be there in the morning. Anyway, this time Rob is not there. I've had no warning. What's going on? I get into the bed and nuzzle up to Ellen's back. Usually I can tell she goes to sleep quickly but this time she's awake. I start to stroke her back. 'Oh, just pack it in, Tom, and go to sleep', she pleads. Then she doesn't get up at half past six as she usually does but stays in bed until eight. She tells me to get up, still in her dressing gown. She gives me breakfast.

I can't work out what's going on and start to cry. Ellen looks at me. 'Tom,' she says, 'Rob has left. He and I weren't getting on. He wants to go and live with someone else.' I stop crying but then she starts to cry, but not a lot. Rob never cried, but Ellen cries quite a lot. This is something girls do, and boys are not supposed to. Karen at nursery tells the boys this if they hurt themselves falling over and start to cry. One or two of the boys at nursery cry a lot but mostly it's the girls.

The day Rob leaves, Ellen says:

'I'm going to take today off. Then there's tomorrow. Amy can have you earlier first thing in the morning, but I'm going to have to work out what to do with you after nursery'.

After a bit we go around to Amy's. They tell me to play with Charlie but I want to stay close to Ellen. She has a long chat with Amy, mainly about me and who's to look after me after nursery when it's time for me to go home. Amy says she will pick me up from nursery, at least for a few weeks. so that's settled.

I quite like the idea of having longer to play with Charlie and watch TV and look at our screens together. There are other good things about Rob not being around. In the morning, I get the whole of his half of the bed to muck around in. I can't do too much of that or I'm told off, but Ellen doesn't seem to mind if I go under the duvet and look at my screen until it's time to get up. She doesn't want me to stroke her back any more. This really upsets me but as soon as I try she shouts at me to stop.

Also, she goes into work later so that she can give me breakfast. Of course, I now have fights with her over breakfast as well as supper. I'm quite hungry when Amy takes me into nursery. Karen usually goes to the kitchen and give me a biscuit. 'You're a lovely little boy', she says, 'And I'm going to make sure you're in a good mood because I don't like you moping around in the corner'.

It's true. If I haven't had anything to eat I don't feel like playing with the others or kicking a ball around. All of us kids have a sleep for half an hour after lunch. When it's time to get up I just don't want to, so Karen give me another biscuit and then I'm alright.

Rob comes around on Sunday afternoons and takes me to the park. I don't really want to go, but Ellen says I've got to. He never used to play football with me but now that's all he wants to do. I can tell he's hopeless at it because sometimes we join up with another man and his son who's a bit older than me and the four of us kick the ball around. Sometimes, Rick, the other man, just plays with Rob for a bit. I can see Rob can't kick the ball straight or keep the ball in the air like Rick. After a bit, Rob gets cross and says we have to go. He wants to take me to where he is living but Ellen says he's not allowed. I don't know why. So, we go to a café quite near and he buys me a chocolate ice cream. That's the other good thing about his not being around at home. When he takes me back, Ellen just takes my hand, leading me back into the house and doesn't talk to him. Anyway, after a month, Rob stops coming on Sunday afternoons. I don't care if that's what he wants.

The next thing that happens is that Amy starts to say she can't look after me in the afternoons after nursery. I think this is because Charlie is such a pain in the afternoons. She says she doesn't want to play with me and just hangs around Amy. When I take the piece of Lego or whatever it is she is playing with, she used to just get on with playing with something else, but now she just starts to cry and goes to Amy complaining about me. This goes on and on until I go home. So, Amy and Ellen had another long talk and have come up with a new idea.

It's to do with Gerry. Since Rob left, Gerry has been in work in Scotland doing TV commercials for paints. I think he has to fall off ladders and get his face full of paint. There is no more work for him, so he's back in London now. He's quite funny when he tells me about his acting.

Ellen has the idea that she ask Gerry to give up work for a bit. She will pay him to pick me up after nursery, take me home or out or whatever he wants, give me supper and stay until Ellen gets back from the hospital when he will have supper ready for her. This sounds a great idea. She hasn't asked me for my ideas on the subject, but I tell Ellen that's what I want.

'Oh, well, that's OK then, if that's what Tom wants', she says in a funny voice. But anyway, she talks to Gerry and it's settled. That begins what feels like the best part of my life so far. Gerry picking me up from nursery is much better than having Amy do it. He's the only man who is at the gate when Karen brings me out. I feel really good about that. The other boys all get picked up by their mothers who talk to them in special baby voices. Gerry talks to me like an equal.

'What would you like to do now, young feller?' he always says.

Quite a bit of the day at the nursery I have spent working out what I'm going to say when he asks me this. In any case, we always go first to the corner shop to buy a Snickers. Usually we also get an orange drink. I'm not supposed to have this as Ellen says it's bad for the teeth, but Gerry gets it for me because he knows I like it. This lot of teeth I've got now will fall out anyway in a few years, so what does it matter?

Ellen hasn't given Gerry money for the drink but, as he's just been working, he's got money of his own. Then we might go to the big shop on Richmond High Street that has a toy department and a games department and a rocking horse that if you put 50p in a slot gives you a three-minute ride. Or we might go to the swing park where Gerry pushes me higher and higher, much higher than Ellen or Amy do.

But usually I choose to go straight home because there is so much to do there. Amy didn't allow Charlie and me to watch TV, even children's TV after school, but Gerry doesn't mind how much TV I watch. I know Ellen doesn't like this. I'm sure she knows about it, but she doesn't say anything. There are all sorts of games to play on the screen. Gerry and I both like playing 'Hop To It' which makes you search for different sorts of food. There are football games at which I often win though I think probably Gerry lets me a lot of the time. Gerry has also built a sort of cardboard theatre and makes up plays with him doing funny voices. But bestest is just turning on the big screen, sitting on the sofa, with me snuggling into Gerry while he tells me what's going on. It's so comfortable, sometimes I go to sleep while we are watching. Time goes quickly and it's a bit of a disappointment when Ellen comes back early and we have to stop so that she can have a catch up with Gerry.

When she gets home Ellen always asks me whether we've 'had a nice time' and what we've done. Usually I just mutter 'Good' and we played some sort of learning game because I know that's what she likes. But this time I said:

'Gerry got me to stroke his widdle again.'

I don't know what made me say this. Gerry has often told me that this is a private game just between him and me. It's important Ellen doesn't know, or he might get into trouble. But I tell Ellen everything. Also, I had asked Gerry for an extra orange drink and he had said no. I suppose I was cross with him. Anyway, it wasn't the right thing to say.

'Gerry what?' Ellen shouts.

So, I am not allowed to see Gerry again. There is a lot of things changes. Ellen gives up her hospital job, so she can look after me more better. She does what she calls something like 'half-time community'. This means we don't have as much money as we did before, but I see more of her. We now have a little car, not a big one, like when Rob was here. We don't really need a car at all, but Ellen has to have one for her work.

Ellen thinks we may have to move to another house, but she has enough money to stay. It is a really nice time, with just Ellen and me. We do lots of things together, playing games, watching TV. I don't have any friends of my own age, so she is my best friend. We often just do sums together. Ellen says she was good at Maths at school and she wants me to be, so we spend a lot of time adding up and taking away. She thinks I'm very good at this. Now, she can pick me up from nursery every day. It isn't as good as when Rob or Gerry picked me up 'cos then I was the only one being collected by a man, but it's good all the same.

I tell her most things I done at nursery. One afternoon, I say about how I think Karen is a bit mixed up about boys being different. They are not supposed to cry, like girls are, but I tell Ellen:

'You know Karen, right. This morning she got all her kids, (that's what she calls us), to play with dolls. The boys as well as the girls. When we boys said we didn't want to, she said it was important for boys to learn how to bring up babies. Just as important as girls. So, we had to do it.'

'Well, what's so bad about that?'

'Mum, I'm a boy, remember. That was the most worstest thing I ever done, washing and dressing up a doll.'

Ellen laughed a lot. I can't see what's so funny in that.

Once a week Ellen goes out in the evening with a friend she knew at medical school called Fiona. Jessica looks after me when Ellen is out. Jessica only comes when I'm in bed. She reads me a story after Ellen and while she's reading it, Ellen says good night and she's off. If I get up after Ellen goes, Jessica just takes me back to bed and goes back to looking at her phone and smiling and then tapping messages into it. She is a bit fat and I don't like her a lot.

Fiona is very smart and has a lot more money than Ellen. Once Ellen takes me at the weekend for tea to a large block of flats called Princess Towers where Fiona lives. It is very big, and I am not allowed to touch anything. You can see St. Paul's and everywhere from the window, so I just do that. There aren't no toys there and all they do is talk, so I get bored and cry, so after a bit, Ellen takes me home. This time though, she doesn't shout at me.

About once every three months we go to Manchester to stay for the weekend with Ellen's mum. We go by train as Ellen says it's cheaper than going by car. Ellen's mum, who I call Granny and Ellen calls Mum, lives in a little flat. It only has one bedroom and she sleeps there. Ellen sleeps on the sofa in the living room, and I'm in a sleeping bag beside her. Granny is very, very old and her room smells a bit. She calls me 'Whatsisname' and just talks to Ellen. She doesn't take much notice of me. When she remembers she gives me a packet of Maltesers which I love. Sometimes she forgets but Ellen always buys me a packet on the station on the way home if that happens. I really don't like going but Ellen says we have to. I know Ellen doesn't like going either 'cos we only stay one night, and Ellen says we should really stay two.

About a year after Rob leaves, Ellen starts to go out two nights a week, once with Fiona and one time she doesn't tell me. Then one Friday, as she is putting me to bed, she says:

'Tom, I've made a new friend I would like you to meet. He's called Justin and he's really nice.'

So, the next day, Saturday, we go out to a restaurant, the two of us, with Justin. This is the first time I've been to a proper restaurant since Rob left. I have the children's menu, chicken nuggets and ice cream, which I like. I don't like Justin much though.

He is a very tall man with a beard. I think Ellen got to know him at his work and they talk a lot about work. Sometimes they moan about not enough money for the health service but it's going to be alright now as someone called Tony Blair has just 'got in'. I can't work out what he's got into, but it seems to be a good thing.

I can see Justin is trying to be nice. He asks what I do in the Reception class where I am now. I don't say much so he stops asking me questions and goes on talking to Ellen. He comes home for tea and goes when I start to get ready for bed.

This happens every Saturday about four times. Then one Saturday, he doesn't leave while I am getting ready to go to bed. I know what is going to happen, alright. I go to sleep, like usual. But next morning, I'm not surprised when I get out of my bed and Ellen's bedroom door is shut and I can't open it. I bang on it and Ellen shouts through the door, telling me to go back to bed. Of course, I'm not going to go back to bed and miss the best part of the day. Not just any day, but Sunday, when we lie in bed for ages. So, I carry on banging. I can hear Justin say,

'Oh, just let him bang, he'll get over it, soon enough.'

'Get over it? Never.' This makes me start to cry. So, I just sit outside Ellen's door for half an hour, really making a noise. Ellen comes out in her nightie in a really bad temper.

'Tom, stop making that racket. This moment. At once.'

'I don't want Justin to stay the night. I don't mind having lunch with him. He's not that bad.'

'Look, Tom, if I want Justin to stay the night, he's going to stay the night. It's just not up to you. You've got me six mornings and that will have to do.'

So, that's settled. Except that the next Sunday, I make the same what Ellen calls my racket, and, if anything, this time I'm even more noisier.

Then, good, it turns out Justin doesn't really want to stay the night all that much. It's a pity, but that also means we don't go out to Saturday lunch with him anymore. I say to Ellen I don't mind seeing him for Saturday lunch but that just makes her very cross, so I shut up about Justin completely.

* * *

The noise of the engines has emptied my mind. As the plane taxies, seemingly endlessly from one side of the airfield to the other, my mind turns over and over. Have I really done the right thing? In the end, just as the plane takes off, I fall asleep. Now, as I wake, I look down on the tiny fields below. They are too far away for me to change my mind now. I have only been on a few flights before.

While I was at school Ellen always said we couldn't afford holidays. We flew once to Dublin to visit an aunt who had invited us over. Then when I was at college and alone, I had never much wanted to travel. In the holidays, I stayed in the flat Ellen left me after she died and saw few people. Once another student, Greg, sat opposite me in the college canteen and started a conversation about where to go in the ten-week summer break. He discovered that I had never been to continental Europe. He had just broken up with his girlfriend and wanted a companion on a trip to Rome. I agreed to go with him though once in Rome we had spent little time together. On all these journeys, I had sat, squeezing my six feet two into a space meant for a five feet two man.

I look around. This time it is different. My seat is well separated from the pleasant-looking woman in the seat next to me. She could be about fifteen years older than me. She's wearing jeans, a white, short-sleeved top, and comfortable looking trainers. She looks better prepared for a long journey than me, in my suit and smart shoes.

When the seat belt sign is off the steward asks what I would like to drink. It seems I can have anything I want. Even though it's ten in the morning, I choose vodka and tomato juice. This comes on a tray with an array of exotic-looking dried fruit and nuts.

I turn to the woman next to me and look at her. She smiles at me and then starts reading her Kindle. I get out my laptop, sip my drink, begin to play a new game I bought at the airport, 'Business Champion'. After some false starts, I start to do well. Suddenly I realise my neighbour is talking to me. With difficulty, I pull myself out of the game.

'Stopping in Singapore? Or going on?' she asks.

'Stopping for six months, maybe longer,' I reply. She waits, clearly wanting me to go on.

'It's work, the firm I'm in. Nothing very interesting.'

'Hm, hm?' She sounds interested. So I continue:

'Yes, my boss said they wanted me to go to work in the Singapore office for a year, maybe longer. I've been with the firm five years and they needed me to get wider experience. It was a difficult decision. I had to break with my girlfriend.'

The woman looks surprised but gives me a sympathetic look.

'That must have been difficult. She didn't want to come with you? Most young women sort of your age would have jumped at the idea of a few months in Singapore.'

'It wasn't as easy as that. Tanya said she didn't want to go with me, indeed couldn't go; something about a passport. I talked to my boss who said there was no choice – I had to go to Singapore.'

'That's odd. Why wouldn't she have been able to get a passport?'

'I don't know really. All I know is that it was going to Singapore for the firm or staying with Tanya.'

At this point, the announcement, a bit late, came over the loudspeaker system and I had to stop talking. 'The seat belt sign is now off. You can move around. But the pilot advises you to keep your seat belt fastened when you are in your seat.'

I smile. The chances of any harm coming to us because our seat belts aren't fastened must be about one in a million.

I look through the window at the tiny fields below. I can't make out where the roads are any more. We must have reached our maximum height by now.

The lady beside me says:

'That's really interesting. You don't have to tell me more if you don't want to.'

But I *do* want to tell her more. I go on:

'Leaving for Singapore or staying with Tanya? It was all to do with risk benefit ratios, just like choosing to wear a seat belt. That's exactly what I'm supposed to be good at. So good that when I left college with a first-class degree in Maths I was snapped up by an investment bank.'

'That means you really must have been *very* good.'

'Yes. I spend my working life modelling different scenarios and making clear to my bosses which they should choose if they want to continue to combine vast profit with minimal risk. It's easy for them. Moderate losses; they will have to find the shortfall. Really big losses; the state steps in. It's a mug's game with the mugs being both the shareholders and the government.'

'It's amazing how bankers seem to come up smelling of roses no matter what sort of shit lake they fall into.'

That set me back a bit. I wasn't used to rather nice looking ladies using language like that. Anyway, what she said was so true I wanted to go on telling her about myself.

'You see, Tanya was my first proper girlfriend. Sex is supposed to be so easy, especially for a man. But it wasn't for me.'

I start to feel awkward telling her all this, but I can't stop now. I go on:

'You see, I'm twenty-six now. I spent all of my teens and my twenties up to a year ago trying to find myself a girlfriend. They just weren't interested. They were supposed to be, but they weren't. Maybe I should have spent more time talking to them before I tried anything on with them. I've never been good at talking to people. Probably that's why I never made friends at school or college.'

'How did you meet Tanya then?'

'I met her in a bar after work. I had only been with the firm for three months. I was on a good salary, earning far more than I needed and owning a flat without a mortgage. Even though her English was not very good, Tanya understood me. She came to bed with me the very first time I took her back to my flat. She did all the things I had dreamed of doing. It was a lot better than doing them in my imagination with porn on my computer.'

'She sounds a very obliging young lady.'

'Indeed, she was. She moved in two or three days after we met, bringing just one suitcase with her. I really had no idea where she had been living before she moved in with me. For the first few days she got calls, I thought from men, on her mobile, but then these stopped. I gave her money. She spent the day reading magazines and talking to her friends on the phone.'

'It sounds as if she had rather limited interests.'

'Well, she was very interested in me and my body. No one else had ever been that before. She and I went out to eat in the evenings when I got back late, often very late from work. At weekends, I watched sport on my laptop and played computer games while she visited her friends who were out at work during the week.'

'Didn't you ever talk about things?'

'You know, I never really told her anything about myself. I didn't tell her about the worst thing. About how, in my last year at school, I came home to find my mother, Ellen, unconscious. She was taken to hospital, but she was too far gone. You see, it was an overdose. She died. That meant I got the house.'

'It must have been very hard for you to leave Tanya behind.'

I think to myself this lady has no idea how hard it was. I had to steel myself to do without what I wanted most in the world – Tanya's hands on my body, her tongue all around me, just the feel of her breasts against my chest. I told her she would have to go. She went, I did not know where. With difficulty, I survived the three weeks before leaving for Singapore without her. Tossing myself off helped but I often sobbed into my pillow. The conversation with this lady brought it all back to me.

So, within a few minutes, I have told her about my dilemma with Tanya, how I hadn't known what to do when I had been more or less ordered to spend time in Singapore. How I had been 'in love' with her. What a wonderful person she was. How I hadn't wanted to hurt her but there was no way out. I talk non-stop for I don't know how long. I start to talk about my mother, then draw back, feeling maybe this is not something I should be blabbing on about. She doesn't interrupt. There is a pause and I wonder if I have bored her and she will go back to her Kindle.

I remember I should be asking her about why she is travelling to Singapore.

'Well, I guess I owe you a bit of my story too. I'm a doctor. I'm going to a medical conference on blood diseases. Usually, it's more senior people who go to these things, but I won an essay prize offered by a drug company. They've given me the cost of business class travel, hotel and registration at the meeting. I've had to leave my partner and five-year-old son for a week, but it's worth it. I'll make useful contacts, maybe learn new laboratory techniques.'

'I think I need to sleep,' she says.

The screen in front of me says it is midnight, local time. She leans back in her seat, puts shades over her eyes and within a few seconds is asleep. I feel left alone. Thinking back, I realise I have never confided before in this way. Something about this lady I can't quite work out has made me want to talk to her in this way. Not feeling at all sleepy, I turn my life over in my mind. I open my laptop but can't concentrate on the game. I turn towards my neighbour and begin to study her. I realise I don't know her name.

I find myself fascinated by her short-sleeved cotton top and jeans. I am entranced by the fair hair on her arms. It is beautiful. For some reason, the look and feel of hair has always fascinated me. I put my hand out towards her and start stroking it. What pleasure! But she wakes at once and stares at me, trying to work out who I am. Then she remembers. She looks at my hand on her arm and pushes it away.

'You can't have a conversation with a man without his thinking you will sleep with him'. She presses the button for a flight attendant. 'This man,' she begins to say to the young man who arrives. Then 'It's alright. Just find me another seat and forget it'. She is led away to another seat.

I feel humiliated and lost. Tears come into my eyes. Then, an hour or so later, I start to feel drowsy myself. The drone of the engines mesmerises me. As I glide into sleep, I hear my own voice repeating 'Forget it, forget it, forget it' until I move into a space where I can do no wrong.

TOO YOUNG TO REALLY BE IN LOVE

It started in the queue at the school gates. I'm standing behind a little group of laughing girls from Year 9, just below me. In front of them is Donovan, being checked by Miss. His shirt is out of his trousers. That is totally out of order. You can't go into school dressed like that.

'But Miss,' he says, 'I washed it late last night and this bottom bit hasn't dried out yet.'

Miss is not impressed. She's short, grey-haired, fiftyish. One of the old school, definitely not like one of our new, young, cool teachers.

'You don't want me to put my wet shirt next to my body, do you?'

Miss seems even less impressed, even a bit impatient.

'You wouldn't want me to come to school in a dirty shirt, now would you, Miss?'

Miss just stares at him, waiting.

'It would be really horrible; it might touch that … you know, that sensitive part of my body, you know. Now you must agree, Miss, that would be really shit.'

The girls behind him think this is *really* funny.

Miss now gets angry. She tells him he has already earned a detention and if he doesn't put his shirt into his trousers pronto, he will be in more serious trouble. Especially if he carries on using bad language. Oh my God, is this boy cool? Donovan or Don, what everybody calls him, says

'Alright, Miss, I'll put it in.'

He gives a little pretend squeal to show the discomfort he is now feeling.

'There you are, Miss, I've put it in. But you must admit, Miss, it's a stupid rule that gives me double pneumonia 'cos you made me put wet clothes next to my skin.'

He walks through the gate, now surrounded by the admiring girls who have followed him in. Odd. Although he has had to do what he's been told, he seems somehow to have won the argument.

That leaves me. And as I walk through the school gate dressed absolutely as the school rules require, I realise something momentous has happened to me. I've fallen in love. With Don. I've developed the biggest boner I've ever had in my life.

I want him. I want Don. Oh my God, do I want him? What is it about him that makes me want him so much? Can I describe it? It's the way he stands when he's listening to Sam and her friends, tall, quiet, confident. It's the gentle curve of his bum. It's his voice when he does speak, a bit husky but sort of like music. It's everything.

I walk into assembly and find a seat with my class about five rows from the front. I've a seat just a row behind Don and a little to one side, so I've got a good view of him. As I sit down and look around at the rest of the class, my boner relaxes a bit, but it hardens again when I look at him.

Is this bad news or good news? I don't know. I've known I was probably gay since my last year in primary school. In Year 6 other boys would talk about one or two of the girls in our class as 'hot' or 'cute' or just 'really pretty'. I felt the same way about one or two of the boys. Also, when I look at ads or porn or films or listen to music, it's mostly young men that turn me on. I get warm feelings and a bit of swelling of my dick when I see them. That just doesn't happen with the girls and young women I see. But I've never had a boner like this one.

Don is in the group I mix with at school. But it isn't a very close group. Just half a dozen black kids and me and sometimes Kevin who is white too, but thick, really thick. Don is a bit fringe in the group. Quite often he's with a group of girls. That's a bit unusual. Nearly always during break, it's boys with boys and girls with girls but there is a bit of mixing. Anyway, a lot more than there was last year.

The girls just love Don. He's a bit older than me. I'm one of the youngest in our class and he's one of the oldest. Also, he's four or five inches taller than me. It isn't that I haven't developed. I've got hair, quite a lot of hair, in all the right places. My voice broke over a year ago, which at thirteen was quite young. If I want to keep the fuzz down and not get teased I have to shave once or twice a week. Dad says he didn't reach this stage until he was a couple of years older than I am now.

But I've just not grown very tall. And I think that's all the growing I'm going to do. Mum and Dad aren't tall, so I guess I have to thank them for being a bit of a dwarf. Well, not a dwarf really. I'm five foot six and a quarter, nearly five foot six and a half. That's taller than quite a few of the Indians or Pakis in my class are going to be.

Anyway, here I am in Assembly, well placed to get a good look at Don and keep him in my sights. Mr. Hargreaves is taking the Assembly. He's youngish but has a nasty thin voice. Like all the others do, he's banging on about how important this year is for Year 10s.

'Now kids, it's your turn. You Year 10s. Don't forget it. It's GCSEs that count in this world if you want to get on in life. We've got two years to prepare for them and that isn't as long as it seems. And it's not just work in school. If you want to get a good start in life, you've got to work at home. We'll do our best for you, but in the end, it's up to you.'

He bangs on for what seems like ages about this though it's probably not more than five minutes.

In fact, it's all rubbish. It's worked out already. When I look round I can tell who's going to do well in GCSE and who's going to do pretty much shit. Old Wang over there is going to get nine A stars. Kevin is going to get a couple of Cs and a D. In my little group, Delroy, Raymond and Barry are going to do like me. A few Bs and Cs, a couple of As if we're lucky. Don is going to do really well but not as good as Wang. I don't know how Don does it, but I've noticed he gets good marks for pretty well everything. His Art is something else. So brilliant! The school only cares that we get at least a C in English and Maths, so the teachers will make sure we get that. That's what Hackney Manor is measured on. After that, they couldn't give a toss.

After assembly, we all file down to the classrooms. I've got Maths and then History. For Maths, we have Mr. Pargeter. He shouts a lot if he sees someone isn't paying attention. I think I would find Maths hard whoever was teaching it but I'm certainly not going to learn much from Pargeter. Mum has fixed a Maths tutor for me who comes on Saturday morning. She's really nice and doesn't seem to mind if it takes me a long time to catch on to something. I think with her help I'll get a C in Maths.

While old Pargeter is trying to explain simultaneous equations, I'm staring at him really hard to give the impression I'm attending to what he's saying very, very carefully. In fact, all I'm thinking about is Don and how I'm going to get him to come home to my place. I've already started to think about sex things I want us to do together. My boner has come back but I've managed to control it so that I think no one has noticed.

Then it's History. A different story as far as teaching is concerned. Mr. Singh really knows how to make a lesson interesting. We're doing World War Two. At the moment, he's onto the Holocaust. Trillions of Jews were killed. Mr. Singh wants to know what we know about it already. He goes around the class to ask if any of us know anyone who's been affected by the Holocaust.

'My Nan is half-Jewish, Sir,' I say.

'Ah, did she have any of her family taken to a concentration camp?'

'I don't really know, Sir.'

Mr. Singh is a bit disappointed when I tell him about my Nan and have to admit I don't really know what happened to her in the war and why she wasn't killed too. I feel a bit of an idiot.

In any case, my mind isn't on the case. I'm still thinking about how to get Don to my place. Trouble is, I don't really know him that well, so I don't know what would interest him. Dad has set up a really good Bluetooth sound system but what sort of music does Don like? I wonder about computer games. I persuaded Mum and Dad to buy me the Cataclysm extension of World of Warcraft for my birthday. I bet no one else has that. If I'm to stand a chance of getting him to my place I'm going to have to find out more about him. Not easy. I'll start this break time.

At break my class divides up into groups like always. There's the three or four Turkish boys who all talk Turkish together. No idea what they are on about. Kebabs and halal, I expect. Then there's the Indian Paki group. They speak so many different languages they have to talk in English to understand each other. Over in the corner, there's a couple of Year 11 boys, Christos and Ivor. I think they're gay. They're showing off dance steps to a boy in my year, shouting the lyrics to the song as they do so. How embarrassing.

Then there's my group, Delroy, Raymond, Barry, me and a couple of others. Often that includes Don but this time he's decided to go over and talk to a group of girls. Sam and Sally and Cheryl and Zehra called him over to tell him how great he was cheeking Miss at the gate. So, no opportunity for me to talk to him. It will have to wait until lunch time.

My lot talk about the TV they've watched last night. There's a programme on at the moment called 'Top Boy' which is supposed to be about gangs in our borough, Hackney. Everyone thinks it's rubbish. Maybe it isn't but they don't want to admit they don't know a lot about what goes on around here. Then there's The Killing. Everyone loves that.

I try to get some interest in football. My Dad is a mad West Ham United supporter with a couple of season tickets. He usually takes a friend from work but once or twice he's taken me. The Hammers are really shit this season, but my Dad still goes. No one in my lot is very interested in football. They are more into Formula One. While we talk, I keep looking over at Don who is not that far away talking to those girls. He-is-so-hot, it's unbelievable. But talking to him will have to wait until lunch.

Then it turns out lunch is no good either. He's gone off to the Art room to finish some work he's been doing. When I pass by the Art room on the way to the canteen I see he's talking to Mrs. Grierson, the senior art teacher. He doesn't appear at lunch, so he must have spent the whole time there. I talk to Delroy and Barry about last night's TV again. Then, after school, I know he's got this detention. It'll be ages before he comes out. I think about waiting for him and walking to his home with him, but he knows it's not in the right direction for me, so he'll be puzzled and want to know what's got into me. I certainly can't tell him.

So, I walk home after school and play World of Warcraft by myself for a couple of hours. Then Mum and Dad come home, and Mum makes supper. I'm normally pretty quiet during supper and don't let on what's been happening at school when they ask me. The three of us sit round the table and Mum and Dad talk a lot together. As usual, they're worried about the election. Like all their friends, they're Labour. Probably Labour is going to win but it's touch and go.

Usually I join in a bit, especially with Dad about West Ham. But this evening I don't say a word. Even though it's spaghetti bolognaise, one of my favourites, I don't eat much. I just don't feel very hungry like usual. Mum asks what's wrong with me.

'Oh, it's just I've fallen in love,' I feel like saying, but no way. So, I just look at her a bit hopeless.

Dad asks me if I want to do some art work on the computer with him. He spends nearly every evening doing this. It's part of his work but he does it at home as well. I think he's pretty good at it. I say 'no' not very politely and go up to my room. I listen to a bit of my music and then go to bed where I have a wank.

I've been wanking most nights for about a year now. Mostly when I wank I've been thinking about Adam Lambert or Ryan Tedder from OneRepublic. Tonight, I start to think about Don. Then I start to think I don't want to spoil my relationship with him and turn back to Adam Lambert. Then I think of sex things I want to do with Don, deep kissing and stuff and come straight away, quicker than I want to.

Normally I go to sleep pretty quickly after I've had a wank, but tonight I just carry on thinking about Don and about how I'm going to get him to come home. I have another wank before I go to sleep and even then, I keep on waking up. Then, about four-o-clock in the morning I have a very, very good thought and go to sleep almost immediately. Mum calls me at 7 and I just about manage to get up in time not to be late for school.

I feel much happier during the day because at least I've got a plan. What I really want to do is get close to Don and talk to him, but I try very hard to keep away from him even though I can't stop looking at him. I just treat him very casual. It's not hard to get through the day. The lessons, Geography, English, Science, PE are pretty easy as well as pretty boring. To be honest, nothing really interests me except History. During break and lunch, I stay with Delroy and Barry, trying to avoid Kevin as much as I can. He is such a pain and seems to think just because he's the only other white English boy he's a right to spend all his time with me.

That evening after supper I tell Dad I'd like to work with him on his desktop and get him to show me some things. He's doing quite a lot about African schoolchildren at the moment so there are a lot of pictures of black kids in bare school rooms with no equipment around. When I go to bed I have pretty much the same sort of night. I have to wank twice to get to sleep and spend a lot of time thinking about things I could do with Don. There's a three-day school journey to Paris in a couple of months. I imagine being in a dorm in the next bed to him and what we might do. Trouble is I know his family isn't well enough off to pay for the trip. There are free places, but I guess he's too proud to ask for one. Again, I'm pretty tired when I get up in the morning but make it to school OK.

That day after school, I just join up with Don and Barry as they start to walk home. I know they both live in council flats on the Brakespeare Estate and always walk home together. I tell them I've got to pass by there to buy some stuff a bit further on from where they live and ask if it's OK to walk with them. I think I'm seen as a bit of a nobody but I'm not one of those nerdy kids it would be really death to be seen with, so that's alright.

I walk on Don's side, so he's in the middle. They talk about school and how most of the teachers are rubbish but Mr. Singh and one or two of the others are OK. I pluck up courage and say:

'I wonder what Mrs. Grierson, the art teacher, is like. I don't have her, but I've heard she's really good.'

Don replies 'Yes, she's great. She can draw really well.'

'Does she do digital art?' I ask.

I didn't know anything about digital art until yesterday evening but I've now talked to my Dad and looked it up on Google.

'No. She doesn't really have the equipment but she's looking into it. I've talked to her about it. It would be great if she did.'

I can't believe my luck.

'Well,' I say. 'My Dad is really into digital art. He's got these programmes called MyPaint, Flowpaint and QAquarelle. He's just bought them. I don't know if they're any good.'

'Oh my God, sick. Your Dad must be rolling in it. That's really swag. That's expensive stuff.'

'Not only that. Now he's building his own 3D printer. It's Makerbots or something like that.'

Don is impressed. 'Yes, I really would like to come back to your place to try my hand at digital art, especially if I could print it off when I'd done it.'

OK, so now I had to persuade Dad to let loose a complete stranger, a kid, on his precious equipment.

So, when Dad gets home I tell him:

'Dad, I've got this new friend called Don. He's really terrific at drawing. I told him about your digital stuff and he would really like to try his hand at it.'

Dad looks a bit doubtful.

'Dad, this kid is very, very responsible.'

Though I had one or two in primary school, I haven't had a friend from this school home before. I've not really made friends. When there has been somebody I just might have invited home, I get worried they're going to think we've got a bigger place to live in than anyone else. There's no worse thing in my school than being different. I can't risk it. In any case, no one has asked me home, so I don't see why I should.

Anyway, right away Dad says:

'It's no problem. What's his name? Why don't you ask him for tea next Sunday and I'll show him how to get started?'

Mum is even more pleased. She's been worried about me not having friends. Now she can't get the smile off her face. Stoo-pid. What does it matter if I ask friends round?

It's Thursday today, so I've only got two days to tell Don about Sunday. I text him.

'Can u come to my place at 4 on Sunday? My Dad could show you how to use his stuff.'

Straightaway he replies

'Sick. Tell me where you live and I'll be there.'

Friday is terrible. I can't think about anything except Don is going to come to my house. How am I going to get him up to my room? I can't think about anything else and get bollocked by Pargeter for not paying attention. The nights are terrible too. I just can't stop thinking about him. Wanking doesn't help me get off to sleep. On Saturday morning, I can hardly keep awake with Mrs. Wedge, my Maths tutor. She has to be extra patient with me. I can't concentrate and don't learn much. Luckily, she doesn't tell my Mum and Dad.

The Hammers are away this Saturday afternoon but it's a London club, Chelsea. Dad has seats through his job and goes with his mate from work. Chelsea are bound to win; the Hammers are rubbish this season, so I don't want to go anyway. What's the point of going to watch your team lose? I play World of Warcraft and listen to music and look at Facebook and the time goes quicker.

Sunday afternoon is a disaster! When the doorbell rings at four-o-clock, it's a big event. No one from school has ever visited before. I do have a few friends I could have asked. But I know my house is much fancier than anyone else's. I just don't want anyone to see it. It's not that we're rich. Mum and Dad go on about how they came to live in Hackney because they couldn't afford to live in Hampstead or Highgate and now their house has gone up so much and so on and so on. Thank goodness, we've still got our Labour poster up with Ed Miliband on it. Anyway, Don is the first kid from school to come around.

I open the door and there he is, dressed in torn jeans and a black T shirt with I ♥ Hackney on it. He looks really hot. Mum and Dad had suggested we had some tea first and then Dad would take Don up to his study to show him the art he could do on his computer. Dad works in the art department of his advertising agency, so he really knows what's what when it comes to this sort of thing.

Dad says 'Hello, Don, I'm Henry Wade. Good to meet you.'

Mum follows with 'Hello, Don, I'm Angie. What would you like to drink?'

'Just a diet coke, please, Mrs. Wade.'

Oh dear, problems straightaway. Mum wants to be called Angie and a can of coke has never dared show its face in our house. I know Mum thinks it's a deeply unhealthy, *American* drink. We only have fruit juice and tap water except when Mum and Dad have wine.

'A coke?' repeats Mum.

'Yes, you know. A coca cola. Diet if you've got it.'

'I'm afraid we don't. Would orange juice do?'

'Oh, just a glass of water would be fine. I've really just come to do some art on your computer, Mr. Wade.'

So, Dad takes Don up to his study and I trail behind after them to watch. I'm shit at computers and worse at any sort of art work, so I just sit in a chair while Dad and Don really get into it. 'Course, it turns out Don picks it all up very quickly and Dad is impressed. While this is going on, I gaze at Don hoping when they've stopped I'm going to get Don to come over to my room.

Finally, after about an hour, Dad says,

'I think that's enough for this afternoon, but you must come back some time and have another go. You've got a real flair for this.'

I ask Don if he would like to come over to my room and listen to some music or play some World of Warcraft. I've got the new Cataclysm expansion. He won't have seen that anywhere else.

'I really need to be getting back, but OK for a bit.'

I can see Don gets a bit of a shock when he sees the size of my room and the stuff I've got to play my music. I have plans for the music we'll listen to: Adam Lambert's 'Whattya Want From Me'. Adam is gay but his music could be straight or gay, you can't tell. But pretty well as soon as Don sits down he gets fidgety and says he's got to go and before I have a chance to say anything, he's off downstairs and out the front door, just about remembering to shout, 'Goodbye and thanks, Mr and Mrs Wade' as he leaves the house.

'Gosh, has he gone already?' says Mum. 'What a good-looking young man. Those eyes are quite something. And his smile. Wow, I bet the girls flock round *him*.'

'Oh yes, they do.' I reassure her, if not myself. Dad is impressed with his artistic skill, so everyone is very pleased, except me.

Monday is a terrible day too, but for different reasons. It turns out that Don always spends Sunday afternoons hanging out with his admiring group of girls, Sam, Sally, Cheryl and Zehra on his estate. When he didn't turn up yesterday, they thought he might be ill so Sam was sent round to his flat to find out where he was. His Mum didn't know. Thought he was with them as usual. Very mysterious. So, when he returned to the estate they all wanted to know where he had been. He told them he had been at my place but not why he had gone there. He didn't want to be thought a nerd, even an art nerd.

The girls, who probably think about sex all the time, assume his visit to me meant we had a thing for each other. And as it is unthinkable that Don is a poofter, it must be me trying to push him into it. Too right, though they don't know the half of it.

Anyway, today I've been the target of the full force of 10B's girlie slagging off. The texts they've sent me really are like acid thrown in my face. The first one went 'Keep your shitty, filthy hands off Don, you dirty poofter,' followed shortly after by 'Get outta this school, u dirty faggot' and 'Bugger off, Jaymie Wade, you got no place in Hakney Manner.'

Knowing I was probably gay from Year 6 meant that, by the time I moved to this school, I was certain. In primary school, we all used to call each other 'gay' whenever we wanted to throw an insult for being fat or stupid or too clever or too cocky or too clumsy or too anything out of the ordinary. It was always 'Oh, he's gay or she's gay.' I knew that gay really meant sexually turned on by boys or men, so whenever the word was used as an insult I felt bad inside because I knew I was *really* gay.

Then, when I came here, kids stopped using 'gay' pretty well entirely and words like 'poofter' and 'faggot' and 'dyke' for girls started to be used. I don't know if Don is gay or not. I don't get invited to parties but at school I hear what goes on at them. After Sam's last party on the estate I heard Delroy say he wished he could pull the birds like Don, but Don didn't seem to do anything about it. I think he must be gay.

'He could have had any of those girls, but he just didn't make any move.'

So, it seemed as if when girls and boys started pairing off, Don just chatted to three or four girls and boys for a bit and then went home. But I know why Don hasn't made it with any of the girls. It's because he's gay, like me. I can sense it. Gays are supposed to have this feeling for other gays and I've certainly got this feeling about Don.

I decide I don't dare go over to Don at break or lunch time to ask if he has had any texts like mine. But at the end of lunch I follow him into the bogs and manage to have a few words with him.

'Have you had any texts, Don? About us, I mean?'

'No. What are you talking about?'

Don looks puzzled. He can't have had any texts. Interesting. I don't tell him about mine. The texts don't make any difference to how I feel. I still want him, to be close to him.

I wonder whether to ask Don if he would like to come back to my place next Sunday. But it turns out there's no need. In full view of everyone he comes up to me and asks if my Dad would be happy to give him another go with his digital art programme. This will certainly mean the girls who've been sending the texts realise it's not me trying to get off with Don. But what good will it do if all that happens is he comes back to my place, spends time with Dad and then scarpers off when he's finished?

That evening I have another word with Dad about Don.

'Would it be OK if Don comes over next Sunday, like last time?'

'Yes, of course. But I've got another idea. I've got two tickets for the Hammers match next Saturday. I can't go because I've got an all-day meeting at work. Maybe you would like to go with Don.'

Going to the match with Don would be a big deal for me, but what about Don? He's shown no interest in football as far as I know. There are just two or three boys in my year who've got Hammers blood in them. Don is certainly not one of them. All the same, I think it's worth a go. Even sitting next to Don for an hour and a half would be great. I tag along with him and Delroy as they leave to walk home after school.

'Don, it's OK to come on Sunday. My Dad said you were really good and he'd be pleased to show you more. He had another idea. He's got two tickets for the Hammers match next Saturday he can't use. He wondered if I would like to go and you could come with me.'

There are a few moments hesitation. Then, he says:

'Yeah. OK. I've never been to a proper match. Cool. I can still come on Sunday, yeah? So, where shall we meet?'

'What about Hackney Central Station at half-past one?'

It's a long journey to Upton Park by tube. We're Hammers supporters because West Ham was Dad's team when he was a boy, living in Romford. He used to go every Saturday with his Dad. So, he's always been keen I should support the same team. Don and I sit in silence as the train gradually fills up with Hammers' supporters. I feel some of them are looking at us as if there's something wrong with us.

Anyway, we get out and walk up Queen's Road towards the ground, passing Queen's Market immediately on the right. Cheap clothes. £2 for a pair of trousers, £1 for a shirt. Don looks at the T shirts but isn't impressed. But he picks one up that has 'Sorry Girls I'm Gay' written on it.

I say to myself 'I knew. I knew.' And now I know for certain. I get a terrific feeling inside me, like I've won a big prize in the lottery. But I can't say anything and we go on walking. There's the Tropical Takeaway after which is the Queen's pub. Outside the pub there's a vast crowd, almost entirely men, holding pints of beer. I realise the deep growling noise I could hear as we got out of the station came from this mob. We buy a couple of slices of pizza at the Pizza Klub and Grill Klub a bit further on.

Still with a bit of time, I get us to walk past the stadium and show Don the statue of Bobby Moore holding the World Cup at the corner of Queen's Road and Barking Road. As we make our way back towards the stadium alongside all these men, I feel good, somehow a man, even if a young man, bonded to this vast group of other men, maybe older, but still the same as me in an important way.

It's only as we queue to go through the turnstiles to enter the ground that I realise with a shock that Don is almost the only black person around. In the market and in the street on the way to the ground, there were plenty of people of all sorts of colour and appearance. But now we're going into the ground it's a very different story. I hope this is going to be alright. There's been a lot in the papers about the Hammers crowd shouting anti-Jewish chants at Spurs and Chelsea teams. Well, at least Don isn't Jewish, but there seem awfully few black faces around. None, to be honest. Has Don noticed? He must have done.

Even though the match hasn't started, it's really noisy. There is a band playing in the middle of the pitch. Almost continuous loudspeaker announcements about future matches, the winning number on the programme, how to become a paid-up supporter, drown the music. There are young kids down there shooting goals past a sort of Mickey Mouse figure. I wonder what Don makes of all this, but, more important, in my mind, I'm celebrating that T shirt.

I find our places in the Bobby Moore Stand and point out to Don where the other stands are and where the Everton supporters are placed. I tell him how the Hammers are having a shit season and might even get relegated. He doesn't understand about relegation, so I explain it to him. Then the match begins. Like everyone else I stand up and shout when the Hammers get anywhere near goal and groan when our players pass the ball to Everton players which they seem to be doing most of the time. Don is watching but doesn't join in the shouting and I can see he is not all that comfortable. Occasionally there is a burst of singing the Hammers song – 'I'm Forever Blowing Bubbles.' I join in until I see Don doesn't, so I stop too.

At half-time no goals have been scored. We sit down and drink from our bottles of water. I sense we are being looked at. I start to feel uncomfortable and wonder how Don is doing. Nearby, one of a group of rough looking young men only a bit older than us, is eating a banana. He points to Don and holds the half-peeled banana out to him, offering it to him and laughing about us to his mates. One of this idiot's friends says 'Shut up, Kev. He's only a kid.' I pray Don hasn't noticed, but he has. Suddenly he gets up, saying 'I'm going. I've had enough. You stay.'

He pushes his way along the row of seats to get out. I follow him. The young man with the banana sees us going and calls out:

'It's OK, kids, you stay. I didn't mean no harm. Honest, I didn't.' Don leaves the ground almost at a trot, with me just behind him.

We walk in silence to the station. All I can think of to say is 'I'm sorry, Don.' Just before the station he stops in front of the Queen's Tropical Takeaway. He reads the list of what's on offer – plantain, roast corn, curry mutton, Jamaican jerk chicken, Jamaican patties. I sense what he's thinking. 'That's my food, not yours.'

It's all very different from school. There, I feel I have more in common with black boys like Don and Delroy and Barry than I do with white Polish kids like Andrej and Krystof and Turkish kids like Berkay and Hassan. Most of them have only been in England for three or four years and still speak with an accent so you sometimes can't even understand them. On the train going back to Hackney I desperately want to touch Don, put my arm round him. No way. But he says:

'It's OK, Jamie. It wasn't your fault.' And he gives me a really nice warm smile. Not exactly sexy, but nearly. I know for sure it's only going to be a matter of time before we get together. We separate at the station as I ask, 'See you tomorrow, Don?' He nods.

The next few days are a roller-coaster. Everything is the same and everything is different. On the next day, Sunday, Don comes around as usual. This time Dad answers the door and they go up together to his study. I take a chair behind them as Don creates more and more amazing shapes. He's also doing portraits now, really life-like, better I think than Dad's. When they've done, he smiles at me but doesn't want to come over to my room. I guess he thinks it would be too risky. We have such warm feelings for each other. He just leaves quickly. I know he wants to get back to the Estate as soon as possible.

After he's gone, Dad and I have a cup of tea. He asks me about yesterday's match. I can't bring myself to tell him what happened, so I make up what we thought about the second half. Then Dad springs a surprise on me.

'How are you feeling about school these days?' he asks.

I don't know where this is going, so I mumble a bit, with a few y'knows thrown in.

'Well,' he says, 'Mum and I have decided Hackney Manor really isn't the right school for you. They just don't have the facilities. The teachers, well, they're pretty good, but they don't have the time to give you. They have so many needy kids.'

I can see where this is going, and I don't like it.

'So, after GCSEs, you're going to Threadneedle. We've made enquiries and your results are going to be just about good enough for you to get in there.'

Threadneedle is a public school. Full of toffs and rugger players. The way Dad speaks I know there's no room for argument, but I try.

'What if I don't want to go?'

'You'll go. Mum and I have decided.'

That's bad enough but then he adds the killer.

'And maybe you shouldn't get too close to Don. You won't be in the same school after next year. He's a bright lad, just brilliant at Art, but we're not sure getting too close to him is going to work out.'

So, they've noticed. Shit, shit, shit. And all that guff about Hackney Manor being a great place to learn about how other people live, is just blah, blah, blah. When they're talking for real, it's all about 'A' level results. And Threadneedle gets a shed load of people into Oxbridge, which is where Dad wishes he'd gone.

That night I go to bed early. One of Mum's favourite expressions is 'You can't have everything in this world'. Not in this world you can't. But the world of wank is different. In the world of wank, you can have anyone you want to and do anything you want to with them. It's just that in the morning I feel shattered and don't really want to go to school.

On Monday I know the texts are going to be even worse and they are. 'U R going to have your dick chopped off if you don't keep your hands off Don.' That was one of the mildest. There was only one threatening to kill me, so that's alright. I've never felt this before, but I've got to tell someone about this. I can't tell Mum and Dad, that's obvious. I can't talk to Don. There's none of the other kids I can tell about this. There's no choice.

At break, I go to Mr. Chalmers' office. He's the Year Head. I know what he'll say when I tell him I want to talk to a teacher about a personal matter. He tells me to go to Ms. Potter. She's called the pastoral head and mainly deals with girls who've got depressed or stopped eating and got thin. I knock on her door and she's free. She looks up.

'Hullo, Jamie, what can I do for you?'

I don't know how she knows my name 'cos she's never taught me, but it's a good start. I don't say anything; just bring my phone out. Fortunately, I've remembered to switch it right off so I'm not breaking a school rule. I switch it on, don't say anything, just show her the dozen or so texts. She takes quite a long time to read them. Then she reads them a second time. She looks up at me. I expect her to ask me if I know who's written them, but she doesn't. She gives me a really nice smile.

'It sounds as though someone thinks you're very fond of Don. Is that right? I don't know Don well, but everyone says he's a bit of a pain but a great kid.'

I nod and mumble something like:

'Yes, he is. He's a really great kid.'

'Well, that's good then. Look, it sounds as if you're gay or you think you are, Jamie. Is that right?'

I nod again.

'It isn't easy to be gay. Even in a school like this one. Especially when there are little horrors like this around.' She points to my phone as she gives it back.

'You just need to know this. There are a couple of gay boys in Year 11, Christos and Ivor. You probably know what they look like. They're not the quietest boys in the school. They've told me it's OK if I give their names to anyone who thinks they might be gay and wants to talk about it.'

I nod. I'm not sure if I want to have anything to do with Christos and Ivor, who always go around together. In fact, I don't. But it's an idea. Ms goes on:

'Getting texts like that. It could really get you down. How are you feeling?'

I know what she's getting at. Am I depressed? Should she send me on to the school counsellor? I don't want that and, in any case, I'm really feeling OK, now I've spoken to Ms.

'Alright,' Ms points again to the phone now in my hand. 'I'm going to have to think what to do about those. But if you get any more like that, you are to come straight here to tell me. Understand?' I do.

At lunch, I see Don talk to Delroy who nods. I realise what that's all about when Don comes over to me and tells me he would like to walk back to mine with me after school.

Not to do any digital art, he knows my Dad isn't there, but to have a chat. The whole afternoon I'm really excited. There will be no one at home when we get back. Oh my God, what couldn't we do?

But it isn't like that at all. I think maybe Don is going to tell me how we're going to be able to meet after school. I keep looking at him, but he just stares straight ahead. We walk for about ten minutes until we've got well away from the school. Then Don opens up.

'Look Jamie. I know what all this is about. You're gay and you've got the hots for me. I'm sorry, but I don't for you. In fact, I know I'm definitely not gay. I had it off with Sam last night. Her Mum was out. I went over to her place. It wasn't her first time, but it was mine. It was brilliant. She really knows what to do. And she's a nice girl with it. She knows some of her mates have been sending texts to you. She's tried to stop them, but they won't. Anyway, I just thought you ought to know.'

He doesn't wait for me to say anything. Just wheels off and starts to walk a different way back towards the estate. I get a dreadful feeling. My stomach feels as if it is going to fall out. Sam's a slag. A real slag. Everyone knows that. Is this what love and sex are going to be like for the rest of my life? Never mind the rest of my life.

Can I get through next week?

FOR SERVICES RENDERED

As I push in there is a cry, but it is not the cry of pleasure I had expected. Instead it is a cry of sharp pain. I pull out. Bloody hell. In more ways than one. I realise I just popped the cherry of what must have been the only forty something fucking virgin outside a convent in the United Kingdom. Well, maybe not quite forty but she must be a good fifteen years older than little me.

'Why have you stopped?' she says.

'Well, it's messy. I didn't think you would want me to.'

'Of course, I want you to. I'm going to clean up and then I want you to carry on.'

Anyway, she goes into what sounds like a shower room off the bedroom. She comes back completely butt ass naked. Goes over to a cupboard and produces a clean set of sheets. She removes the bloody ones and puts on the new. I go and clean up a bit myself. Then return and watch her making the bed.

'Come on. At least you can tuck in your side'

I didn't know there was a 'my side' already but she seems to know her own mind. Then, we're both back in the bed.

After the briefest of stroking, she makes it clear I'm to go back in again. I do and this time she moves fast against me. After about thirty seconds, I can't stop myself and come inside her. She puts my hand on her clit and moves it. I do my best to make her come, but she doesn't get there. After three or four minutes, she pulls my hand away.

'Forget it. I won't come. I never do when I do it myself. Just lie there and let me hold you. And you hold me.'

I do what I'm told, and we lie in silence for about half an hour. I feel I should be leaving but she holds me too firmly.

'No. Stay.'

I don't feel like arguing. It's a comfortable bed and looking around I can see her flat is quite something. Fucking classy looking furniture and pictures on the wall.

I'm going to need to explain to Hassan why I've not returned ready to pick up my next delivery. Otherwise, I'll get asscanned. He's given me one warning already. That one wasn't my fault. If he hadn't packaged a Margherita when he'd been asked for a Four Seasons the customer wouldn't have complained. This time though it would be up to me and no excuses. So, I reach out for the floor and my jacket and pull out my mobile.

'Max here. I'm really sorry, Hassan, I'm not coming back in. I've had a fucking accident. Yes, there's blood all over the place.'

I look up. Fiona, for that, she has told me, is her name, is giving me an eyeful. I can see she's not pleased with the way I put that.

'Well, it's not quite all over the place. Just some bleeding. No, I won't be going into A and E but I'm not going to be able to make it back to you. Yes, the scooter's OK. It's still working fine. You'll just have to make do with Sammy. You're not all that busy, so it'll work out. Yes, I know you're not insured if I have an accident. Don't worry. I won't be putting in a claim. It's not that bad. Oh, shut the fuck up, Hassan. I'll be in again tomorrow morning at 10.'

This is fucking bizarre. A great deal more than I bargained for when I rang her doorbell only an hour or so ago. Of course, getting it off is always a possibility when you're delivering stuff and someone new opens the door. But I've been pushing pizzas through people's front doors for two years now and nothing like this has ever happened before.

In fact, the opposite. Not all that often, but from time to time a good-looking bird opens the door and you think you might try it on. You say something about how pepperoni is your favourite pizza too and how it's better if it's *really* spicy and you give them a wink and ask what other ones do they like and all that. In no time at all they've tumbled to what you're really on about and you're out the door thinking about your next call.

There's only once someone's taking an interest in me that way and it wasn't at all what I wanted. This perfume-smelling guy opens the door, looks at me and asks me in. He sits me down and starts to chat me up. Tells me I'm really amazing looking and had anyone told me before I was the spitting image of some actor called Lawrence Oliver who it turns out lived about a hundred years ago. Had I ever thought of being a model? He worked in an agency and could get me a test, no trouble at all.

I knew what all this was about. Malcolm in the children's home had about ten boys but he didn't have me. No, thank you. And then there was the man in the foster home, one of five I've been expected to call Dad, who tried it on. Anyway, I thought being a model would be a great idea. So, when this foul-smelling guy put his hand on my knee I left it there and said, yes, I would like a test and when could he get it for me? I didn't let him go any further than hand on knee but that was enough.

I went for this test and they took dozens of pics with fantastic gear. The man said I was good-looking alright, but I didn't have the hard looks they were after in the men they took on. I was the right height, middling to tall, and I wasn't fat or anything, but my face was too soft and my nose was a bit small. So that was that. I always arranged for someone else to deliver to the smelly guy and never met him again. Disgusting geezer.

Anyway, when Fiona opened her front door about an hour ago, getting it off with her was very far from my mind. It wasn't she was bad-looking exactly. A bit pudgy maybe and face not great. It was the grey suit, no make-up and the rimless specs. No nonsense there was my first thought. I seemed to remember I'd delivered to this front door a couple of times before, but I do a lot of deliveries in Princess Towers, so I wasn't sure. Anyway, I wasn't at all ready for what happened next.

'Why don't you come in for a moment?' She had some sort of an accent, northern, I think. Not posh, anyway. Well, why not?

'I've just opened a bottle of red wine. You could have a glass if you'd like one.'

'Fucking hell. There's something going on here,' I say to myself.

'Been doing this job long?'

I tell her a bit about it and the hours I work. Also, that I've had loads of other jobs like being a model (nearly true) and working for a contract cleaner. I've been in other flats in Princess Towers.

'Some have been slag heaps. This is a nice flat, though.'

'You like it? It's got a fabulous view. Come and look at St. Paul's.'

So, we go over to the humungous window.

'Look, you can see the Shard over there. That's the Gherkin, and around there, the Cheese-grater.'

As she points these out, she moves closer to me and within fifteen minutes of my ringing her doorbell, her hand is on my thigh, moving upwards. I turn to her and we kiss. Except she clearly hasn't a bleeding clue how to kiss. Tongues are out of bounds for a start. Then, it's into the bedroom next door, her bed and a horror show on the sheets, never mind my dick.

After I'd put my mobile back in my jacket, I reach into another pocket for my packet of fags.

'No, you don't. Not in this flat. I'd rather you didn't smoke at all, but if you really must, there's the terrace over there.'

I decide to stay in her bed. It's cosy alright, and it looks as though I'm here for the night, so the fag can wait.

'And another thing. I don't want you to use the f-word, or, for that matter, the c-word.'

She's certainly calling the shots here, but if that's how it is, that's how it is. I don't protest. I think of saying, as a bit of a joke:

'Well, I don't know who you think you f-ing are, you stupid c,' but decide against it. She's a bit frightening.

After an hour or so, she goes to sleep. But I don't. I lie awake thinking whether to get dressed and leave or stay until the morning. Hassan won't be expecting me back so why not stay?

Then, a few minutes after she's asleep I get the feeling there is someone else in the flat. There is a sort of scuffling sound. I get really anxious. Her hubby back when she's not expecting him? Bloody hell. No, not very likely, given that she was a virgin until less than an hour ago. I don't have to wait long before all is clear. There is a sharp whining noise followed by some insistent barking.

The shape on my left side suddenly comes to life.

'Oh God, it's Louis. I'd forgotten about him.'

She jumps out of bed and goes into another room. It sounds as if she's feeding the bleeding animal, whatever it is. At any rate, the sniffling and barking stop. Then she comes back in and lies down beside me again. We lie awake, not talking. Suddenly I realise she's crying. I turn to her and see tears running down her cheeks. It's an ugly sight and she's not much of a looker at the best of times.

'What's all this, then?'

'I don't know. I feel I've let myself down. After all these years … It's so humiliating. I feel I've given in. Wrong place, wrong time, wrong man, wrong thing to do anyway.'

I might feel insulted about the 'wrong man' bit, but let it go. It's not the first time that I've had a bird sobbing afterwards. Usually though it's when they've been pissed. Indeed, the more pissed they are when they come to bed the more likely they are to turn on the waterworks later. Fiona is not in the slightest bit pissed. I don't know what to say.

'The problem is I want to make love again. It's crazy. I've never done it before. You hurt me. Now I want to do it again.'

Bollocks to this. I tell her I can't. It's too soon after the last time, but we'll do it in the morning if she still wants to. The fact is she doesn't turn me on all that much, but I know I'll be able to have it off with her again in an hour or two. After a few minutes, I go to sleep. I've no idea if she does too. It seems only a few minutes later when she wakes me up, stroking my back.

'Max, it's six-o-clock. I want to make love again. I've got to take Louis downstairs for a few minutes, come back here and leave to go to work at 7.15. So, what about now?'

This time, with a little instruction from me to go slow, it lasts a bit longer, but she still doesn't come. That doesn't seem to worry her.

She's clearly the sort of person who is run by the clock. At 6.30 she says:

'Right. I've got to get up now. I'll be out by 7.15. Look, I want you to deliver me a pizza again this evening.'

'If you ring Hassan it'll be a one in two chance you get me. But I can probably fiddle it that it's me. In any case, I certainly won't be able to stay the night again or it'll be ta-ta and thank you from him and I don't wanna see your ugly mug again. I'll get the push. An hour max is all that it'll be.'

She says that's OK and she'll show me round the flat. Then I can be off when I want to. There's a second bedroom where Louis is during the day. She tells me not to go in there or he'll go mad. Then she shows me what she calls her study which has papers all over the place. Not just the desk but on the floor and all over the bleeding place.

Bloody hell! That's four rooms and a kitchen just for one person. She takes me into the kitchen and says I can help myself to anything I want before I leave. The door is self-locking so when I go, all I have to do is make sure it's shut. There's just one thing. If I move her papers or even touch them, she'll murder me the next time she sees me.

The front door shuts with a slam and she's off to wherever it is that she goes to work in a white top, grey jacket and skirt. They make her look like the banker I assume she must be to afford this place. I shower, dress and make myself a Lavazza.

Then I wander round the flat. It crosses my mind to do a major nicking operation. But she knows where I work and could trace me easily enough. All the same, I can't help casing the joint to see what she's got that's worth the take. Not much obvious. There's a couple of locked boxes in a drawer of the cupboard in her bedroom. That's where she must keep her bling.

Hassan's pretty busy that day. I'm scooting around all over the place for him from mid-day onwards. It doesn't surprise me that I miss Fiona's call. But the next day Hassan asks me to do the delivery to her flat at around eight in the evening. I tell him I might be a bit longer than usual as I've a mate I want to have a drink with before my next delivery. He's not too busy and buys that, so there's no problem.

After I arrive at the flat, there's the same performance. Offer of red wine, shufti through the windows, hand on my thigh, bed and sex at the end of which I come. Like last time, she doesn't. It's sort of become a ritual already. This time though I can tell she's enjoyed it – a lot. But there's the same show of waterworks afterwards. I feel assed out. Don't know what to do about it. When she's Kleenexed her eyes she asks me how much I earn a week. I tell her around £400 for a sixty-hour week plus another £30 or so in tips. Most people, including her I want to say but don't, never even dream of giving a tip for pizza delivery. She looks thoughtful and says she wants to make me a business proposition. We'll talk about it next time.

'Oh, will we?' I say to myself. That surely is up to me as well as you. But I turn up the next day with a Norwegian and a Pepperoni and a big question on my mind. I've sweetened Hassan to give me the evening off (unpaid, of course), after which I've bought the pizzas off him to sweeten him up a bit more. I ring her doorbell, assuming she is going to be at home.

She lets me in and we go through the ritual with even more enthusiasm on her part. After she's dried her eyes and dressed, we sit in her living room. She pours me a glass of red wine. Then she remembers something, goes into the kitchen and comes back with a plate of crackers with some rather tasty spread on them.

Then, she puts it to me.

'Look. You're earning about £400 a week. You've done cleaning jobs. What about moving in here? I'll give you £500 a week for living here, doing the cleaning, taking Louis for a walk every day, maybe even twice a day. He'll never have had it so good. You'll share my bed and.... all that. I'm not that bad-looking. It doesn't sound as if you have a regular partner but if you want to… make love with someone else from time to time it wouldn't worry me. No house rules apart from smoking only on the terrace and, of course, the swearing.'

I look around the flat. It would be a fucking lovely place to live. The gig sounds a good deal less sweat than what I'm doing now. I'd give up my room with Pete. She'd buy the food. I might even be able to save a bit and buy myself a scooter. Bloody hell. I'll do it.

'This is a bit sudden, isn't it? I don't even know you. You can't just start living with someone you hardly know. It won't work out. I don't even know what you do.'

'I work for the NHS.'

'You what? I thought nurses got paid peanuts.'

'I'm not a nurse, Max. I'm a consultant surgeon. And I have a private practice. I can well afford this.... and you. Anyway, I'll be saving a bit on the cleaning and the dog walking. You won't be cheap but if that's how I want to spend my money, well …'

'Hold on. If I give up my job with Hassan and you decide to boot me out after a week, he'll have got someone else. There's queues of Pakis and Poles and whatever wanting to earn what I earn.'

She's obviously thought about that. 'I'll put you on a month's notice. That means if I ask you to go, I'll give you £2,000 as a parting gift. You'd have to trust me about that. I hope you'd give me a bit of notice too.'

I really want to do this, but I just have to say:

'Look, we hardly know each other. Fucking, sorry, excuse my French, but I've got to say it, is just one thing. We'd have to eat together, watch TV together, talk for goodness' sakes. It's a bit insane, this.'

'I don't watch television. Max. It's true you don't know me, but I know you a bit better than you think. You've obviously forgotten, but you had delivered here about half a dozen times before last Thursday. It isn't sensible of me to admit this, but you turned me on the first time you came here. It's got worse or better, I don't know which, every time since then. You just turn me on. A lot.'

I don't quite know what to say about this. Usually, if some bird says I turn her on, and this is not the first time, I manage to pay the compliment back. At least to say something pretty meaningless, like:

'Well, you're not bad-looking yourself.'

But this time, I'm struck shit mute. Don't know how to react. I don't need to. She just goes on:

'Besides, I seem to have got to the stage when I quite like the idea of some company in the flat. The sort of company I don't have to worry about. I don't want some barrister or business person. I'd have to do too much thinking and there's quite enough thinking to do at work. Don't be offended, Max, but I won't have to do too much thinking with you. I just want someone who's going to be around. What do you think?'

Offended? I'm not at all bleeding offended. No one's every accused me of being brainy. Didn't exactly win all the prizes at school, except perhaps for being a prize pain in the ass. Now it seems like being a bit thick is a fucking advantage.

So, it's settled. I'll move in on Friday. I've got to get to know Louis. It seems that getting to know fucking Louis is going to be more important than getting to know Fiona. He won't take to me at once and by Monday I've got to be able to take him for a walk. She'll show me where and what to do over the coming weekend.

I give Pete a week's rent and tell him I'll be moving my stuff out on Friday. I tell Hassan that Thursday is my last day. He says he doesn't think my mind's been on the job recently, so he won't miss me. Thank you, Hassan. There's no one else who needs to know. There's one or two blokes and one or two birds I see every so often, but it looks as if I'll still be seeing them. I don't think I'll be telling them about this arrangement.

So, on Friday evening I move in. I borrow a van from a mate. One journey is quite enough to move my stuff. The TV is Pete's and all the rest fits into a couple of suitcases. I'm to keep my stuff in her room for a couple of days until Louis gets used to me and then I can use the cupboards in his room. It's clearly not going to be my room. Louis, who, Fiona tells me, is named after some French geezer who discovered bugs caused infections in wounds and made surgery safe, is going to be a real pain. He's apparently a Boston terrier, very affectionate. I've never known a dog be affectionate to me, but we'll see.

Over the weekend I get a crash course in living in Princess Towers. She tells me she's on call one weekend in three and this is a weekend off. Her machines and cleaning stuff are all pretty standard. I've seen them all before when I was working at my cleaning job. She has a vast freezer which is full of expensive looking stuff. There must be about twenty bleeding packets of prepared dishes in there. She's not vegetarian, thank God.

Then we go out with Louis on a lead. First, she introduces me to the old, uniformed geezer in the entrance hall downstairs. She tells him I'll be staying in her flat from now on. Could he tell the others on the desk? The bloke gives me a long eyeful and just maybe the trace of a wink and nods.

Then we go to the local Waitrose and she tells me what she buys for food. Apart from the prepared meals which she gets delivered, it's all salad and fruit and not much else apart from cans of dog food. She says she's going to pay and I can buy anything I want. I pick up several tins of baked beans, some spaghetti rings and a few large packets of barbecue flavoured crisps. For old time's sakes, I buy a couple of pizzas, taking trouble to get the same ones she has ordered from Hassan. At the checkout, she's very short with the girl at the desk when she can't find the bar code on the cucumber.

'There it is. In front of your eyes,' she almost shouts at her. I feel sorry for the girl. Doesn't seem like a shouting offence to me. We walk back carrying our bags along the side of a so-called lake along a route she tells me I should use when I'm taking Louis for a walk. Louis seems to be familiar with most of the trees along the way. She scoops up his poo and puts it into a bin along the way. I'm meant to watch but turn my eyes away.

On the way back to the flat, I ask her what sort of surgery she does. She tells me it's ear, nose and throat. In fact, it's mainly cutting out cancers in the head and neck. But it's also sorting out the messes other surgeons have made in that part of the body. She's obviously got a pretty good opinion of herself and thinks a lot of other surgeons are fucking rubbish. My words, not hers. I like the way she talks to me about her job. She seems to have made up her mind that if we are going to live together she will have to treat me like a human being, or at least a lot better than that checkout girl.

Back in the flat, she shows me where all the food goes. Our first meal together, lunch, is a bit of a laugh. She cuts up lettuce, tomatoes, cucumber and makes herself a salad. I heat up a tin of baked beans. She tells me she's going to work for the afternoon and evening. Have I got any plans? When I had my own place, I was so whacked after my delivery work I just used to flop out and play on my screens or listen to my music. Now I'm not at all tired, but there's nothing else I want to do.

Most of the time, I play Grand Theft Auto V on my phone. I gradually learn how to pull off more and more fantastic heists without getting nicked. The time goes pretty quickly. When I get bored I watch a few quiz programmes on the shit telly she's bought me. I have the idea maybe I'll be able to talk to Fiona about more things if I learn the answers.

Over the next three or four months we sort of get used to each other. There's a lot of getting used to for both of us. I feel I've found myself a very comfortable little number here. I've no intention of leaving. But I can see that really the only reason she keeps me on is the sex. She just loves it. She still doesn't come but she's stopped turning on the waterworks afterwards. She won't try anything new, but she wants it to last. Christ on a bike, does she want it to last? After fifteen or twenty minutes, I'm totally hacked off, but she pleads.

'Don't come. Don't come yet.'

I murmur I'm unable to hold back and there's a grunt of disappointment after I come as I pull out. After two or three weeks of this, she starts to stroke my belly after I've come.

'What's all this then?', she says.

'What's all what?'

'Your tummy. You've got more than a bit of a pot here. You're only twenty-four, for goodness sake. You've been doing too much sitting around, playing games on your phone. It'll just get bigger, you know. You've got to do something about this.'

So, it's agreed I go to the City Lights Health Club up the road. She pays, of course. I go every morning apart from Sundays and spend a couple of hours on the machines. Thirty lengths in the pool, lifting weights, treadmill. I've never been so fit. A coffee and then a repeat performance. The pot shrinks; the muscles start to bulge. Every night before we fuck she does a sort of inventory of my body, just to check it's all moving in the right direction. I feel a bit owned, like I'm one of her fucking collections.

We settle into a routine. She leaves to go at 7.15 every morning apart from Sunday. Mondays to Fridays she goes to the hospital; Saturdays she goes to the private clinic. She does her what she calls her private operating on Friday afternoon and goes in to see the paying victims, as she calls them, the morning after. She gets home around 7 in the evening, apart from Tuesdays and Thursdays when it's later. She tells me Thursday's the evening she goes to the pub with her 'team' after work.

Except on Tuesday evenings, she doesn't ever go out or watch the box. We eat together. I've given up the tinned stuff and eat the same as her. Once you get used to it, it tastes OK. She tells me about some of the things that have happened at her work. Not the cutting stuff, but all about the paperwork which drives her mad. The bloody (her worst word) managers. The way they mess up her lists, so she can't operate as often as she wants to. The porters who can't speak English and push trolleys to the wrong operating theatres. The paper work is all the fault of the bloody government which keeps reorganising things. Now they've got this new man, Blair, in. But it's not going to change anything. One long moan.

I tell her about some of the conversations I've had at the health club. There aren't many as I keep myself to myself in case anyone asks what my job is. I don't tell her about the birds I chat up while I'm there.

In the afternoon, I take bloody Louis for a second walk round the lake and sometimes a bit further. He's already had a little trot around the lake before I go to the Health Club. I must say I've grown to quite like Louis. He's always glad to see me. It's a new experience. With him sitting on my knee, I watch a bit of horse racing. Occasionally I put a bit of money on which I lose. But it doesn't matter. I'm saving quite a bit from what she gives me. The purchase of a scooter is in sight.

Then, after supper, she goes to her study and works until about 10.30. She seems to be editor of some sort of an ear, nose and throat magazine. This means she has to read papers that have been sent to her and decide which are good enough to be published. Not many, I gather. I hear her muttering about them. 'Can't even spell.' 'What rubbish', and so on.

Sunday afternoons she spends on her 'collections'. She gets out her two display boxes, one of Georgian butterfly brooches and the other of Victorian thimbles. Then she's on to her laptop looking for new things to buy. She's shown me what she's got. You can keep the thimbles, but the brooches are quite something. They're not cheap either. She shows me two or three worth several k.

She doesn't seem to have many friends, but there is this one woman she sees on Tuesday evenings who is also a doctor. Someone called Ellen she met at medical school. They just go out for a meal. It's not a long evening as this Ellen has a young son she doesn't want to leave with the baby-sitter for too long. Fiona tells me she goes walking in Scotland with a group for a fortnight once a year. Her Mum lives in Hull but she only gets a fairly short phone call a week.

A month or so after I arrive, she gives a drinks party for her team in the flat. She tells me this is something she does every six months or so. I suggest I clear out for the evening. But for some reason she doesn't want this.

'No. I'd like you to be around. Maybe you could serve the food and drinks. I always have it brought in.'

'They're bound to realise I live here.'

'No, they won't. It won't cross their tiny minds. They don't know this, but *I* know they call me the Iron Virgin.'

And indeed, they don't seem to cotton on. They're a strange fucking mixture, her team. About twenty of them. Germans, Poles, Pakistanis, anything you can think of. Only two of them British. They're not all doctors and nurses. There are one or two speech therapists and a man who tests hearing. She's the only woman among the five consultant surgeons. After eavesdropping a bit between keeping them tanked up, I understand why. They're all bloody frightened of her. I hang around a little group talking about her.

'You know that man who was brought in with glands all over the place and his tumour blocking virtually everything in his neck? He'd been turned down for surgery by pretty well every ENT surgeon in London. But his wife was desperate, had heard about Fiona and pleaded with her to operate. And she bloody did it. It took her ten hours and fifteen pints of blood, but she did it. Her dissection. Amazing.'

As the drink and the food she's had brought in circulate, the groups start to get more lively. Especially when they don't think she can hear what they're saying.

'Bloody rude though,' I hear someone else say when she's well out of earshot. 'The way she talks to the students! Especially the women. She made two of them cry on the last ward round. And in theatre. 'If you can't hold a retractor for an hour without shifting from foot to foot all the time, you should be a shop assistant; you certainly shouldn't be doing medicine'.'

'Yes,' says another in this group, who might be a nurse. 'She didn't make too many friends during the junior doctors' strike. Told her own juniors that if they wanted a reference from her at the end of their jobs, they'd better stay at their jobs. They did, of course. She told them she worked 70 to 80 hours a week when she was training, and they were lucky to get every third evening off.'

There was something else I learned from an interchange in the kitchen, while Fiona was in the living room.

'Have you noticed? I never thought of her that way, but I think she's become a bit more of a woman. I caught her looking at Ronaldo the other day. For one wild moment, I thought she might be fancying him.' The young man who made this remark, probably a junior doctor, one of the few Brits there, seemed to me a bit full of himself.

Another, older man, didn't agree.

'Bollocks. She's the sexless bitch she always was. I know she loves gossip, so the other day I told her about how Charles is probably having it off with Sue. She said she just didn't understand how a man like Charles could let himself down like that. She obviously hasn't noticed how half the nursing staff, never mind all the women medical students who aren't lezzies, are gasping for Charles.'

So, maybe my little Fiona is having a bit of a sexual waking up. Lucky for her she's got me around now her hormones are beginning to trouble her.

When the guests have left, she's really pleased no one seems to have picked up I'm living here. It's as if she's played a trick on them and it's worked. She's really chuffed with me too for not having let on.

'Let's just leave this stuff,' she says, pointing to the dirty glasses, crumbs on the carpet, plates with half-eaten food on them. 'You can clear it up in the morning. Let's go to bed.'

So, we do. And, for the first time, she gets there. Jesus wept, it's about time.

It's about a fortnight after the drinks party she suddenly appears in the middle of the day. She goes straight to her study without even looking at me, let alone doing any explaining. In the evening, she turns up for supper but again, not a word. She comes to bed at 10.30, the usual time and, as usual, I fuck her. No sounds of pleasure this time, also no waterworks. But after, instead of just giving me a hug and turning over, she wants to be held for much, much longer before finally she releases me and turns over the other way.

In the morning, she doesn't go off to the hospital, just lies in bed while I take Louis out for his walk, come back to the flat and go off to the gym. She doesn't want any lunch. At supper, we eat in silence. She just toys with her food. Bed is the same as last night except this time after sex she holds onto me until she goes to sleep. I can't sleep like this and eventually extract myself from her and turn over. For fuck's sakes, what's going on?

In the morning, before I leave for the gym, she's in her dressing gown. It's long after she should have left for work. I decide I want to know what's up.

'Well Max, I've got to tell you. I've been suspended from the hospital. For the time being anyway, they've stopped me working there.'

'But you're supposed to be this bloody brilliant surgeon. How can they do that? What you done? You've not been caught having it off with one of the Polish porters?'

She doesn't think this is funny.

'Come on then, Fiona. Hand in the till or what? You can tell me. I'm sure I've known worse. It's a bit of a relief to find out you're not all that perfect, after all.'

'It's nothing to do with any of that. Last Thursday, I shouted at a patient. I was supposed to operate on her that morning and she changed her mind and withdrew her consent. It was going to be a three-hour operation, and it was too late to call for anyone else. We've a six-month waiting list for routine operations. It meant a whole morning wasted. What was I supposed to do?'

'Sounds to me as if you had every right to freak out. Anyone would've done.'

'Well, it wasn't quite like that. I really did lose my rag. Called her all sorts of names. Even used some of those words I've told you not to use here.'

'All right. Maybe you did wrong. But why can't they just give you a bollocking. Tell you it mustn't happen again.'

This time she gets pissed off with me. Her voice goes up a bit.

'Max, that's not the way the NHS works. Some nurse, who isn't my most ardent fan, wrote to my Medical Director. Probably exaggerated a bit. Told him this wasn't the first time by a long chalk. It didn't help that the woman in question was black. I … er, I might have brought that up when I was on at her.'

There is a long pause while I take this in.

'So, what's going to happen?'

'The Medical Director has to decide whether there is a case to answer. He'll probably decide that there is. Then he has to set up a panel to decide if it's all true and if it is, what the penalty ought to be. The whole process lasts for ages. The Medical Director doesn't come back from holiday until the end of next week. Then there's all sorts of ways they can string it out.'

'What might they do?'

'In the end, I've been told I'll probably get what's called an oral warning. That's really what you call a bollocking. But they could give me a written warning. They might even dismiss me, though I don't think that's likely. Frankly they can't afford to. I'd appeal and probably win.'

'What about your patients? Do they just have to wait until you come back, or don't come back?'

'Oh, they'll bring in a locum. He'll be able to do the routine stuff, but he won't be up to the more complex work. That will just have to wait.'

'How're you going to manage? Financially, I mean.' To say I'm thinking of myself would be a bleeding understatement.

'There's no problem there. I'll be on full pay while they sort out what they're going to do. They haven't decided if I can carry on doing private work yet, but I expect I can. And

even if I can't and they dismiss me I'd still be able to get work in the Gulf. Plenty of it.'

So, we settle down to a slightly different routine. Instead of the hospital she sits and works in her study. After a week or so, it turns out she can continue to work at the private clinic. Indeed, she now does an extra half day there. So, she's earning even more dosh.

We carry on more or less as before in the day. It's just that she's in her study not in the hospital. The nights are a bit different though. I've fucked her every night for the past five months except when she's got the painters in. Now, more than occasionally, she doesn't want it. I'm a bit alarmed.

What's all this? It's a relief not to have to perform every night, but if I'm not performing, what am I doing here? Also, she's losing her rag with me quite a bit more often. It's mainly over fucking Louis. I don't see why she shouldn't take him out a few times if she's at home in the flat. She thinks I've got a 'bloody nerve'. I suspect it's being stopped from operating that's affecting her temper. Whatever it is, I don't like it.

After about six weeks she gets a letter saying she's got to come in to see the Medical Director who, it turns out, will give her the bollocking he could have given her right at the start. Then she can go back to work. I'm pleased for her, but things are not the same. She's not a happy bunny anymore and it's me that's suffering. I can see that it's not going to be long before I get my marching orders with two thousand quid and a kick up the arse. That's not good enough.

My thoughts have already been turning to Izzy at the Health Club. A website designer who seems to be doing pretty well for herself at a City firm where she goes in the afternoons. She uses the gym most mornings and we've had chats. One or two afternoons at her place quite a bit more than chats. The sex with her is a lot more interesting than it is with Fiona. She's clearly been around. She's not a great looker, more than a bit chunky. Could do with losing a couple of stone which she's trying to do at the gym. She isn't with anyone and clearly won't be while she's the shape she is.

Over mid-morning coffee I've spun her that I'm an estate agent, so successful I only need to work in the afternoons. I make her laugh telling her stories about clients I've made up.

'There was this old dear, not bad-looking but old, old.

I was showing her the bedroom in this two-million pad in Knightsbridge. She nods at the bed and says, 'That looks like a useful bit of furniture.' 'Oh yes' I say, 'What do you think it could be useful for?' 'Oh well,' she says, 'If you really don't know, perhaps I should be looking at some other place to buy.'

I told her it was my time of the month. She laughed and said well, maybe we should look at the flat again in a few day's time.' Next time, I got one of my mates to show her round.'

Izzy thinks I'm living at home with my Mum and Dad after a bad break-up leaving me too skint to buy a place. I hint things at home are awful and I'd be glad to move out. She soon swallows that one and says why don't I move in with her? She's got an extra room but maybe, just maybe I won't need it.

So, one morning, I just scarper. I pack my stuff; it still goes into a couple of suitcases and get a cab to Izzy's. I decide I'll do without the two thousand grand but make up for it another way. So, I nick all her brooches and take them with me. I leave the thimbles; probably rubbish any way.

I can't put the brooches on e-bay. Fiona would soon be on to me if I did. But I've a mate who specialises in back of the lorry deals. He'll see me right. As I see it, I've earned what I get for them. For services rendered, you might say.

I have a picture of Fiona getting back that evening and hearing fucking Louis scrabbling around in his room. I've not left a note, but she'll realise soon enough what's happened. The first thing she'll do is to go to her boxes and find her brooches missing. She'll be bloody furious. Lose her rag completely. What will she say to herself? She's so loaded it's not going to be a big deal for her. I suspect she'll think:

'Cheap at the price'.

As I hear the key turning in the lock and Izzy returning home, maybe that's a bit how I feel about myself too.

LIVING WITH GOLDIE

Our wedding. It was such a happy event because nobody came. Well, hardly anybody. Just Naomi's aunt, Rita, and my cousin, Sam, Kebir's son. Sam only came because he hadn't understood from the rest of my family that he wasn't supposed to. Aunt Rita came because she loathes all the rest of Naomi's family. She wouldn't have dreamed of coming if she had thought they would be there. Anyway, we had our two witnesses, so all was well.

My Mum and Dad would never have come. When I told them, I was getting married to Naomi, I thought I had given them both heart attacks. They had tried to hitch me up to so many Hindu ladies, but I had always refused them. Now, they both clutched their chests, groaned and then put their arms round each other as if they were saying their last goodbyes. When my Dad, a small man with a droopy moustache, regained the power of speech, it was only to say:

'Look, Adi. When my brother paid for you to come with us over here from India, he wasn't just offering to give you a training and a job with him. Your uncle wanted to bring you back into the family. He did want you to be part of *us*. Do you have to do this to us, Adi?'

What could I say? I said 'Sorry, Mum. Sorry, Dad. I'm going to marry Naomi.'

After all the hoo-hah signing was over, we went to a pub around the corner from the Registry Office. Aunt Rita told us she had been to a bar mitzvah of one of her great-nephews the previous week. She is only going because she is especially fond of the young man in question. She told us that the guests seemed to have nothing else to talk about but Naomi's marriage.

'Marrying a schwartzer,' her mother had moaned. 'How could she do this to me? It won't work out. That girl hasn't got a brain in her head.'

'Trouble is,' her father had said, 'She's got too much brain in her head. If she hadn't been to University, she would never have met this man.'

'Yes,' Simon, Naomi's osteopath brother had added, 'From a little girl, Naomi always wanted to be different. She wanted trousers when all the girls were wearing skirts and skirts when all the girls were wearing trousers. Her hair went from orange to green and then back again. I called her my traffic light sister.'

I am never knowing any of this. For me, it wasn't Naomi's brains or lack of them that were the big attraction. It was her face and her body and the energy, the bright light in her eyes. She was so alive. Her brains were a bonus, but only a bonus. It isn't just Naomi's looks. I find all ladies – well, nearly all ladies between sixteen and fifty-five, attractive. As I get older, the ages of ladies that turn me on go up. It seems that there's a moving ceiling, twenty years or so higher than whatever my age is at the time.

It's hard to imagine, but that means when I'm sixty I shall be looking at eighty-year olds in this way. Maybe it's not so hard. I think my 70-year old father still finds my Mum desirable. And they had an arranged marriage. Amazing to think he could still want her when they only got together in the first place because their two families knew each other in Delhi all those years ago and their families thought it would be a good idea for them to marry. All the same, no such arranged marriage for me, thank you very much.

I find it difficult to understand why all men don't have the same fascination. I'm walking along the road and this good-looking young lady is coming towards me. As she approaches I can't take my eyes off her. As she passes I want to swivel round and continue to gaze at her. Yet I can't help noticing other men don't seem to give her a glance. They just carry on walking not even seeming to notice her. It's as if this heavenly being doesn't exist for them. I look very hard to see if there are even just faint flickers of interest. Not a bit of it. What has happened to their hormones, for goodness' sake?

It isn't that I want to make love to all these ladies. Even if there was the opportunity (and there never is), I wouldn't want to do that with them. But in my perfect world I would want to stop them, and perhaps ask them if they would have a cup of coffee with me just so I could chat to them and carry on looking at them. I would have been happy not to make love with Naomi. When we got together, it wasn't me who made the first moves for that. She did; indeed, in the end with what seemed like some impatience as she could see I wasn't going to get around to it. Then, not long after, it turns out she wants a baby. So, of course, there's no option. Otherwise I would have been quite happy just looking at her, maybe what the boys at school called 'stroking the salami' from time to time, but mainly just looking.

Although I have this idea of myself that I'm attracted to all ladies under the age of fifty-five, I do have my ideal lady. She's blonde, with long fair hair flowing halfway down her back. A bit below average height, like me, and slim, not all that much like me. I love these romantic American movies from the 1970s on; I could watch them forever. Indeed, before Naomi, that's just what I did most days when I got home from work.

My favourite, the one I could watch, indeed the one I do watch over and over again on Youtube or on DVDs when there are any, is Goldie Hawn. She's just my type. Blonde, petite, cheeky, full of fun. I like her especially when her part makes her a control freak, the boss. In *Private Benjamin*, she's an army recruit who leads her battalion to victory in an army exercise, even though she's just a rookie soldier. I get a real thrill out of that. Then, in *Overboard*, she's a stinking rich wife on a cruise with her husband, lording it over the crew. She even manages to tame a rotter who chases ladies all the time, in *There's a Girl in my Soup*. I don't like her nearly as much when she's a doormat, like in *Shampoo*. I can hardly watch that. Then, nearly as good as *Private Benjamin* is *The Baby Sitter* in which Goldie plays a con-artist who outwits

Steve Martin, a not very smart architect. It's when she's the one calling the shots that I am liking her the best.

I seem to be the only person who thinks Goldie is a really, really great actress. She didn't get nearly as many awards as she should have done. But she did win an Oscar nomination for her part in *Cactus Flower*. And Steven Spielberg did cast her as his heroine in his very first film, *Sugarland Express*. If she hadn't been such a terrific actress in that, maybe no one would have given him his second film, which just happened to be *Jaws*. When Naomi told me she was Jewish, it clinched it for me. You see, Goldie is Jewish. A Jewish blonde like Naomi. When your dream girl turns into your reality girl, you are having luck. Mum and Dad would say it was in my stars to be lucky like this. I think they curse those stars of mine. I don't believe in the stars but I'm happy to be so lucky.

The way ladies are dressed is important too. What I most love to see is three or four inches of bare skin below a short blouse, like the yellow one Goldie wears in *There's a Girl in my Soup*. Maybe this has something to do with me being brought up a Hindu. We believe ... no, they believe because I'm certainly not a believer, ... the navel is the source of life and creativity. In the winter, I can't wait for the spring to come so that ladies' navels will be unveiled. Seeing this midriff, this delicious band of flesh just above the waist is somehow what makes a lady a woman for me. You don't see men dressed like that.

The other day, I am walking towards the bus stop from where I catch the bus to the train station. My eye is caught by a very attractive back view. Her appearance just right, fair hair falling to halfway down her back, slim figure, ticked all my boxes. I quicken my pace to pass her, giving her a sideways look. Wow, a lovely face to add to it all. This is a lady I would really like to get to know, maybe have a coffee with. And my luck is in. We catch the same bus, both get off at the station and I manage to enter by the same carriage door. She takes a seat and I sit opposite her.

I'm just about to make a remark to her about the train being emptier than usual when I suddenly notice she has unusually large hands and feet for a lady. I look more closely at her hair and realise it is probably a wig. The words I was about to speak disappear into the back of my throat. The 'lady' has been looking at me and I realise she has guessed that I was about to speak but have changed my mind. She gives a little smile as if she is quite pleased she does not have to talk to me. It must happen to her all the time.

Naomi knows about my fascination with ladies who look, well, a bit like her. Perhaps even as much like her as possible. She teases me about the description of myself I gave on the dating site on which we met. She knows what I wrote by heart and says she finds it funny.

'Indian gentleman, 34, a little below average height, would like to meet English lady about same age for LTR and possibly marriage. Would prefer lady with fair hair but not essential. Occupation: Accountant. Wears spectacles for reading.'

I am not knowing why she finds this so funny. As I was settling up the bill for the dinner we had at the Indian restaurant where we had our first meeting, she said:

'You know, Aditya, when I read the description of yourself I thought you would be about five foot tall. All men put on an inch or two and some a great deal more. But you really are only a bit below average height. What are you? About five feet six. Well, that's a perfectly respectable height. As you can see, I'm very small myself, so I wasn't looking for a giant. Your height is perfect. Everything else, I'm not so sure. But let's meet again and we'll see.'

When I wrote my description, I felt I had to be honest. After all, if a lady is going even to think of spending the rest of her life with you, she needs to know what you are really like. Naomi sometimes points out I hadn't, in fact, been anything like totally honest. If I had I would have written: 'would prefer any lady with fair hair'. That's true but I realise this might have put many ladies off.

Naomi's description of herself was a good deal less honest than mine. She's not 30 years old, as she said, but a bit older than me. She didn't say anything about the colour of her hair but when we started to live together I realised that she must have dyed her hair before we met for the first time. Collars and cuffs didn't match. She did say she was English and wanted to meet a man 'of colour'. A bit unusual and I liked that idea. An English lady who would actually prefer a man like me. Also, she didn't say that what she really wanted from her LTR was at least one mixed race baby. If I had known that, things might have turned out differently.

There was just one thing neither of us mentioned and, if we had, it would have maybe clinched things more quickly. Both of us were keen to get away from our families. Not only to get away from them, but to free ourselves in a way that made them realise how angry we were with them. I had always lived with my mum and dad. Naomi had been living with her parents for the last three years since she broke up with a boyfriend she had had for some years. For years they had been trying to fix her up with what she calls a 'nice Jewish boy'. She makes a face when she tells me this.

We are meeting for the fourth time in the late afternoon for a coffee in a Costa in the High Street. After we have talked a bit about our families and how we want to get away from them, Naomi suddenly gives me a surprise.

'I have a friend,' she says, 'She has a flat here, just up the road. She works in London and lives there during the week. She says she is happy for me to use her flat during the week whenever I want to. We could go there now if you like.'

'How do you mean? 'What would we go there for?'

Naomi looks at me as if I'm stupid.

'Well,' she says after a bit, 'We could get to know each other better, couldn't we?'

Of course, I realise what she means. I don't say anything.

'When we met last time, I thought you found me attractive. But maybe you didn't.'

'Oh yes, I did. *Very* attractive. I just thought we could meet like this and talk for a few times. Maybe next time or the time after that we could go to your friend's flat.'

'OK. If that's what you would prefer. I just thought all men ....'

What Naomi didn't know and what I couldn't tell her was that I would have been quite happy to carry on meeting her in coffee shops for ever. She was so lovely to look at and even lovelier when she was talking. But clearly this wasn't her idea of a future together. I realised that if I wanted to carry on seeing her (and I certainly longed to be carrying on seeing her) I would have to make love to her. I didn't know if I could do it. I hadn't ever made proper love with a lady before.

So, the next time we are meeting in Costa I say to her:

'Let's go to your friend's flat when we meet again. We come here first, and then we go together.'

'Yes, that's fine,' she says. 'It will be a treat in store.'

I think she is trying to make a joke. To be honest, I don't really see why we have to make love. We have plenty to talk about, our families, our jobs, our pasts. But if that's what she wants I know that's what's got to happen.

So just a week later we go together to her friend's flat. It's only a few hundred yards away on the first floor of an old house. It's a funny feeling as she puts the key in the lock of the front door and we go into this strange place. In the living room, there are photographs of what must be her friend's mum and dad and many others of her friend with the same man. This man is always smiling; is he really happy all the time? There isn't time to look around. Naomi obviously knows the place well and takes me straight into the large double bedroom. We sit on the bed and kiss.

She removes my spectacles, undoes my tie, takes off my jacket and then my shirt. Then she feels for me. I was really worried it wouldn't work, but as soon as she touches me I know it is going to be alright. She looks at me down there and says:

'Oh, A., I'm so pleased you are not circumcised.'

I am not understanding why she says this, but do not dare to ask her to explain.

I have brought a condom but so has she. We laugh as we discuss which one I am to put on. I tell her how I had to go to the chemist four times before I got round to buying mine. I now have four packets of paracetamol.

It is really a good feeling when we do it. She teaches me how to give her pleasure and when she comes at the end she makes the same noises as Goldie in 'Private Benjamin' when she has sex with that French doctor who turns out to be such a heel, so I know I've done the right thing.

Afterwards she looks at my body.

'You're such a gorgeous colour. And your body is in pretty good shape,' she says as she strokes my back.' Of course, I just love the way *she* looks. I tell her that looking at her body all over is better than just looking at her bare midriff. I didn't think I liked tattoos on ladies, but I do love the golden butterfly on Naomi's right shoulder blade. I would never have seen this if we hadn't gone to bed together.

After making love, we make coffee for ourselves in the living room. Because it is someone else's flat, it feels like having a picnic. After an hour of chatting, we are feeling maybe we can make love again, but Kate is coming home soon, so we have to leave.

Time passes. We get into a routine of seeing each other two afternoons a week in Kate's flat. After six months and it has always worked out well, I say I would really like next time just to have a coffee with her in Costa. There is a coffee machine in the flat which makes perfectly good coffee, but I feel I want a bit of a break from all this love-making. I don't tell Naomi, but I prefer to be in Costa with her than in the flat. I can't tell her that because I know she would be upset.

When we meet in Costa, after a bit she says:

'Look, Aditya, we are getting to the point where we have to make a decision about our future together.'

I don't want to talk about the future. For me, Spring has come and I have talked Naomi into wearing a short blouse, showing her gorgeous skin above her skirt. I am so happy as it is now. She says women of her age shouldn't dress like this, but I point to the street outside Costa where there are Indian women walking by, a lot older than her, wearing saris and showing their midriffs. Why can't we carry on meeting in Costa, maybe going to her friend's flat from time to time, if that is what she really wants?

Anyway, it turns out that meeting in Costa isn't such a great idea because it means that Naomi has time to push me into a corner about her plans for our future together. When we are meeting in Kate's flat, I can always stop her talking by doing a bit of love-making. No such diversions in Costa.

'Look, Aditya,' she starts off, 'I expect you guessed. I'm a bit older than I said. I'm 37 and I'm not getting any younger.'

I look at her. She is wrong, but I don't say anything. I had thought she was younger than me.

'I really do want to settle down with someone. If it works out I would like to have at least one child. We find each other attractive. I think you would be a great dad.'

I can't work out why she thinks I would be a good father. I've no interest in children at all. All I am wanting is to carry on seeing Naomi like I've been seeing her over the past six months. So, I don't say anything.

'We can afford to buy a little house together. Property prices in Radford are really pretty low at the moment.'

I am getting a bit anxious, but I still don't say anything.

'To be honest, I don't know how you are placed financially. But I've got enough for the mortgage. The salary of a primary school teacher isn't great but even on that, we could get by.'

I'm thinking that I have quite a big saving in the bank. Thirty thousand I've put by over the last four years since I joined Singh and Co. Uncle Kabir doesn't pay me a large sum to be his assistant, but it's quite enough for me to add to whatever Naomi can afford. Money isn't the problem. It's whether this is what I really want. Half of it certainly is; the other half certainly isn't. Again, I say nothing.

'Come on, Aditya. Say something. You must have had some thoughts about our future together. You put in your ad you wanted an LTR. Well, I'm sure you know, a long-term relationship means living together and, for most people of our age, children. So, what's it to be? I really like you. I think I sort of love you. I miss you when you are not around, and I look forward to our meetings. But I need to know because I can't go on if you don't want to commit.'

Commit. Dreadful word! I do want to commit to seeing Naomi for all of my life. But the rest ... I don't have any option.

'Naomi, I love you. It's what I really want. I can't think of anything I am wanting more than to live all the time with you.'

It isn't a long speech, but it's enough. We leave Costa hand in hand. It's the first time we've done this in public. As we walk together along the High Street, I realise it's a beautiful day. It's rained in the night and the puddles are glinting in the sunlight. Just now, it wouldn't matter if it were pouring with rain, it would still be a lovely day. We pass an estate agent and then stop and look at each other. We go back to read the advertisements. Then we look in the windows of others – each second shop seems to be an estate agent. There are at least four three-bedroom houses we can look at.

Claibourne Road is not in the nicest part of Radford, but it's not the most slummy either. There are other couples who are half and half. Indeed, when I look at the kids coming out of St. Jude's C. of E. school around the corner, I think there are more mixed-race than anything else. Our neighbours, the Patels on one side, and the Hendersons on the other are definitely not mixed. Neither of them seems to want to have much to do with us, and that's fine by me.

The Patels are older people. I think they are Ugandan Asian and came over in the seventies. He spends a lot of time in the garden. Fond of his roses, the only time he speaks to me is when he complains about the state of the fence between us that he says is our responsibility. The Hendersons are another matter. I suspect they don't like the idea of a 'mixed' couple next to them.

They decide to replace the front garden fence between us (their responsibility) on the very day that we are moving in. I say maybe it could wait a few weeks so that the man who is moving our stuff in will have a clear path into our house. Mr. Henderson says he will take out an injunction against us if we do not allow his fencers free access to our front garden on that day. It seems neighbours are all about fences.

The house is empty of furniture when we buy it. Even after the house purchase, there is quite enough money to buy some, left over from what I've saved, but we don't find it easy to agree when we go to the department store.

'Yes, I know this sofa looks good, but I want to have some comfort, Naomi.'

'That one over there you want looks like it's come out of a brothel, all purple tassels and ghastly brocade. I couldn't live with that, A.'

So, we are buying the modern one and we don't have the rugs I like on the floor or indeed any rugs at all and Naomi chooses everything in the bedroom and the kitchen, except I'm allowed a tandoori cooking pot and anything I want in the room that is to be mine to watch things on my computer. She wants all white walls and I am wanting red and blue stripes wallpaper. We have white walls everywhere except in my study room which, I must admit, turns out to be a bit of a mess with red and white wallpaper, a gold door knob and aluminium frame windows.

It is easier to decide what to cook for Sunday lunch as we can do a bit of each. We both like cooking at the weekend. So, maybe we buy a chicken and I do a very tasty tandoori. To start the meal, Naomi makes what she calls a chicken lokshen soup which is noodles and chicken broth. Pretty tasteless unless you put spoonfuls of pepper in it but of course, I tell her how delicious it is. She certainly likes my tandoori.

Naomi doesn't seem to have much spare time in the week. She takes an hour off when she comes home and then starts marking the kids' homework and preparing the next day's lessons. I get home after her, sometimes if we are busy at Singh and Co., a lot later than her. We are usually having a lot of prepared meals in the freezer. When she has finished her marking, if I am home we have one of those in front of the TV or she waits for me. She doesn't mind if I am late which is just as well as Kebir doesn't ask me if I want to work late. He just expects it and I don't get paid overtime either.

Sometimes, while we are eating our dal at supper, she is telling me about the kids at her school.

'A. I just have too many in the class. Twenty-nine seven year-old kids with just me and Penny. It's too much.'

I don't know too much about this, but I make sympathetic noises. I don't tell her that there were fifty in my class in Delhi when I was seven years old.

'And when I started to teach, A., I had some say in what I taught my kids. Now, it's all laid down. Fractions and decimals when they're seven. It's ridiculous. They have to pass tests all the time. It's this awful Gove.'

'Surely that's a good thing, Naomi. Otherwise how will you know whether they have learned anything?'

'Yes, but they're all different. I've got one poor little mite who just can't sit still. He really needs to have someone with him the whole time. The Head has been trying to get him a statement or something so that he can have more help. But it takes ages.'

'Sounds to me as if he should just be expelled. Where I come from the teachers wouldn't have had a kid like that in their school.'

'Oh well, A. At least we've moved on a bit from that.'

We agree to disagree.

She has some friends she sometimes sees at the weekend. There is another lady teacher at her school about her age, who also has an Indian partner. Duleep is quite nice, a real gentleman, but Frances is really ugly. A vast nose and no chin at all. I just shut up when they come around which luckily is not often. Mostly Naomi goes around there or sees her by herself. I know I'm not supposed to think of ladies just the way they look. Naomi says:

'A., Frances is a really lovely person. She's very, very bright. She's wonderful with the kids. They adore her. I know she's not very good-looking but that's not important. Well, I know it is to you, but it ought not to be the only thing.'

She goes on:

'Anyway, you ought to have some friends of your own. At least you ought to see your brother. I know Sanjoy has written to you since the wedding to say he would be happy to see you. Why don't you meet up with him, at least?'

'I wouldn't mind meeting Sanjoy, but he's too busy. With his wife and two little girls and his job and everything. Besides, I know all he wants is to tell me how upset our mum and dad are by what I've done. I don't want to listen to that.'

I don't tell Naomi but I've no need to see anyone else. I'm very happy with my life with her. Just as it is. The love-making is different from before now we are in Claibourne Road. Now we can do it any time. She's on the pill so that needn't stop us. Before it was maybe once or twice a week. When we go to bed all I really want to do is to look at Naomi's face and body. She wears short nighties. If I come to bed even a few minutes after her she is asleep, and I can just gaze at her. Her pretty legs, toes, it is all so good. This is the best part of my day. I don't want to touch her; that would spoil the way she looks.

But she wants to do it three or four times a week.

'Come on, A. It's time for bed. I'm just too tired to stay up and I've got to be up by quarter to seven to get to school on time.'

I know what she really means. I was worried I wouldn't be able to make love as often as she wants but it turns out this isn't a problem. As soon as she touches me, I'm ready to go. Of course, I would never touch her first. Sometimes we lie there, and I know she wants me to, but I would never do that. I could lie there forever just looking at her, so in the end, she gets impatient, comes over to my side of the bed, touches me and we do it.

When Naomi is at the end, she shouts and screams with pleasure. She does this more now we are in our own house. This gives me a really good feeling. I know I am pleasing her. The love-making all goes well unless she uses bad words, like the f-word, which she does from time to time. Or she gets me to do things to her with my tongue. I don't really like this. She stopped doing this when she realised it made me lose my stiffness so that I couldn't go into her again. I want to tell her these are things Goldie would never do, but I think she would be upset so I haven't done that.

So, all is good, but after a couple of months Naomi tells me what I knew she was bound to tell me at some point. We are lying in bed after doing it one Sunday morning.

'A., I think I ought to tell you. I've come off the pill. I've got to get going now or it will be too late.'

'Yes, you must get on with it. A good idea.'

'Do you really think it's a good idea? You've not suggested it yourself. And you always remind me to take my pill if you think I've forgotten.'

'I think it's a good idea, Naomi.'

But really it is a thoroughly bad idea. When my uncle boss, Kebir Singh, is giving advice to clients about investing their money, he always asks if they are more interested in short-term gains or in building up for the long-term. For me, Naomi having a baby is a rotten idea in both the short-term and the long-term. When she gets pregnant, in no time her tummy will lose its lovely shape. She will look fat and ugly. And then when the baby comes it will make a pest of itself. When Sanjoy's little girls were born it took three years before he had a decent night's sleep. I really like my sleep. But what can I say?

So, now our love-making is different. Before it was just for pleasure. Now it has a different purpose and pleasure is not enough. Naomi has to stop having her periods because this will show a baby is on the way. But it doesn't happen. The periods keep coming. Sometimes it seems as if they have stopped but after three or four days, it turns out they have happened after all. Naomi tells me we must do it at certain times of the month only but that doesn't work either.

After a year of trying and failing, Naomi is going to the G.P. The doctor says she really needs to see me as well. I am not seeing the point of this. After all, I am doing my part; it is Naomi who is not getting pregnant. So, we both go to see Dr. Hammond, a pretty young woman about Naomi's age, but dark-haired. She asks if we smoke or drink a lot of alcohol. We don't. Difficulty having a baby is sometimes because the lady is unfit. But Naomi is quite slim and goes to the gym once a week. We are having it enough times and at the right time of the month. Dr. Hammond is puzzled. She says she would like to refer us to the Radford Hospital where there is a clinic for infertility, but this is only for couples who have been trying for three years without success.

Naomi has another six months trying and I do my bit, but her periods keep on coming. Then she is telling me that she has been to see her Aunt Rita who has agreed to pay for private treatment which will give a baby. Her aunt has been married twice, both times to quite rich men who have divorced her and been made to give her a lot of money. She has no children of her own and Naomi has always been her favourite niece. I cannot believe how expensive this is going to be, several thousand pounds.

The next month Naomi spends looking at the different clinics on the Internet. They all claim high rates of success, some more than others. Of course, I want her to go to one with a low rate of success, but that is not her idea. So, she ends up fixing on a clinic in London, not far from Euston. Once again, the letter of appointment says I have to go with her for the first session.

The Viaduct Clinic is a really plush place. The waiting room is nothing like the one at the local Radford Hospital where I went a couple of years ago with some skin trouble. Only two people in the waiting room. Comfortable chairs. Expensive-looking splodgy paintings on the walls. And we are seen five minutes after the appointment time. The lady doctor, an older Indian lady, seems nice. The only difficult moment is when Dr. Patel asks how keen we are to have this baby. Naomi says:

'Oh, it's what I most want in the world. I've always wanted babies. When I see a pram in the street I walk to the other side of the road so that I won't be tempted to peep inside and be made to feel green with envy. But I don't really know about him ...'

There is a silence while the two women look at me, accusingly. I feel that I'm a bad, bad person. There is no way out.

'No. I know this is what Naomi wants so I'm all for it. I really am.'

That seems just about good enough and Naomi is given the go-ahead. She is given a spray that will stop her usual eggs from working. She is told when to come back to have some tests and to begin some injections that will make loads of new eggs inside her. Then I shall have to come in to give what Dr. Patel calls a 'specimen'. I know what that means.

Unfortunately, the spray has very bad effects on Naomi. She starts to get headaches which she's never had before. Maybe it's the headaches or maybe it's the spray that make her lose her temper so quickly. At school, she says the kids are really getting at her. She knows they're only kids, but she says she can't stop shouting at them. She's even beginning to put on weight so her slim tummy is beginning to lose its shape.

Things get worse when she's on the injections that make her lay more eggs. She has to have a lot of injections, four a day. She starts to ask me if I will do them but one look at my face and she knows that's not on. No way. She seems to sprout eggs in her belly like there is no tomorrow and this makes her feel bloated and miserable. We've been told we can do it, have sex, if we want to, but neither of us, not even Naomi, wants to.

Then it's my big day. I have to go up to London to give my 'specimen'. Naomi has to see the doctor at the same time. After she has been called by the doctor I'm left waiting. There is another man in the room. He is friendly and talkative. Turns out he's a minicab driver in his fifties. He's already got two children by his first marriage. Then he divorced to marry one of his regular passengers, a younger woman.

It's his second wife who wants kids; he's not so sure, so we have something in common.

'No choice,' he says. There is a companionable silence between us.

'Going off to the wank room too, are you?'

I smile at him but don't say anything.

'Your first time, is it? Well, I tell you, there's loads of good porn in those two rooms. It's my only chance to read porn magazines. My wife would kill me if I brought any of those home. Thank God for the internet and free porn sites, I say.'

The lady at reception calls me over, gives me a little booklet of instructions and a labelled pot which is completely clean but looks as if it might have had hummus in it. She tells me which room to go to. It's comfortably furnished with an easy chair or two. There are indeed porn magazines. As well as *Playboy* and *Penthouse*, there's *Loaded* and *Front*, that I've never seen before.

But I can't do it. I just can't do it. Not a flicker. After a bit, I go out, back into Reception. Luckily the man has gone and there is no one in the waiting room.

I feel an idiot. I decide I have to ask the receptionist what to do.

'I'm afraid no luck. Would it be alright if when she comes out of seeing Dr. Patel, my wife comes into the room with me?'

'Yes, of course. That's absolutely no problem. Don't worry. It happens to lots of men.'

When Naomi appears, she understands. As soon as she touches me, I'm erect but that's all. I know what I have to do. I shut my eyes and think of Goldie and, sure enough, in less than a minute I've come and all Naomi has to do is direct the stuff into the hummus pot.

It turns out I don't have as much sperm as I should. I've got twelve million of the little tadpoles and I should have a minimum of fifteen million so I've got what's called a low sperm count. This means the lab has to look at my tadpoles, pick out the very best and put them one by one into Naomi's best eggs. That's another £1,000 hole in Aunt Rita's bank account.

After they have put the egg back in her, they tell us they will do a blood test in seven days to see if she is pregnant. At five days she is sure it has worked. She is really excited and pleased, but it turns out it hasn't. A relief for me. So, it's all a waste of time and money. Naomi continues to have her periods. She has another go with the IVF. This time her misery and discomfort are even greater than the first time. I am feeling really sorry for her. I don't want this kid, but she does. I realise it means so much to her. Even Aunt Rita can't take any more of this spend, so we decide to look at the possibility of adoption. The Social Service Department that arranges adoption says we should have no problem if we are accepted. They have a real shortage of mixed race couples wanting to adopt. We can't decide.

Then, after what seems months and months, an amazing thing happens. One day, Naomi says to me:

'A. I'm pregnant. I'm really pregnant. I haven't told you before because I wanted to be quite sure. But it's ten weeks now. I've been to the Clinic. It's going to happen.'

I say how pleased I am and notice that I think, for goodness sake, I *am* pleased. It is so much what Naomi wants.

'But A. This isn't what *you* really want, is it? I just know. A., it would break my heart, but I would have a termination if you really weren't happy about being a Dad.'

'You mustn't think of it. Not for one moment. I'm delighted, not just for you, but for me.'

She knows I mean it this time and she comes over to me and looks me in the eyes. I look into hers. We have our first real kiss, ever.

IF YOU'VE GOT LEMONS

I hadn't met with Rick for maybe five years. We'd been close, very close at Columbia in the early to mid-eighties. Then, after we graduated, we joined up for a drink after work every few weeks. We married around the same time and for two or three years we came together a couple of times a year as a foursome. It didn't work out. I was working night and day, building up a massive future. Rick was plodding along in a district attorney's office, earning little and with few prospects. Our wives were very different too. My Beth, outspoken and opinionated, Rick's Kate quiet and always looking to him for what to say next. We were just too far apart.

So, I am not surprised at the hesitation in Rick's voice when I suggest that we meet for a drink after work. He would know I had made it to partner in Palmer and Palmer. A senior position in the DA's office in Queens is a long way behind that. We are probably even further apart than we had been. But we had shared many good times all those years ago. I know there is still a bond. I guess he would feel that way too. I think about arranging to meet at the Metropolitan because it's quiet, but Rick might think I am trying to impress him. He might not even own a tie. Oh, come on. He must. Even a young or junior DA … Still, I have a better idea.

'Let's meet at Tommy's for a drink after work,' I say. 'You probably know it. It's on East 43rd and 7th. Not too far away from you, I guess.'

'Right, Henry. So long as I'm not too late home. The kids mostly put themselves to bed now, but I like to be back to say goodnight before they're asleep. Could you make it at six? Then I'd be OK until 7.30.'

Rick sounded very much as he had in the past. A bit holier than thou. I can't imagine any lawyer at Palmer and

Palmer admitting he had to be home to see his kids before they were asleep. I guess he's reading them bedtime stories.

When we arrive at Tommy's ten days later there must be hundreds of people in the bar and spilling out onto the sidewalk from the surrounding law firms, - partners, associates, paralegals, secretaries and other parasites of the legal system, all drinking and shouting to be heard, making conversation impossible. It's a typical six-o-clock Manhattan scene.

'I can't talk here, Rick. I noticed a Starbucks just up the road. Let's go there.'

We sit down, me with my macchiato, him with his americano. He can see I need to talk.

'What's the matter, Henry. You in trouble?'

Rick has changed a bit since I last saw him. I'm tall and he's three or four inches shorter than me. He has a rather featureless face. His thin, fair hair has now receded so that a larger forehead now adds to his bland appearance. That makes him sound unattractive, but, when we were at Columbia, women had always been drawn to him. He was quite a player and, unlike me, had no problems in that direction. Maybe it was his sad mouth, drawn down at the corners, which made him look vulnerable and in need of someone to look after him. In theory, my height, broad shoulders and firm chin should have made me the magnet, but somehow it didn't seem to work out that way. At parties, he was the one with girls all round him. I would be on the edge of the crowd, wondering how he did it.

I ask about Kate and his kids. He has a boy of fifteen, and two girls about two and three years younger.

'They are all fine.' Rick says. 'James, my oldest has had some problems reading but is getting out of those now. Beth and Lucy are just great. Lucy's gone into a bit of a quiet phase but nothing to worry about. Thirteen-year-old blues, I expect. She seems to be doing well at school, indeed extremely well.'

I tell him about Beth, how she is as active as ever, chairing the local charity that helps dyslexic kids. There is a pause.

'So?'

'Rick, I just feel I need to talk to someone about the crazy life I'm living at the moment. I suppose I could have booked myself in to see a psychiatrist or counsellor or whatever. I can afford it, goodness knows, but I don't feel there's anything wrong with me. I really don't. On the inside, I'm great. Work has its boring moments and doesn't go well all the time but I'm earning very decently. You might think, working at Palmer and Palmer, I must be making a fortune.'

'Well, you're with one of the big players, Henry. You must be into the big time, bucks-wise.'

'I'm not. I decided the really high-earning fields, - litigation, corporate, mergers, tax and so on -were not for me. Real estate doesn't bring in as much but it's not as competitive. The funds for buying property just seem limitless. There are tricks to make money grow called derivatives I can't begin to understand, but whatever they are, they shoot up the value of real estate to an incredible degree. I make my 350 K without trying all that hard.'

'Jeez. A third of a million without trying. I won't tell you what I make. So, it's trouble at home then?'

Rick's clearly impressed by my income, but he doesn't sound as envious as I thought he might be. He seems more interested in what's going on at home, with Beth.'

'No. It's not that. Beth is just great. I still find her very attractive. Our sex life is well, less, maybe quite a bit less, but in most ways as good as ever it was. I don't have all that much time for socializing, but at the weekends she has built a good life for us. Tennis, friends in the church, people to dinner, the occasional play and concert.'

'Well, Beth always was great at the social side. I remember those parties she made up at Columbia. Anyway, all that doesn't sound so crazy to me.'

'No. That's the hard bit. I find it embarrassing to tell you about it, but it's the other women, Rick.'

I look round to see who might be listening. There's just two men in the place, one on his laptop and the other reading *The New York Times*. The guy reading the paper isn't all that far away, but he looks pretty engrossed in the article he is reading. In any case, the noise of the coffee machine means it's probably hard enough for Rick to hear me, let alone this stranger. I carry on, with Rick cupping his hand to his ear to hear better:

'At the moment, I'm running three as well as Beth. That's pretty average for me. And they're not one-night stands either. I have real relationships with all of them.'

This time there is a long pause.

'Real relationships? But Henry, you're forty-three. You're married. You're only allowed one real relationship at a time and that's with your wife. We're not college kids anymore. What are you in to? Hook-ups?'

Straightaway it sounds as if he is going to be critical. This is not what I want. Maybe I should have gone to see a psychiatrist or a counsellor after all. I'll give him another chance.

'I'm not trying to make excuses, Rick, but this is how it happened. As you know, at a place like Palmer and Palmer when you're an associate, you have to work 24/7. I was expected to bill 2,500 hours a year. That meant an 80-hour week, and, when you're a beginner, you're not talking easy stuff. It was a tough life, non-stop conferences and meetings.

'Oh, I know about all that. That wasn't the life I wanted. I'm a lot happier in the DA's office. Apart from which, I feel it's really worthwhile work. I must tell you about it some time. You'd find it interesting. It's a million miles away from what you're doing. But carry on.'

'Well, as you might guess, I had to leave home at 6.30 and usually didn't get back until after 9. Weekends I was at it too. That lasted ten, twelve years. Then, when I made partner six years ago, all that changed. It was the associates that did most of the hard grind. I wasn't free to come and go as I chose, but if I wanted an afternoon off, no one was going to ask any questions. And, of course, I was now making mega bucks. Well, when you've got lemons, as the saying goes, you make lemonade.'

Rick looks puzzled.

'How do you mean, you make lemonade? What's that supposed to mean?'

'Come on, Rick. I suddenly had opportunities. My first little venture into the extra-curricular was five or so years ago with a woman I met at an ABA real estate conference in Houston. She was from Chicago. Very attractive, married. We found ourselves sitting side by side at a bar. We had a lot in common. She'd just made partner too. We didn't talk about our marriages, not at all.'

Rick was really listening now. It's almost as if he's there with me, in Houston. He leans forward, intent on not missing a word. I look over at the man with the laptop to make sure he's not hearing what I'm about to say.

'Anyway, after an hour or so shooting the breeze, she yawned, said she was going to bed but added that, if I wanted to come by, her room number was whatever. I couldn't pass that one up. You won't believe this, but the only woman I had ever slept with before was Beth. I still see this lady every year at the ABA and we make sure we see each other at another law conference or workshop at least one other time during the year.

'Well, I guess conference trysts of that sort ....'

'Yes, but it doesn't stop there. I'm seeing one of our paralegals about once every two or three weeks. We go to a hotel and spend the afternoon there. She buys a salad lunch and I bring the wine.'

'Now that does sound a good deal more complicated. Practically. Doesn't your secretary notice anything? And emotionally, how do you cope with that and Beth and all?'

I knew Rick was always fond of Beth. It's typical of him that he should think of her now.

'This woman Alison, the paralegal, is married too. She has two kids. The idea of our getting together is, well, just never raised. Once or twice, she's said 'This is great, but Henry, if you think I could ever live with you, it would never work out. I have a really good marriage. Why should I want to move on?'

'But what about you? Have you ever tried to stop?'

'Stop? Never crossed my mind. Why should I stop? This and the rest I'm going to tell you are the most important parts of my life. A few times, Alison has said she's not sure she can make it one afternoon, maybe because one of her kids is sick, and I find myself actually praying, yes praying to a God I only half believe in, that we will be able to spend the afternoon together.'

'I'm not sure God would be very sympathetic to a request of that sort.'

I'd forgotten Rick was an enthusiastic church-goer. He says this in an ironic tone. Well, I can put up with his irony so long as he's willing to listen to me.

'I don't know if God is or isn't listening, but I can tell you it's very unusual for our meetings to be called off. And that isn't all. There are the one-offs. You can't call them one-night stands, not only because they're not at night but because they often go on for months, even years.'

'Tell me more. As if I could stop you.'

'A couple of weeks ago, I met a girl, early twenties I should think, at a client's party to celebrate some deal or other going through. It turned out we were both New Yorkers and neither of us had ever been to Staten Island. I could see she was flirting, so I said why didn't we go to Staten together one afternoon and maybe we could think of something interesting to do when we got there?'

I'm rather proud of my pick-up lines. This one or a variation of it, I've been using for years. I go on:

'Well, this girl was up for that, so we met at the ferry. I discovered it only takes 25 minutes and it's free. She knew I was married all right. I never make any attempt to pretend I'm not, but it didn't trouble her. I was a bit worried I'd be spotted on the ferry, but I told myself the chances were remote. Have you ever been to Staten, Rick? No, I thought not. Well, let me tell you. Don't go in February. The blood froze in my cheeks as it did in hers. We actually couldn't speak. But we had thawed out by the time we got to the Hilton Gardens, where I had booked a room. It went well. I'll probably see her again.'

'I'm sure the Statue of Liberty waved her torch approvingly at you both as you went by. You know, you really do sound like a college kid. Only a college kid with too much money.'

'OK. What about this, then?'

I'm warming up now, but I can't work out if I'm telling him all this because I want to impress or because I just can't keep it all to myself. All I know is that it's a great relief to share the life I'm leading. I've found it really hard to keep so many secrets in so many different parts of my mind. It's been worth it, very much worth it, but it's been tough. I suppose it's ridiculous to feel sorry for myself, but the fact is I do. I go on:

'About six weeks ago, I flew to LA to negotiate a property deal. It was big, big. I went with a finance woman from another New York firm that was putting up most of the money. We flew together and clicked on the plane. It was a very competitive field and we had to stay two nights. You don't need much imagination to work out how we spent the evenings and nights together.'

'Aren't there any downsides to this? What about Beth? Does she know? She must at least suspect?'

Rick looks concerned. He's obviously worried I'm going to make Beth unhappy.

'Downsides? Hardly at all. You know, I think Beth does have some suspicions. But she has never said anything. After one of my afternoons I'm hardly ever late home. She knows my work involves overnight trips. We get on well. The sex is not spectacular or very frequent, but it's OK.'

'Don't you ever have any trouble, er .. er .. you know?'

I can't see what Rick is getting at. Then it occurs to me that he's curious about my virility. Probably has a bit of difficulty in that department himself. I help him out.

'You mean, don't I sometimes have trouble getting it up? Well, I don't want to go into the sordid details, but, yes, it does involve a certain amount of calculated planning when, for example, I have sex with Beth. Nothing that's impossible. I think Beth and I have a very good marriage. We like each other. We respect each other.'

Rick sounds a bit shocked, but his only response is:
'Hmmm.'

There is a pause while he considers what I've said. He doesn't sound convinced.

'What about work? I know you said you didn't need to try too hard. But it sounds to me as if your partners might notice you've not exactly got your eye on the ball a good bit of the time.'

Rick looks at his watch. I look at my Rolex with a certain sense of pride. He's going to have to go soon.

'Oh, I think they're happy enough with me. As a matter of fact, after the LA trip, one of the senior partners did take me aside. It had come out that the successful bidders had spent the evenings buttering up the sellers, while I had been, so to speak, otherwise engaged. I had to explain myself and might not have done too well. But I'm not in any real danger. There are quite a lot of deals still to play for. They know that.'

'Seems to me you're going to have to watch it. Look, I've got to go now. Are you going to be OK?' Rick sounds solicitous. He's a nice guy.

'I'm OK, Rick. But it's been good to talk to you. Can we meet again in about a month or so? I haven't heard about your news. I'd like to catch up on that.'

'Nothing as dramatic as you, I'm pleased to say. But yes, let's meet again in a month. It's been interesting, to say the least. I'm not quite sure if I'm deeply envious or grateful I don't lead such a complicated life.'

So, we fix a date, and he goes off. I pick up the check and go back to the office for an hour or so before taking the commute home from Penn.

I get home around ten. I always have a sense of pleasure as I walk up the drive to my house. Even the garage, housing the Cadillac and the Jeep, is stylish. Just that extra touch of luxury in the oak timber frame. It's Beth, the architect and Jemima, the sexy interior designer she's found, who should take the credit really. But if it wasn't for my bucks, none of this would be here.

I get my supper out of the freezer and put it in the microwave. Beth has had hers with Lucy a couple of hours before, but usually joins me for ice cream and sometimes coffee after I've finished dinner. This time though she comes into the kitchen before I've started to eat. It looks as if it's she who wants to talk. I wonder if this is it. Is she going to start accusing me? What does she know?

No, it's about Lucy.

'Henry, you know I've been taking Lucy to the pediatrician every week or so.'

'Every week? Why, what's the matter with her? I thought you went a couple of months ago, because she was being so fussy with her food, but he said everything was OK. What's all this about once a week?'

'No, Henry. I didn't say he said everything was OK. You heard what you wanted to hear. What I said was that he found nothing physically wrong with her to account for her not eating and losing weight.'

'So, what is wrong with her then?'

'Well, if it's not physical, I guess it must be emotional. Anyway, that's what Dr. Lederman thinks. I don't know if you've noticed because the three of us only sit down to eat on Sundays and sometimes you're not there even then. But basically, Lucy hardly has anything to eat. She's even lost more weight over the past month since we've been going to see Dr. Lederman.'

Beth is obviously worried. In my view, she's always been a bit over-protective towards Lucy. Taking her to the doctor over the slightest little thing. Naturally, the pediatrician isn't going to tell her to worry less. He's always going to carry out investigations and they always come back negative. But he's got to live too, I suppose. Beth goes on:

'Well, I've done what Lederman said. Told her she can't leave the table until she's at least eaten something. Offered to get whatever she wants to eat. But it hasn't made any difference. Now he says he thinks she should see a child psychiatrist. There isn't one in West Addington, so he's referred her to a Dr. Stark in Princeton.'

'A psychiatrist? You must be out of your mind. It'll go on her records. She'll have to declare it when she applies to Yale or wherever. She'll never be able to get a job. Come on, Beth. She's just a normal teenager.'

'Normal teenagers don't lose weight, Henry. You've got to face it. We have a daughter with anorexia.'

'Look. Lucy is a really nice, normal fourteen-year-old. She's doing brilliantly at school. She's not very sociable; I wasn't at her age. But she does have a good friend, that girl with the squint, whatever her name is. And Lucy's great looking. She's going to be a stunner. What do you want to ruin her life for?'

'Obviously I don't want to ruin her life, Henry. I want her to start eating normally and have periods and *really* be a normal girl whether she's stunning, as you put it, or not. Anyway, I've heard from this Dr. Stark's secretary. He's offering Lucy an appointment at two next Thursday afternoon. We're lucky to get the appointment. They've had a cancellation. And I'm afraid the letter says it's necessary for both parents to come with her.'

'You know I can't come at such short notice, Beth. I can't remember what appointments I've got, but I'm sure I'm tied up.'

In fact, I can remember very well. Thursday is an afternoon I've booked out to meet Alison. I've a mass of other appointments next week but I wouldn't be able to say when any of them are without my secretary to tell me. The only one I'm absolutely sure about is the one with Alison.

On my way to bed I drop in to Lucy's room. I stand by her bed for a few minutes. She's asleep and looks just lovely. Her room is immaculate. Her clothes are laid out for tomorrow. She has put her homework just beside her school bag so that she can have a last look at it before she goes off to school tomorrow. I'm proud this child of mine is so bright and well organised. How can there be anything seriously wrong with my lovely daughter?

I don't like Dr. Stark from the moment I meet him. He's fifty-ish. Everything about him is small. He's about five feet four, has a little goatee beard and a tiny high-pitched voice. He talks to Lucy in a different, sort of oily voice, from when he's talking to us. I'll bet he couldn't make it in a proper branch of medicine, like surgery or medicine or even pediatrics, like Lederman. My own Dad was an orthopedic surgeon and he certainly wouldn't have had this man on his team. He does have a decently furnished office with a couple of expensive looking pictures and, I will say this for him, his receptionist is quite a looker.

'So,' he starts off, addressing all three of us, 'I'd like to hear first from each of you why you think you're here.'

Lucy looks out of the window; I look at Beth and she begins. She says she thinks it would be better if Lucy told her own story, and waits a bit, but when Lucy doesn't respond, she tells Stark how Lucy has gone off her food for the last six months and is losing weight and how Lederman has thought she needed to see a psychiatrist. She has this idea she's fat and you've only to look at her to see she's not. She's doing well at the private school she goes to which has high standards. She doesn't have many friends but there is one girl her age she likes.

She stops and asks Lucy if she's got it right.

Lucy doesn't reply so Stark, in his oily voice, asks her himself.

'Sometimes it's hard to talk, Lucy, especially when you're with your Mom and Dad. But we do want to know what you feel about coming to see me. We don't want to make mistakes because we don't know how you feel.'

Silence.

So, he turns to me.

'How do you feel about your daughter coming to see a psychiatrist, Mr. Lansley?'

'I don't feel at all happy about it, if you really want to know, Dr. Stark. I think girls of her age go through phases. She's obviously not happy. I wasn't at her age. But teenagers come through it the other side if they've got supportive parents and Beth and I are doing our best. This is not going to look good on her CV. What more can I say? I know I've got to go along but I don't want to give the impression I'm happy about it.'

'I absolutely understand your position, Mr. Lansley. You want to do your best by Lucy and I'm sure you always have.'

'Lucy,' he goes on, 'would you like to say something? No? OK. Well, I always like to begin by finding out a little about where you've come from, so to speak. So, Mr. and Mrs. Lansley tell me please about your childhoods, how you met and so on. But before we get on to that, I wonder if we could rearrange the seating a bit. Mrs. Lansley, could you just move away a little from Lucy, and Mr. Lansley, could you move your chair a little nearer your wife and daughter. You seem a bit out of it over there. Good, good.'

This man seems to fancy himself as a bit of a theater director. OK, we'll play along but I'm going to be very, very careful. I can see where this is going and I don't like it, not one little bit. There are too many cans of worms this man could begin to open. Lucy doesn't know that Beth's parents divorced shortly after she was born and the man she calls grandad isn't really her Mom's father.

Lucy doesn't know either that Beth got pregnant shortly after we met and that Beth wouldn't have the abortion I tried to talk her into, so that, somewhere or other, Lucy has a sister who has been adopted into another family. And Lucy doesn't need to know. It would just upset her. Then there's the largest can of worms of all - the one to do with my playing away from time to time. I don't really know if Beth has rumbled me on this one, let alone Lucy.

Luckily, Beth seems to have come to the same conclusion as me. There's no point in telling this man things Lucy doesn't know and that are obviously irrelevant to her problem, if indeed she has one. So, there's no mention of her parents' divorce and nothing at all about the adoption. Beth paints a rather rosy picture of her childhood and, as far as I know, that is indeed accurate.

I tell Dr. Stark about seeing rather little of my Dad in my childhood as he was always at the hospital. All the same, I think of him as a good father. After all, he made enough to pay for me to do law at Columbia and that can't have been easy. I try not to sound self-pitying, but the fact is my Mom constantly suffered from headaches and misery and I can't hide that completely. Nor that my older brother was a sadistic bully. I say far more than I mean to about my childhood. Somehow when I get started I can't stop. It all just flows out. I even get a little tearful. It's a lot of stuff even Beth didn't know.

As we get near the end of the ninety minutes we have been told this first appointment will last, Stark opens up a bit. He's hardly said anything for half an hour. Now he talks a basinful. He addresses Lucy, not us. He says: 'Lucy, you've heard about your Mom and Dad's early life. You've probably learned things you didn't know before. Is that right?

Lucy, still looking out of the window, nods.

'You've heard how your Dad had a hard time as he was growing up. What struck me as he told us this story of what sounds like a thoroughly rotten childhood, is that he didn't really seem to show any anger to his Mom and Dad or to his terrible brother. Yet you must agree he has every right to. From the way he spoke, I think he's really sad about his early life. Maybe even sad now. And pretty angry too. Angry with his Dad but especially his Mom.'

He's really got into his stride now. I can't make up my mind if this is your typical psychobabble or if he might be onto something. He goes on:

'I think it's hard to be angry in your family. Sometimes girls I see who can't bring themselves to eat. They tell themselves they're too fat. That's maybe the case with you. But, you know, I think also you just might be angry, even angry with *your* Mom and Dad, and find it hard to show it. Next time, I hope you might be able to tell us what you're so angry about. Please think about it, Lucy. We'll meet again in two weeks. And Mr. Lansley, I know this isn't going to be easy for you, but it really is important you make it to that appointment.'

So, there's no choice. We're hooked.

The three of us leave, not saying anything to each other at all, not a word. I drop Lucy off at her school and then drive home. We still don't speak. I feel angry, humiliated at having exposed myself in this way. What right has this man, Stark, to poke his nose into my life? I drop Beth off at home telling her I'll be late this evening, but not how late, and drive to the parking lot at the train station.

When I get to work round about six, knowing that I've about two hours paperwork to do to catch up on the day, there is a note from my secretary telling me that Hank Gardner, one of the senior partners, wants to see me. I know he'll still be at work. Hank never goes home before eight. So, I go up to his swanky office, old mahogany desk, old master paintings on the wall. It's on the thirty-eighth floor with a panoramic view of the Chrysler, the Rockefeller and the Brooklyn Bridge. His secretary isn't there but he's still around.

'Ah, Henry. Thanks for coming up so promptly. Good to see you. How are things? How's Beth? And your daughter?'

He's only met Beth twice so it's clever of him to remember her name. Probably looked it up when he sent for me. But I know he's not asked to see me for a social catch-up.

'Henry, there's a couple of rather disagreeable matters I have to discuss with you. The first is pretty minor and I'm sure you can clear it up in no time. The second will be more worrying for you. Let me tell you about the first.'

'Uh huh?' I'm worried about both. Does he know about Alison? No, it turns out.

'Henry, one of the associates in your department, Sarah Johnson, has complained about your attitude to her. She says she feels uncomfortable at the way you look at her. She feels almost attacked, sexually, by you. She says you haven't touched her. It's just the way you look at her. Do you have any comments about that?'

Oh, I know who Sarah is all right! She's the pretty associate that came into the department from taxation about three months ago. No sooner had she arrived than she started to come on to me. Bringing stuff to me when she could have chosen any one of the five other partners in our department. What a nerve to complain about me. I had, of course, put her name down on my mental list for future consideration, but she couldn't know that. Now it looks as if I shall have to cross her off.

'Hank, I can't think what Sarah's on about. I've not given her any more attention than any of the others. I don't even find her particularly attractive. Now you've brought the matter up I'll take particular care not to have anything to do with her. It won't be a problem.'

'That's reassuring, Henry. You know we had a really nasty case of sexual harassment in corporate and mergers last year. It cost us a lot of bucks. We can't afford any more of those. The other matter is more serious.'

'Now you really have got me worried, Hank.'

'Yes, and I'm afraid you've reason to be. You must be aware that the real estate division isn't bringing in the income we are looking for.'

'Well, it's around 15% of the business. That's substantial.'

'Yes, it is indeed about 15% of the business. But it's about 80% of the bad business. The real estate department just isn't sufficiently profitable. What's more, the future of real estate itself is in serious doubt. All this sub-prime business looks as if it's growing, getting out of hand. There's even talk, as you know, of one or two of the major banks going under. You must have heard of the rumors about Lehman's.'

'What does all that mean?'

'It means, Henry, that we're thinking of closing the real estate department. I won't say we've come to a definite decision, but I have to warn you, I think now it's more likely than not.'

'Hell, Hank.'

'We're having a Board meeting of senior partners next week. We may even make a decision then. Either way, I'll need a paper from you and the other partners in the department two days before the meeting so that I can circulate it.'

'Well, you'll have your paper. It won't be difficult to make out an excellent case for the department to survive.'

'If that's the case, there'll be no problem. I look forward to reading it. See you then.'

And with that I leave his office, take the elevator down to the sixteenth, go to my room, sit at my desk and stare out the window at the blank, windowless wall of the building directly opposite.

I get home at ten, drained. I've virtually exposed myself in front of a bloody shrink. Then I've more or less been warned that I may be out of a job in a few months. My God, if they make me go, they're going to face a massive compensation bill, the bastards. They're not going to know what hit them.

I warm up a carbonara in the microwave. As I start on it, Beth appears. I don't know what to expect from her. Any more flak and I'll lose it. But no, it turns out she's full of compliments.

'Henry, I just want you to know that I thought you were very brave this afternoon, talking to Dr. Stark like that. I didn't know the half of what you told him about your childhood.'

'Well, I seem to have hit the right button, even if almost by accident. Stark asked and I told him, that's all. How's Lucy been?'

'Oh, not much different. She hardly ate any of her supper this evening. And she didn't say anything about the session this afternoon. But after supper, I heard her crying in her room. She's not done that before. I went into her room to see if I could comfort her. She pushed me away. I don't know what all that means, but maybe it means something.'

'You did well, Beth.'

'I don't know if I did but thank you anyway.'

She stops as if she has something to say but doesn't want to say it.

'I'm afraid there's another bit of bad news I've got to tell you about. It's about me this time. About three weeks ago, I found a lump in my breast. I went straightaway to Dr. Keen. We seem to be seeing a lot of doctors recently. Thank goodness for Palmer and Palmer's health insurance plan. Anyway, I had a scan and it'll have to come out. They don't think it's the worst sort of cancer, but it's not just a benign lump. These days it's likely to be curable, but you can't be sure. I'm going to have the op next Friday.'

I go over to her and put my arms round her. It seems the right thing to do.

My next drink with Rick is due the next day. I think of cancelling but decide not to. I'm really not sure what I'm going to tell him, but, in any case, when we meet at Starbucks, after we've settled for the same coffees as last time, it is he who seems to want to talk.

'Before I forget, Kate sent her love and asked to be remembered to you. I told her I had met you and we were going to meet up again.'

'You didn't tell her why I wanted to see you, for God's sake, did you?'

'What do you think? No, of course not. But I would like to carry on where we left off. At Columbia, I never thought of you as a risk-taker, but you're taking a helluva lot of risks, cheating to that degree. You know eventually you're going to get found out. Beth surely will. Then you risk losing her, Lucy too maybe. Or one of your women will want more than you can give and will turn nasty on you. Or things will catch up with you at work.'

'As a matter of fact, it already has.'

I've made up my mind I'm not going to tell Rick everything that's happened since we last met, but I am going to talk to him about my interview with Hank and about Beth's lump. Who knows? I may be looking for a job in the DA's office before too long, though I'm not best qualified for that. I begin by telling him about that flirt, Sarah Johnson, and her ridiculous accusation.

To my surprise, Rick doesn't accept my version of the matter.

'Henry, I suspect you don't realize just how you do look at women. I was watching you last time we were in here. Whenever a halfway attractive woman walked in you didn't seem to be able to take your eyes off her. I can't help asking myself if the life you are leading is really worth it?'

'Worth it? If you're talking about the sex, of course it's worth it. Rick, you have no idea. I can't begin to describe the intensity of the experience of sex with a woman who freely, yes, completely freely takes the decision she wants to give you pleasure and to receive pleasure from you.'

This is something I've thought about. It comes from the heart. I go on:

'Yes, freely. Not as part of some contract, in which sex is part five of the deal you've agreed to x years ago; with part one to stay together until death do you part, part two to have children and look after them properly, part three to share all your money and part four to put up with any sort of nonsense your spouse wants to throw at you.'

'Who are you trying to convince? And when it comes to consent freely given, is that really the case? What about the paralegal in your firm you meet in a hotel room? Isn't she just a bit frightened what a partner could do to her career if she said she wanted to stop seeing him?'

'As a matter of fact, last time we met I asked Alison whether she felt harassed by me. She just laughed at me. I'm here because I want to be here, she said. And if I want to stop, I will.'

'Well, I don't know about her, but it seems to me you are sort of addicted. You're a sex addict, Henry. You're addicted to sex with as many women as will have you.'

'I thought it doesn't count as an addiction unless whatever it is you're supposed to be addicted to is harming your life. Well, sex isn't harming; it's improving my life.'

'It will catch up on you, Henry. Sure as fate, it will.'

I decide not to tell Rick about the possible closure of my Department. But I do tell him about Beth's breast lump. I can see he's very shocked, more than I would have thought. I'd forgotten that the four of us spent so many evenings together all those years ago. He must have gotten fond of Beth then, more than I realized.

We talk about other things, about Kate thinking she will get a job when their kids are older and what she might do. I can't see that happening. They're going to have to struggle on with Rick's salary.

I have finished my coffee and have to go. Rick says he'll stay a couple of minutes. He has one or two calls to make. We arrange to meet again.

As I am on my way out of the bar to get back to the office, something makes me look back. I see Rick pull his cell phone out of his jacket pocket. I'm curious why he should want to make a call before finishing his coffee and making his way home to say goodnight to his precious kids, I hang back behind a pillar to listen. Ringing home to tell Kate he is on his way, I expect. Well, no.

'Beth, darling, I've got to talk to you. You won't know because he won't have told you, but I just met Henry for a drink. He's told me about your growth. What terrible luck. I couldn't just text; I had to speak to you.'

Am I hearing right? I can't make out exactly what he's saying but it sounds like:

'Tell me … Yes … No … No … Yes, of course I understand we won't be able to meet next week now. But I'm shattered. I just hope it won't be too long. You too? Oh, my love, my darling…. Well, I expect Henry will keep me in touch with what's happening. He and I are meeting again in a month. I'm *really* sorry but I've got to go. Au revoir, my love.'

He carries on listening. She's obviously saying something to him, not letting him go. But I don't want to hear more. I slip away. Confrontation was never my style.

NOTHING LIKE FAMILY

If you'd told me a month ago I'd be at fucking Sydney airport waiting to go through immigration, I've never have believed you. I've never been further away from south-east London than this place near Benidorm we go every August. For me, abroad *is* the Costa Brava. I've never wanted to go anywhere else for a break. The sun, the beach and the bacon, egg and chips at San Felipe, this little place just up the road from the flat we always stay in. Unbeatable. Never lets you down. So, Sydney Airport is quite a change.

It began about three weeks ago when Karen and me was having our tea, sausages and chips. We was in the kitchen just about to start watching *Gogglebox* when Karen says:

'Ken, I haven't told you, but I got the sack from my best cleaning job, the one with the doctor in Princess Towers. I been doing it for five years, five fucking years and then this morning, out of the blue, this bitch ring me and say she found someone else and can she have the keys back this afternoon.'

'Hope you didn't take them back without having copies cut. She must have some valuable stuff there.'

'She does, and I know where she keeps it all. But it's no good, Ken. She'd know soon enough who done it if she had her stuff nicked by someone who had the keys and got through the front door.'

'So, what you going to do?'

'I just took them back. Some young bloke answered the door. Looked a bit of a wide boy to me. Anyway, he just took them, winked at me, said 'Thank you, I can really do with those', and give me an envelope with fifty quid in it. That's a bit more than one week's pay. Then he shuts the door in me face. That's all the thanks I get for five years cleaning up her shitty place.'

'Fucking bitch. So, what you going to do.'

'Well, there's nothing much I can do, Ken, except go to the manageress at Domestic Dreams and ask for another regular job. Trouble is they take twenty per cent. And they don't have good paying jobs on offer. It's ten pounds an hour max. So, all I get is £8. That's twenty-four quid for three hours. The doctor's job I found myself in an ad in a newsagent. I got paid fifteen an hour and didn't have to give no one nothing out of that.'

I want to cheer Karen up, so I says let's go up the Three Horseshoes. They got a new stand-up there. I just been paid for a job, so I've got enough for a few pints.

It's true I've got enough for a few pints but what I don't tell Karen is that I got a lot more than that. It's a really big job I got paid for. A couple who's just bought a new house who's got me to put in a heating system, boiler and all. With a bit of tiddlywinks on the invoices, I've made a couple of grand out of them. I shan't be telling Karen about that; you never know when a bit on the side might be more willing with a little present.

So, after supper, we give up on *Gogglebox* and go up the Three Horseshoes. There's a good crowd up there but only one other couple we know. Fran and Brian are good for a laugh, so we have quite a few pints with them. They're about the same age as us. Fran's a manageress in Sainsbury's and Brian works in a betting shop. Brian's always good for stories of people who've come in with betting slips they think they've won a fortune and turns out they got the name of a horse wrong. I think he must have his hand in the till from time to time. Probably quite easy in that sort of caper. Anyway, he seems to have plenty of dosh to throw around.

The stand-up doesn't start until half past nine and then it turns out he's dreadful. But by the time we've realised he's rubbish, it's half past ten before we roll home. Both of us is pretty pissed so we turn in. I only got one thing on my mind so when we hit the sack I start stroking Karen's neck which is my way of getting her going.

'What you doing, Ken?' she says. She knows fucking well what I'm doing. I've been doing it for nigh on thirty years.

'I don't think I want it. I'm too pissed. Maybe later.' And she turns over and starts to go to sleep.

But that's not what I want. Not what I want at all. I got wood like a fucking oak and I want it, I want it now. So, I carry on stroking her neck and then put my hand down to her thighs and move up a bit. So, she give a sigh and then turns over in my direction but she's hardly awake. I push myself in. She starts to get excited but she's really half asleep. Then it happens. She starts to murmur the name 'Tony'.

'Oh, that's lovely, Tony,' she says, slurring she's so pissed.

'Just keep going like that.'

I pull out sharpish.

'Why you stop, Tony?'

I shout at her. 'Why am I stopping? Because my name's not fucking Tony.'

She wakes up suddenly then and looks around as if she doesn't know where she is.

'Who is this fucking Tony?'

She's fully awake now and scared.

'Come on, admit it. You're screwing some geezer called Tony.'

'I'm not, Ken. I'm really not.'

'You can't expect me to believe that, you fucking bitch. Why don't you just tell me who he is?'

'Don't hit me, Ken. Just don't hit me.'

But I can't help it. There I was, all ready to fire her one and she calls me by this other geezer's name. So, I do clock her on the face. I hit her harder than I mean to. I can see she's really hurt. There's blood on her cheek and one eye's half-shut.

'You bastard. You fucking bastard, Ken.' She's sobbing and can hardly speak but she manages to go off to the bathroom where she stays. I turn over and fall into a heavy sleep. I am *so* pissed. I could sleep for a week.

But I don't sleep for a week. I wake at about nine the next morning and go for a piss. I nearly fall over on my way. I can hardly stand, and my head is like it's full of whirring and popping fireworks. The first thing I discover is that Karen isn't in our bed as I expect her to be. She's not even taken herself off to one of the other two bedrooms as she sometimes does after we've had a bit of a barney. She's not in the living room, kitchen or bathroom and there's nowhere else for her to be.

The place is a tip. There are blood stains leading from our bedroom into the bathroom. Our dirty crocks, knives and forks are still on the table in the living room in front of the TV where we'd had our supper. Two of the greasy plates have a lot of fag ends on them and one a half-eaten sausage. There are dirty glasses and potato peelings in the kitchen sink and a half-cooked sausage in the frying pan on the stove.

Not only is there no sign of Karen, but a quick shufti under the bed and I can see she's gone off with one of the suitcases. She must have taken some of her clothes. There are none of her wash things in the bathroom.

She must have gone to her mum's in Peckham, as she's done before, so I ring Bet. I know I'll have to crawl to get her back.

Bet answers and I ask to speak to Karen.

'I don't know how you got the nerve, Ken. Of course, she bloody well won't talk to you. She got here at one-o-clock in the morning. I had to take her straight to King's A. and E. They had to put five stitches in her cheek. Her face looks as if it's been hit by a bulldozer and she's lost a tooth. Lucky for you, she told them she'd fallen down the stairs. They could see she was still half-pissed so they believed her. I told her to go to the Police or the social, but she wouldn't.'

I told Bet to tell Karen I was sorry and I'd be round later in the day in the car to pick her up. She could get the bus. It's only a couple of miles away, but I don't want the neighbours to see what she looks like.

'In your dreams, Ken, will she come back to you, today or any other day. You've gone too far this time, you have.'

I've made up my mind I'm going to get to the bottom of this Tony business, so this time I start to go through Karen's things seriously. She doesn't get many letters but those she does and wants to keep she puts in a cupboard drawer on her side of the bed. Nothing there. It's more likely that she's hiding letters in her clothes drawers, so I get her stuff out, pants, tights, tops – again nothing there.

We're not brilliant on the computer but we do share an email address. I look it up, but I know there won't be anything there because we see each other's messages anyway. I give up. I need to talk to somebody.

I should really go see a customer I've got an appointment with, but I decide it's more important for me to talk to Brendan. I know where he'll be, sitting in a pub in Forest Hill, so I make my way up there. He's at the bar, talking to the barman and he's the only fucker in the place. The Mitre is not one of your fancy pubs, it's plastic chairs, plastic tables, two fruit machines, one at each end, and nothing to eat apart from little packets of peanuts at a quid each.

I get Brendan to come down off his bar stool and sit at a table, where the barman can't hear us. Brendan's a little bloke, Irish, and a bit of a lush, but sometimes I use him if I need an extra pair of hands to do a job. He's always around if I need to bend someone's ear.

'I got problems again with Karen,' I say. 'She's started talking about some geezer called Tony in her sleep.' I don't tell him the exact details about when Karen has talked about Tony.

'I just don't know what to think, Brendan. She must be screwing him, but I don't know when. She goes off to the City to do office cleaning jobs at 5 in the morning. Then she does other jobs in people's homes till she gets home at 4. She brings home good money, so she must be working all the time. Unless he's paying her, of course. I hadn't thought of that.'

'Nah, Karen's not that sort of bird. She wouldn't do that, Ken. And, to be brutal, if he's got the money to pay for sex, he's going to do himself a lot better than her. She's got, well, what they call in Galway quite a full figure.'

'So, what do I do? I can't have her screwing around, making a fluffer out of me like this.'

'If she won't tell you, Ken, there's not much you can do. Anyway, maybe he's someone she knew years ago and isn't around now at all, at all.'

'Nah, I got to know her when she was 19. She'd had her cherry popped, all girls had at that age, but I knew her well enough to know she'd never had a regular bloke.'

So, there's nothing doing there. It's too late to go around to the lady I was supposed to do her drains today, so I give her a bell and say I'll be there tomorrow. She's pissed off with me. Says she can't empty her sink. What's she's supposed to do? I tell her to call one of those big firms, but she knows they'll charge her twice what I do. She says no, she'll manage. She'll expect me tomorrow. She's quite fit, and I've a feeling she might be up for it, so I don't want to lose her.

I've still got a thick head from last night, so I go back to the flat. The lift's still not working. Bloody council not onto it, like always. Anyway, once I got inside, I switch on the telly, get myself a beer or two from the fridge and start watching *A Question of Sport*. I can get quite a few of the answers this time. Then I order a pizza and it's *Big Brother* night. Usually I watch this with Karen and we tell each other who we fancy and who's going to get kicked out next and all that. It's not so good watching it by myself, so I give Bet another ring. They're watching it, all right, but she won't talk to me and won't even ask Karen if she'll talk to me.

I got to talk to somebody, so I give Meg a bell. She knows all about what happened last night. Karen has made sure of that. As soon as she knows who it is she starts blasting me off, defending her mum and saying whatever she done, she don't deserve that.

'Dad,' she says. 'What got into you? You love Mum but you're going to lose her. If you haven't already lost her, carrying on like that.'

'Look, I can't tell you what your mum done to me. But it's bad, it's real bad. And she won't tell me the half of it. Maybe you could tell your Nan to get your Mum to come clean.'

'I don't know what you're talking about, Dad, and, in any case, I got my own worries. They just kicked Archie out of school, said he can't come back until Friday. That's three days I've got to find someone to look after him. And I've got to go to work. They want me to go up to the school tomorrow afternoon to talk about what they call the 'next steps for Archie'. I can't think what they're on about. He's fine at home.'

'I'll come up with you, Meg. I've got a job, but I'll have finished by three. He's a normal seven-year-old, Meg, and don't let them tell you anything else. I'll pass by you at three and we'll go up together.'

'OK, Dad. That could be helpful. Provided you don't lose your rag. You know what you're like. We've both got to be calm. Do you think you can do that?'

'Course I can. I'll see you at three tomorrow.'

I don't sleep too well. Too much beer, too much telly and no Karen in the bed. But I wake at nine, get myself a large coffee, pick up my rods and motor over to Clapham to do this blocked drain. It's a pretty nice place but I can see there isn't money to throw around or she would've got Thames Drains or one of them big firms to do it.

The lady wants me to get on with it straightaway. It's an easy job really. Would take me half an hour if I pushed it, but I make it last an hour and groan a bit about how hard it's been. She's pleased when I tell her what I'm going to charge her and offers me a tea. So, I say I'll have a coffee if that's OK and I hope she'll join me. She looks a bit surprised but says she will.

I look round. It's a big house but neglected. One or two places in the living room with damp showing through. I notice there are pictures on the wall, but some blank spaces where it looks like some have been recently removed. I ask her how long she's been living there, and she says five years, but it won't be much longer. She and her partner have split up. He's left and taken half the furniture. She points to where the pictures he's taken used to hang.

She can't afford to keep the place up, so she'll have to sell it and move out.

'Well, I'm sure it won't be too long before you find someone else. Someone looking like you? No problem.'

'Come on,' she says. 'Flattery won't get you anywhere.'

She's wrong about that; very wrong. I'm really not sure now if she is up for it but, in my experience, the chat-up lines that make them laugh have the best chance of success.

'No. I'm sure it won't. But you don't look like a lesbian to me.'

She laughs. A good start.

'Tell you what, I bet you don't think of plumbers as poets.'

'No, you're right. So what sort of poetry do you write?'

'Well, all sorts. In fact, I write mainly about plumbers.'

'At least that's original. Try me with one.'

'OK. What about this?

A maiden who lived by the sea,

Met a plumber who plumbed her for free.

'Said the maid, 'Cease your plumbing.

'There's somebody coming.'

Said the plumber, still plumbing, 'It's me.'

Remembering all that is a big effort for me. Them's the only words I've ever got by heart. This time, it's not worth it. She gives me a funny look.

'Well, if it's that sort of plumbing you have in mind, I'm afraid you've come to the wrong place. In fact, I think it's about time you were going. I've a few things to do.'

You can't win them all and I clearly wasn't going to win this one, so I pick up my rods, get in the motor and drive back to the flat for a kip before I go up to Meg's.

Meg has arranged for Archie and Liane to be looked after by a neighbour, so just the two of us go up to St. Martin's. Archie is in the Junior part of the school and Liane in the infants. We go to the lady at reception and she tells us we're seeing Mrs. Purcell, the Deputy Head.

We have to wait for half an hour which doesn't improve my temper and then this bint arrives. She's about fifty, a hard-faced bitch, bit like some of the teachers I had in my school. She doesn't say she's sorry she's kept us waiting. We follow her into a room where there's four chairs, a table, a display cabinet with cups the school has won and a lot of charts on the wall. There's another, younger looking woman in the room. Not a bad looker, either.

Mrs. Purcell says:

'Good afternoon, Mrs. Langley, and this is ....?' (indicating me as if I'm an unwanted add-on). Mrs. Langley, you know Archie's class teacher, Deborah … (the good-looker gives a smile).

'Yes, my ex, left about two years ago. He's in Scotland now and doesn't see Archie. This is my Dad. I hope it's OK for him to be here?'

I am looked at suspiciously as if I might cause trouble. I'm a big bloke and they probably don't like the look of the snake tattoos on my arms.

'That's fine. Now, Mrs. Langley, you will want to hear why we had to exclude Archie temporarily the day before yesterday. As you know, because you've been up to the school quite a number of times to see Deborah, we've been finding Archie very difficult since the beginning of this school year. It's June now so that's over two terms.'

Meg says, 'Yes, he's not got on with Deborah. Nothing wrong with her, I'm sure, but somehow the chemistry isn't right. He was alright last year.'

'Well, his behaviour wasn't great last year either. Anyway, the fact is that for the whole of this academic year, he's been a very disruptive influence in class. He keeps shouting out when it's not his turn to speak. He just can't sit still in his chair. So, when the class is given a task to get on with by themselves, he gets up and interferes with children who are just trying to get on with the work they've been set.'

I say: 'I bet he's not the only one.'

Meg gives me a look to shut me up and says: 'I do know his concentration isn't great.'

'Yes, he needs more attention than we can give him. He's really making very disappointing progress. As you know, he's not yet able to recognise letters and short words. He should be at his age. But we'll come to that in a moment. The really hard bit for us is his behaviour in the playground. Archie finds it difficult to play with others. Sometimes when he doesn't get his own way, he hits out. We've had three complaints from parents of other children, two girls and a boy, who say their children are frightened to go into the playground because of him.'

'Well, he complains he's been hit.'

'We have teachers and teaching assistants in the playground. I'm afraid there's no doubt where the trouble starts. On Tuesday, he hit a little boy who wouldn't give him a ball so hard he had a nasty bruise on his shoulder. Luckily his Mum didn't want to take it further, but we just had to exclude Archie. It's what's called a 'fixed term exclusion' for three days. We've got to work out together what to do when he comes back on Monday, so that this doesn't happen again.'

Meg asks, 'So, what's going to happen?'

'I think the first thing is we can't let Archie play with the others at break time. If we've got a spare teaching assistant, he can stay with her in the classroom or the school library, or he'll have to sit in the secretary's office.'

'Well, that's going to make him worse. The part of school he enjoys most is the break. He's good at football. Other boys look up at him for that.'

Hard-faced bitch says:

'I'm afraid there's no option. We just can't take the risk of him hitting another child. It could be worse next time. Then we have to think of the future. You see, Mrs. Langley, we think that Archie needs specialist help. You've probably heard of ADHD.'

'Yes, I've heard of it. I don't want him on no pills.'

'Well, he may not need pills. The first thing is to get him assessed. Not just his behaviour but why he isn't making more progress from the point of view of his education. We need to have your consent to make a referral. The waiting lists for CAMHS, the child and adolescent mental health services, are very long these days. It may be months before he's seen, so the sooner you agree, the better.'

At this point I can't hold back no longer.

'Look,' I say, 'Not so fast. You're trying to make out Archie's not right in the head. He'll be seeing a psycho whaddyacallit before you know where you are. Archie is a perfectly normal boy. He's tough. He can stand up for himself. I've made sure of that. Given him some lessons in how to defend himself, I have. But there's nothing wrong with him.'

'I'm afraid there is something wrong with him, Mr …
Langley, is it?'

'Yes, it is. Just let Archie be and he'll grow up fine. I know
because I was like him. I was slow to read. To be honest,
I'm not all that clever at reading now. And I got into a bit of
trouble as a boy. But I was left to grow up my own way, and
look at me, I'm fine. I've got a decent job. I've brought up
three lovely kids. Well, two lovely girls, and one lad I had a
bit of an argument with. Anyway, I've made my way. And I
got no psycho help. Archie don't need it neither.'

The two teachers look at each other with little smiles on
their faces, as if I'd agreed with them rather than saying what
they've been claiming is rubbish.

Meg says: 'Come on, Dad. You know that's not quite
right. You told us yourself you'd had to go to a special school.
Approved School, wasn't it called? You're always telling us
that and five years in the Army made a man of you. But you
wouldn't have had to go to this school if you'd been all that OK.'

I don't know what to say about that. Meg's right, of
course, but I don't see why she's got to bring all this up. In
the end, I say:

'Look, I grew up fine, like I said.'

'Well, even now, you've got a terrible temper on you.' I
thought she was going to bring up what happened a couple of
nights ago with Karen, but she didn't. It was something else.

'You just can't hold it. That's what happened with Douglas
when he was fifteen. He was staying out late. Time and again,
you lost your temper with him and hit him bad. He buggered
off and hasn't been seen since. You've been a great Dad in
many ways, fair enough, but if we can help Archie to be a
more normal boy by getting him to see someone now, that's
what we've got to try to do.'

So, it's agreed, Archie will return to school on Monday
and Meg will agree to his seeing a shrink. I'm completely
pissed off but there's nothing I can do.

We drive back to Meg's place not saying much. I expect
she's sorry she asked me to come along but I felt I had to
make my point.

I go back to my place, sit and watch the box for a bit. I feel I want something to eat, but there's next to nothing in the fridge. Next thing I know there's a ring at the bell and it's Bet. She says she's come to get her daughter's things. She's got two suitcases with her. She says Karen is too scared to come herself. She looks around and makes disgusted noises.

'Ken, you dirty bugger. You haven't touched a thing since Karen left. The dirty crocks still in the sink. And what have you done to her things? You've pulled all her clothes out of the drawers and just left them on the floor. Look here, her dresses, her skirts, what the hell were you thinking of?'

'What you going to do about it anyway, Bet? If she's not living here I've a right to do what I want with her things.'

Bet starts clearing up. She can't really want to do this for me. It must be a sort of woman's thing, not to be able to see dirty crocks without washing them up. I have a thought while she's drying.

'Look, Bet. I need to talk to you. I know that Karen has been screwing around. Don't ask me how I know, but there's some geezer called Tony she's seeing?'

Bet stops what she's doing straightaway.

'Tony?' she says, and then 'Christ Almighty.'

She obviously knows who this Tony feller is.

'Well, come on, tell me, Bet. Just tell me who he is. You know, don't you?'

But by this time, she's got herself together.

'Tony? No, no idea, Ken. I've never known no Tony.'

'Don't be a bloody liar. Just tell me.'

She won't say another word. She puts all Karen's clothes in the suitcases she's brought, calls a minicab and she's off like a cat that's had water thrown at it.

I feel I need a bit of advice, so I go up The Mitre to see if Brendan's there. Sure enough he is and I drag him down from the bar to a table. I explain what's happened and how I'm sure Karen's mother-in-law knows who this Tony is.

Brendan is silent for a bit. Then he says:

'Look. Karen's already made it clear she's not going to tell you. I think your best bet is to frighten her mother-in-law.

Suppose you tell Bet that unless she tells you who Tony is, you're going to follow Karen no matter where she goes and you're going to do her face in so bad that punch you gave her will look like nothing. If she does tell you about Tony, then you'll do *his* face in and you promise you'll never lay your hands on Karen. That way she can be sure her precious daughter is safe.'

'Why should she believe me, Brendan?'

'Oh, she'll believe you. You got history. Not for a few years, it's true, but you got history. Years ago, you glassed that bloke you didn't like the way he was looking at Karen. You got away with that. He wouldn't bring charges for fear of what might happen next. But you got put inside for nine months when you slashed that geezer who didn't pay his bills when you knew he had the bread 'cos he was lashing it around. Bet and Karen'll remember. It's not the sort of thing you forget. You got history, Ken. They'll believe you.'

This looks like a good plan, so the next problem is how I'm going to get to talk to Bet by herself. I know she's not well off, so I decide to give her a bell and tell her I've got a load of dosh and want to give some to her and Karen to make life easier for them. But to do that I need to talk to Bet by herself. You know Karen doesn't want to talk to you and that's OK. Can you meet her, Bet, in the Nero just around the corner from hers? Karen won't stop Bet coming to talk to you if she thinks there's some dosh in it.

It works and six-o-clock that evening I'm sitting talking to Bet.

'Look, Bet, tell Karen I'm sorry I bashed her. I can understand she won't come home now. I'm not too skint now, so I'll give her some dosh to keep her going.'

'You can't buy Karen off, Ken.'

'Well, I got a monkey in my pocket.' Bet's eyes widen.

'But she's got to tell me who this Tony is. If she doesn't tell me, I swear I'll watch your place until she comes out and then I really will do her face in if she won't tell me. I won't do her no harm, I promise, if she tells me but I swear I will do that fucker, Tony, in. He won't know what's hit him.

I can see Bet is really terrified. She says I've got to give her some time to think. I say no, it's now it's got to be decided. She thinks for a bit and then says:

'Look, Ken. It's a bad story but I think I've got to tell you. Christ knows what Karen will think but it wasn't her fault. It really wasn't.'

Bet is having difficulty getting her words out. I can see she's really choked.

'You know Karen's got an older brother, Steve, who's three years older than she is. Well, what you don't know is that Steve has an older step-brother, five years older than that. My first, from another bloke. He's called Tony. You wouldn't know him because he wasn't around anymore when you first got to know Karen.'

'Christ, Bet, what you telling me?'

'Tony was a difficult lad. He didn't get on with his step-dad who could be a pretty hard man. And he didn't get on with me. He thought I didn't love him because I made such a fuss of Steve. He'd never do what he was told. Even in primary school, he was in trouble for all sorts of mischief, even interfering with little girls. When Karen was twelve, Tony, who was seventeen, started to have sex with her. I mean, proper sex. Not just fooling around.'

'Bloody hell.'

'Let me finish, Ken. It must have gone on for about six months. Then Karen got pregnant. Well, of course, it all came out then. Karen wouldn't say who it was had got her in the family way but in the end, she had to tell us. There was an almighty row. Bob, their Dad, you never met him, Ken, beat the living daylights out of him.'

'What happened then?'

'Tony ran away from home. We didn't hear no more from him, until five years had gone. Then we got a letter from Australia asking if he could come home. Bob wouldn't even have us answer it.'

'I should bloody hope not.'

'I think all this killed Bob. He died of a heart attack just a year later. That's why I've been by myself for nearly twenty years now. Anyway, somehow or other, Tony must have got the money to go to Australia. We've never heard from him since. He must be over forty now.

'What happened to the pregnancy?'

'Well, Karen was only just thirteen. She had to have a termination. But she didn't want it. You won't believe it. She actually said she wanted Tony's baby. Of course, she didn't know what she was talking about. The doctor who saw her put the fear of God into her about the chances the baby would be deformed in some way with a brother and a sister the parents.

'Poor little bleeder.'

'Anyway, she had the termination. But even though Tony had done her so much wrong, I know it was a terrible blow for her when we discovered he was in Australia. She really wanted to carry on seeing him.'

There was a pause while I took all this in.

'So, there you go, Ken. That's the story. That's who Tony is.'

'Fucking bastard. What a fucking bastard.'

'You see why I've told you. Now you've heard the story you won't want to do anything to poor Karen. You've promised not to, anyway. And Tony is in Australia. We've no way of knowing where he is. So, you can't do him. And I wouldn't want you to. He did wrong, yes, he did. But it's a very long time ago. And he was only a lad at the time.'

I give Bet a couple of hundred quid and go back to the flat. It's a lot to take in. It means when we have sex, Karen at least some of the time is thinking of her step-brother. It's disgusting. But it's not her fault. It's that fucking step-brother of her's.

I got to track him down. I got to hunt down the bastard. By Jesus, he's going to pay for this. How in hell's name am I going to do it? Bet must know more than she says. I could go back to her. I google Tony Parkinson Australia and nothing useful comes up. Lots of profiles and bloody Linkedin but they're not going to lead me anywhere.

Then I have a brainwave. Leopards and spots. I google Tony Parkinson paedophile Australia. Instant success. A report in the Sydney Morning Herald about a man called Tony Parkinson who was given six years in 1994 for being part of a paedophile gang targeting young girls. He'd be out now, but a web site called MAKO/Files online gives me the place he's living: Whitefern, NSW. That's as far as I can get. No addresses. I look up Whitefern and it's in Sydney. Right, I'm going out there. Old Tony's not going to get away with it.

I start checking out on the fares to Sydney. You can get an economy class return for £600 travelling next week on Malaysian Airlines. That's OK. I've still got nearly two grand. I've nearly bought a ticket when I discover you've got to have a visa to get into Australia.

You can get an instant tourist visa for £20. I start to fill in a form. Do I have any criminal convictions? Yes, I do. Lucky, I was only inside for nine months. If I'd been inside for twelve months they wouldn't give me a tourist visa and I'd be buggered. I need a contact address. That's a problem until I remember Brendan has a married sister in Sydney. A quick bell to him and he calls me back with the address in half an hour.

Six days later and I'm on a Malaysian Airlines plane from Kuala Lumpur to Sydney. The first leg from London I had an empty seat next me but this time there's a gabby old couple. They're visiting their daughter in Sydney. She's got two children and they visit her family once a year. 'What about you?' they ask.

'Oh, I'm on my way to visit my brother-in-law,' I tell them. 'Haven't seen him in many years, so it'll be quite a reunion.'

'Nothing like family,' the old biddy says. 'Friends are OK, but you can always depend on your family.'

I remember what my Dad used to say. 'Never trust no one. Especially members of your own family.' Cynical old bastard. But he was right. He should've known. My mum scarpered off with another bloke when I was nine. That left my dad, my brother and me. Then, when I was sent away to this special school, he never came to visit me. When I got out he'd paired up with another bird and didn't want to know me. Proved himself right about who you can trust.

Luckily the old couple don't ask any more questions. They both go to sleep for most of the journey. I'm left to enjoy the flight looking at the stewards, one man and two slim Malaysian bints with their dresses, slit up the sides, giving you a good eyeful of leg. A lot better looking than the girls you get on the Ryanair flights to Alicante. I don't sleep a wink.

I get to Sydney quite early in the morning. First thing I do is walk through a large duty-free area. I think maybe I'll buy Karen some perfume but then I remember I might not see her again. That takes me to Immigration. This is what I'm really worried about. What if they ask me about Brendan's sister whom I'm supposed to be visiting? I don't know nothing about her.

Anyway, when I get to the immigration, it's a man who just asks me what I'm visiting for and I say there's been a death in the family and I'm just coming for a few days for the funeral. The guy's very sympathetic and just says 'Sorry about your loss, mate. Welcome to Australia anyway. Have as good a stay as you can.' And I'm away.

I don't have to go through the baggage claim place because I didn't have no cases in the hold, so I was quickly through to the arrivals hall and the fresh air. Fresh air? Not a chance. Hot air. I'm hit by a wave of fucking heat like I've never known before. Much hotter than Benidorm. I make straight for the information place that has a big I sign in front of it. I know about this from an announcement on the plane. I ask about how to get to Whitefern.

At the desk a nice grey-haired old lady in a blue uniform tells me I can either get a taxi to Whitefern or a train to Central Station and then get on a different train and it's only one stop from Central to Whitefern. She tells me me it would be about 50 bucks for the taxi, so I decide to go by train. It doesn't seem that difficult. I ask the lady whether she knows of any cheap hotels in Whitefern. She tells me they don't keep that sort of info but there's another information place at Central Station. They'd be able to help me. A blue uniformed bloke next to the information desk hears what I'm asking. 'Yes, mate. I can't think why anyone should want to go to Whitefern, but there are cheap places to stay there.'

'Just go past Macdonald's to the escalator which takes you to the train ticket office,' blue uniform says. I pass Macdonald's which looks like every other Macdonalds I've ever seen and get myself some local dosh at a counter marked Exchange.

Then I fight my way through the Arrivals Hall to the rail ticket office which seems full of little yellow people. I wonder if I've got off at Shanghai by mistake. The bloke in the ticket office tells me I can get an OPAL card for nothing and put some cash on it. So, I spend my first fifty bucks on the card.

When at last I get to the platform and the train to Central Station comes in, it's a double-decker. Never seen a double-decker train before. It's very clean and quiet. Only four stops to Central. It's fucking enormous, but I find the Visitors Information place. By now I'm getting really whacked. It's the heat and it feels as if I haven't slept for a week. I ask about a cheap hotel in Whitefern.

The Indian chappie at the desk gives me a list and I ask if they'll ring a place called The Suffolk. It looks about the right price. He asks why I want to stay in Whitefern. Second time I've been asked in an hour. There's obviously something wrong with the place.

I find the train to Whitefern. It's only a five-minute journey. The pub, well it calls itself a hotel but it's really a pub, is just ten minutes from the train station. It's a hundred dollars a night. That's about fifty quid, so I reckon I'll be OK to stay here for a fortnight if necessary. I should be able to find the bugger in that time. I undress, go straight to bed and sleep for about ten hours.

When I wake up there's a sort of scratching noise round the bed. I look down and it's nasty-looking little beetles. I get shaved, dressed, go down to the reception place where the man laughs and says it's cockroaches. They'll send someone up with a spray. In the meantime, don't leave any food around.

I haven't got much time and I've got a plan. Straight after breakfast, I buy a couple of local newspapers. There's the

South Sydney Herald and the *Sydney Morning Herald*. Sure enough, in the *South Sydney Herald*, there's a story about a guy who's just been done for child abuse. There always is. So, I go back to my hotel and sit in one of the chairs next to the man at the reception. After a bit I look up and interrupt him in what he's doing. I say:

'Hey, listen to this. I didn't know this sort of thing happened here. It's all over the place in England, but here? Terrible story in this paper about this man abusing little boys. What do you think? Do you get much of this sort of thing over here?'

The foreign-looking guy doesn't look very interested.

'Ask me three years is nothing for a bastard like that. Ought to lock him up and throw the key away. You get people like that around here? You can find out where they live now.'

The foreign-looking guy looks up.

'No, mate. I've never heard of anyone like that around here. You're right though. It's a terrible thing to do.'

Well, he's not much help, but at least he doesn't approve of men having sex with children.

That morning, I start going around bars in Whitefern. It isn't much of a place. In the paper, I read it's supposed to be going up in the world, but you wouldn't know. There are some houses that have been done up, but mainly it's a bit like the Old Kent Road. There's loads of graffiti, mostly telling abos (the slang word they have for blacks here) to stand up for their rights.

Bars are open all day, and I mainly go when there's hardly anyone there - mid-morning and mid-afternoon. I talk to the barman and read my paper. I pretend to find the piece about the paedophile.

The barman always agrees. That's their job.

I draw a complete blank on my first two days. The evenings I spend in The Suffolk. It's a busy place. The first evening there's what they call a Craft Beer party. It's all pretty good ale. I knock back quite a bit. With the jet lag, this makes me feel I'm hanging out of my arse. The third evening

I just go to bed early. Can't get to sleep because of the noise downstairs.

On my third day and what must be about my tenth bar, the barman at the Parkside Bar turns up trumps.

'Yes, we've got one living just up the road. Sad sack. Bloke about fifty. Comes in here by himself about once a month but you can see he's dead scared someone will recognise him. Keeps looking round him. Most times he doesn't even come in here. Just goes for a walk in the park around the corner, over there. I know it's him. His picture's been in the paper. No, I can't remember his name.'

It *must* be Tony. He's the only one on the web site listed in Whitefern and the age is right. The barman tells me what time he goes for his walk and which part of the park he walks in.

I thank him and go back to Whitefern's High Street. I can see this is where the money is. There's a lot of smart-looking couples having lunch outside classy restaurants. Look like University types. But lunch is not what I'm looking for. There's a hardware store. I go in and there's a section called 'King of the Knives'. I find an assistant.

'Can you give me a bit of help, mate. I've been given a half a sheep. I'm getting it out the freezer this afternoon. I'm going to want to carve it up.

'Seems to me, cobber, what you need is a butcher's knife.'

'Yes. That is exactly what I want. A butcher's knife.'

GAME SUSPENDED

'Blast', I roar. The noise creates a major local disturbance. A couple, wheeling a pram on the path running alongside the tennis courts, stop to see what has happened and stare at us before moving off again. Three pigeons, perched on a nearby tree, take off in a flapping flurry in the direction of the ornamental lake.

The four gay men on the next court stop in the middle of a point. They agree to play the point again. On the court the other side of us, two teenagers, a boy and a girl, knocking balls back and forward to each other, see what has happened, look at me and giggle. Leonard, on the other side of the net to us glances at his wife and picks up the ball that has hit the back netting with some force. My wife, behind me, expresses strong disapproval.

'Oh, Victor.' The tone of her voice is sufficient. She does not need to say more. It could have been worse. I'm not sure if she noticed, but I only just managed to stop myself shouting out the f-word.

What has happened is that I have hit an overhead smash over the baseline and out of court. It is the last point of today's game. Our hour is up and there is a couple waiting to come on. The score is 6-4 to us in the first set and three all in the second. Whether the smash went in or not makes absolutely no difference. The four of us, our friends, Leonard and Hetty, my wife and myself, walk silently over to the bench at the side of the court to pick up our things.

It is an awkward moment. I say: 'Sorry about that. A bit over the top.' My wife begins to speak.

'Victor,' she begins. I interrupt her.

'Marie, if you say, 'Victor, it's only a game', I shall murder you. I have the murder weapon in my hand.' I say, brandishing my racket. 'And, at the trial, I shall get off on grounds of provocation. I shall hire Tony Blair to defend me. He could get me off anything. This will be child's play for him. I shall walk away a free man and sell my story to *The Moon* for millions. There is nothing like a crime passionel for selling newspapers.'

Marie is silenced. Leonard and Hetty smile and we are able to move on. At the same time as we leave, the four gay men pack up too, gathering their gear from the other bench. Like us, they always play from 9 to 10 on Sunday mornings. As usual, two of the men leave together and the other two move off separately in different directions. Before they part there are affectionate, noisy kisses all round. One of the couple shouts after one of the others:

'Now, have a good week and don't do anything I wouldn't do.'

'We all know what *that* might be,' says one of the others, and all of them fall about laughing.

The four of us walk back to our place. It's only five minutes away. We take it in turns to host the post-tennis breakfast. This ritual of Sunday morning tennis followed by a chat over a late breakfast has been going on for nearly twenty years. We met Leonard and Hetty all that time ago. They were playing singles on a court next to ours and seemed to be about the same standard, so we linked up for a foursome and have been playing as such ever since. They're about our age. He's a tallish solicitor, a bit better than me, but as Marie plays a stronger game than Hetty, who's really pretty hopeless, it balances up. Although he's no Federer and I'm very definitely no Djokovic, it always irks me when he returns a shot I've been confident will win the point. It's odd. I know that in his work, he's immensely competitive where I've been happy just to jog on in a regular job, but it's the other way around on the tennis court. I really hate it when it's me receiving and he serves an ace. Hence, probably, my loss of temper when my volley went so badly wrong. But it's not just that.

To book one of the public tennis courts in Greenbridge Park, one of us has to ring the Council promptly at 8.30 on the previous Thursday morning. Just occasionally, we forget to book, or someone has got in before us. If this happens, we can usually arrange to play later in the morning, but we prefer this earlier time. It means that by 11 we can start to get on with the rest of the day and our lives.

Over croissants and coffee, there is no mention of my outburst. Hetty and Leonard will probably discuss it on the way back to their place. Leonard will be impressed with the monumental extent of my rage. Hetty will just regard me as a bit childish. She's right, but I know why I've been so out of control this morning. Nobody else does. Nobody at all.

After they've gone Marie says:

'Well, you certainly are on a short fuse these days. I know you told me not to tell you it's only a game. Well, it is. And you very nearly used a word that might well have got us chucked off the courts in future. And I don't need you to lose your rag just because I've forgotten to buy milk and we have to make do with yoghurt with our cereal. And it would be good if you could keep your swearing down whenever you get a call from work. And … and … and … What the hell's got into you?'

I mutter something about how maybe work is getting to me. She knows the number of natural disasters in the countries we 'look after' has never been as high. I don't need to say more.

In mid-afternoon, she takes the car and goes off to her book club. I go to the window of my study to watch the car drive off. I have to be sure she really has left before I click onto 'gay pornhub'. I begin to watch a total of about thirty men, mainly in pairs but sometimes in threes, kiss, hug, cuddle, mutually masturbate, enter each other's anuses and suck each other's penises. That's about it. They always make the same groaning noises, with shouts of pleasure when they come. I avoid the ones involving teenage boys.

No violence apart from the occasional gentle smack on the bum. Nor are there any expressions of affection. This is gay sex, not gay love. The whole thing is so formulaic and repetitive, I'm amazed I don't get bored and switch over to something else within five minutes.

But I don't. I start to get an erection almost immediately. After about fifteen to twenty minutes, I allow myself to come, go to the bathroom to wash and tidy up generally. Then I go downstairs to carrying on reading *The Warden*, the Trollope I'm on now. If Chelsea were playing, I would watch the match, but that isn't the case today.

When Marie returns, she finds me as she left me. She tells me about the discussion of the book her group has been reading. It's the latest McEwen, *The Children Act*, and they've all liked it, especially because this time, she says, there wasn't any neuroscience in it, like in so many of his previous novels. We make supper together, me the sauce for the pasta and she the salad. She's forgotten to buy the parmesan again. This time, I manage to suppress my irritation.

After we've eaten, we watch the latest episode of *Wallander*, the headlines of the BBC news and then go to bed. Sex used to be for Sunday evenings but not for the last ten years. Now we read in bed until we tire, turn out the light and go to sleep. But I know there is unfinished business that will have to be faced before too long.

I wake at seven and consider my options.

Next day, soon after arriving at the office, I go to the usual Monday morning senior staff meeting. There are half a dozen of us there, with me as head of fund-raising. We review the situation and the week ahead. Malcolm, our CE begins:

'Right. As you all know because it's been the fifth item on the news the whole weekend, the floods in our part of the world have caused more damage than we thought was going to be the case.'

Our part of the world is central Africa. He goes on:

'I've heard from Luanda, Brazzaville and Kigali that some of the country areas have been really badly affected. Of course, their schools are not their top priority, but I've already had calls from five of our schools that they've virtually been washed away.'

It's clear the floods in Central Africa are creating the biggest humanitarian crisis the continent has known. He goes on:

'Many more of the schools we're helping have been forced to close temporarily. They are going to need new equipment and expertise to get going again.'

I know what this means for me. This is going to require far more funds for next year than we had planned. Clearly, as head of the fund-raising section, it is my job to up the ante. We discuss strategy and I go back to my office to work out who to approach first and how.

But I just can't concentrate. Images of naked men having sex seem to be taking over my mind. I think of myself, naked, having it off with the best-looking man on the tennis court next to ours. I don't even know what his name is. By eleven, when I'm due to meet our freelance web-designer, Henry Wade, I've made no progress at all. I fiddle with my computer, tempted to pull up a porn site. I manage to resist until he arrives.

We work together quite productively for a couple of hours. He has some new equipment at home and has a number of bright ideas how we might attract new donors with different images from the ones we have been using up to now. I have no ideas at all but am able to pick up on his. At one-o-clock we go out to buy sandwiches and bring them back to my office. We chat as we always do about our weekends. I've been working with Henry for two or three years now. We know quite a bit about our respective families. Henry tells me about his new stuff. Then quite unexpectedly, he says:

'I've had a bit of a shock, Victor. You know Jamie, our fourteen-year-old. He brought a schoolmate home. A black boy. Very bright. Things came up. I'm beginning to think Jamie's gay or at least going to be gay.'

'Oh my God. How are you going to cope with that?'

'It was a shock. I haven't been able to talk to Angie about it yet. I don't know how she's going to take it. But somehow or other I've persuaded myself it's no big deal. We know two or three gay couples. They seem to live a pretty good life. I'm just a bit worried Angie might have a bad reaction.'

I pause for a bit and then take the plunge.

'Well, Henry, you know one more gay than you thought you did. I've been gay all my life, pretty much.'

Henry looks shocked, incredulous. It's as if I'd told him I was just about to go to prison for embezzling Africa Ed funds. He was speechless for a bit. Then:

'You, Victor, come off it. You're married, got a daughter, I thought. Nurse, isn't she?'

'Things aren't always what they seem. I've known I was gay since my very early teens. Of course, I pretended to be straight. Later, in my mid-teens, I'd even boast of screwing girls I'd never even spoken to. Some of the gay men at college guessed I was like them and made advances. I always managed to avoid getting physically involved. I had a very full social life, but it wasn't until my third year, when I met Marie, that I had a full sexual experience.'

'What do you mean, a full sexual experience? How can you have a full sexual experience with someone who doesn't attract you?

'Well, we went out regularly, shared a number of interests – Third World charities (we had both done VSO), competitive sport (she ran marathons and I played badminton). We greatly enjoyed each other's company. I really liked her, though she had no sexual attraction for me. But she had quite strong sexual urges.'

'Yes, but you haven't answered my question.'

'Fact is she seduced me, and we began to have sex regularly, with me fantasising about men but not telling her. She was delighted with our sex life, said I gave her the best she had ever had, and maybe I did. I really liked her. I suppose I was in love with her. I certainly missed her when she wasn't around. I desperately wanted to please her. A few years ago, she didn't seem to want sex anymore. For me, it was a relief not to have to, well, carry on doing it. Now, thirty-five years on, with our daughter in her thirties, I thought I had, well, got away with it.'

'So, what's changed?'

'You know, I had never watched any porn. Then, about a week ago, I started to look at gay porn. It's an amazingly easy thing to do. Problem. Big problem. Watching it has made me desperately want what I've never had. Sex with a man. I've begun to think this is 'the real thing'. I sort of think that I've got to be true to my real self. But I love Marie, I really do. I hate the idea of hurting her.'

And with that, I put down my half-eaten bacon, lettuce and tomato on brown. My eyes start to water. I pull out a Kleenex and dab my eyes. If Henry comes over to me and puts his arm round me I will probably start to sob, but he stays in his chair.

'Do you have to tell her? She's been OK all this time. Why do you have to?'

'You're right, I don't have to. But if I go ahead and find some man to sleep with without her knowing, I shall just be telling a different sort of lie. Oh, God, I don't know what to do. Come on, let's get on with what we're supposed to be doing.'

So, we plough on, in fact rather successfully, devising new, powerful images that will pull at the heartstrings of rich people and get them to dig deeper into their wallets and purses.

By the end of the afternoon, I've been able to persuade Malcolm to spend another ten thousand pounds on the website. 'A good investment,' he agrees.

On the train back to Greenbridge, strap-hanging as usual, I make a definite decision not to open up to Marie. She isn't at home when I get back and I remember Monday is the night she swims and doesn't get back until 8.30. She's pretty athletic, a tall rangy woman. She dyes her hair and looks very youthful for her sixty years. But it's no good my trying to tell myself how attractive she still is. I go to my study and immediately put up the gay porn. It seems I never tire of watching the same couples go through the same routines. It's pathetic but I can't stop. Don't want to stop.

By the time she gets back I've made a definite decision to talk to her. After spaghetti carbonara and fruit, I tell her I need to talk to her about something. We each carry our coffees into the living room.

'Marie,' I begin. 'This is hard. It's pretty well the hardest thing I've ever had to do.'

Marie does not look sympathetic. I can see she is already beginning to look angry.

'Look, don't start trying to win me over by telling me how hard all this is for *you*, Victor. It's pretty obvious you're seeing another woman. Just get it over and tell me what you want to tell me about it. How long has it been going on? Ten years? Since we stopped having sex? Just tell me.'

'No, Marie. I'm not seeing another woman, or indeed anyone else. Maybe that's the problem. There is something about myself you don't know. Or maybe you do. Sometimes I can't believe you haven't guessed?'

I want to laugh. The idea of having sex with yet another woman strikes me as comic. It's been difficult enough having sex with Marie. Trying to have sex with yet another woman would be really punishing myself. But it isn't a laughing matter, I tell myself. I look at her questioningly and can see that indeed she hasn't the faintest idea.

'Marie, I'm gay. I always have been. Right from the start. I've been sexually attracted to men. And I've begun to want to have sex with a man. Not any particular man. Just a man.'

There is a long, long silence while Marie takes this in. There must be hundreds of questions on her mind. But there is one big question and it doesn't take long before she asks it.

'So, Victor, all those years we made love. You seemed to enjoy it. But you weren't thinking about me. All the time you had some man you were thinking about. Is that right?'

There is another silence. Then I nod. There isn't much else I can do. I now just wish I had kept quiet.

'Well, I must say, you're a pretty good actor. Maybe you ought to get yourself a new job as a gay porn star. There's probably a demand for, what do they call it, mature gay men.'

There is a pause. She doesn't know it. But there is nothing I would rather do more.

Marie gets up. I can see she doesn't want to carry on the conversation. Would find it too painful. 'Well,' she says, 'I'm not sleeping another night in the same bed as a man who must find me repulsive. You can sleep in your study. There's a sofa there. You know where the sheets are. Tuck yourself up nicely. I'll see you at breakfast. Maybe.' And she gets up and takes long-legged strides out of the room, banging the door behind her.

I sit in silence, thinking what a complete idiot I am. I haven't told her how much I love her. I haven't told her how I don't want this to make any difference between us. I haven't even told her that, in spite of everything, I really enjoyed the sex we had together. Because I did. It clearly wasn't fully what I wanted but I did indeed, in most ways, find it pleasurable.

I sit pondering all this for about half an hour. Then I decide I need to tell Marie all the things I have failed to tell her up to now. I go up to our bedroom and wonder whether I should knock on the door. It is after all still my bedroom as much as hers. I go in without knocking. She is in bed in her nightie. She's red-eyed and has clearly been crying.

'Marie, I haven't told you half of what I need to. I just want to tell you …'

'Victor, just get out of this room. Go on. Bugger off, will you?'

'Marie …'

'You heard what I said. Just get out. Get bloody out of here.'

So, I make up the sofa bed and try to sleep. I probably don't get more than two or three hours. In the end, I sleep quite soundly between six and eight. When I do finally wake I discover Marie has already left to go off to work.

I feel terrible. What I've done is despicable. I've just deeply hurt the person in the world to whom I feel closest. I don't deserve to live. Now I've got to go into work. No, I don't. I ring the office and leave a message with reception saying I've got some sort of a virus and won't be able to come in today. I leave another message on the answer machine of my number two, telling her of the images Henry and I devised yesterday, how to access the stuff and what she might do next. In any case, Alison really ought to be running the fund-raising department – she's way more competent than me.

I spend the morning in a state of dithering despair. I certainly don't want to watch any gay porn. I pick up *The Warden* and then put it down again. I walk to the local newsagent, buy *The Guardian*, go to the park and sit on a bench reading it. There is an article about floods in Central Africa, but I can't be bothered to look at it.

I think about finding someone I can talk to about what to do. There is no one. Our friends would not be in the slightest bit sympathetic. Take Leonard and Hettie. Leonard had bad experiences at school. He was badly bullied, possibly even sexually abused by older boys. We've never talked about it, but I get the impression he's at least mildly, possibly even seriously homophobic. There's Henry. But I really hardly know him. It's only because he mentioned his son that I confided in him yesterday.

I return home about noon and there's a message from Joanna, our daughter, saying she's tried to get me at work but I'm not there so she supposes I must be at home. Please will I ring her back? I guess that Marie has been in touch with her and told her all. I don't want to ring her. I've always been close to Joanna, probably closer than Marie. Joanna and I can talk to each other. Now I've let her down too. But I've got to ring her, so I do.

'Dad, Mum rang me earlier this morning.'

'I'm glad she did. Jo. I'm really sorry about this. I've been a complete idiot.'

'You mean you're not really gay. You made it up?'

'No, of course, I didn't. But I didn't need to tell your mum.'

'But you did need to. You wouldn't have told her if you didn't have a deep need to.'

'Well, it's nice of you to say so. But I still wish I hadn't.'

'Look, Dad, I think it's good to talk about these things. I'm going to tell you something that will surprise you. You remember when I went up to Leicester to work there for a year? You wondered why Leicester. Well, I fell in love with a woman doctor who got a job there. We actually shared a flat together for six months. Then she decided she wanted to have children. We were both really bisexual, but we loved each other alright. So, we split up. She is married now. A few months after Rachel and I split up, Brian and I got together.'

'So that's why you insisted we never came up to Leicester. You didn't want us to know.'

I notice on my desk there's a photograph of Joanna, Marie and me, taken at her wedding to Brian. I've always thought how attractive Joanna is and how lucky the man would be who managed to hook her for his wife. I suppose a lot of fathers think like that. Never for one moment did I think of her as attractive to other women. Yet why shouldn't she be, it suddenly struck me. I realised she was still talking to me.

'Well, it wasn't difficult to persuade you not to come to Leicester. You're such metropolitan animals. But yes, that's why I always came down to London to see you. I really didn't want you to find out. I just didn't know how you would take it.'

'So, you understand a bit about my being gay?'

'Yes, of course I do. And I told Mum to get a grip. I told her she had had thirty-five years or so of a pretty happy marriage. You've done masses of wonderful things together. That is as well as bringing me up and not making too much of a mess of that.'

As she's talking I'm looking at the photograph of the three of us. Yes, we, Marie and I, have done pretty well together.

'So,' Jo goes on, 'She's had about twenty years more than the parents of most of my friends. You've had great times together. Obviously, I didn't know about the sex, but even that she tells me was very good until it stopped a few years ago. You must have been well over fifty then. What's she got to gripe about?'

'That's very generous of you. But, for all that, Mum is going to find it incredibly difficult to take in. And I would if I were her. Suppose it turned out she'd been fantasising about some woman all the time. I'd be more than a bit pissed off.'

'Look, it's up to you two to work things out the best you can. All I'm telling you is that I'll carry on loving both of you whatever you decide. Now I've got to get to work for the afternoon shift. The NHS needs me.'

I think about going into work in the afternoon but decide against it. Instead, I fiddle about on the computer, looking at the images Henry and I worked on yesterday. I know Marie will come home, if she comes home as usual, at around 6.30. I make another pasta sauce, this time puttanesca, one of her favourites.

As I'm chopping the chili peppers, taking care to avoid touching my eyes while I'm doing so, I think about how I'm going to handle her anger. I say to myself that this time I must get in how much I love her, however much she tries to stop me or tell me that she doesn't care how I feel. But I know it's her move.

She nods as I tell her what I've made. All she says is:

'We'll talk about this after supper.'

We eat the pasta and fruit in silence. I can't work out how she's taking it. After supper, we take our coffee into the living room. The first signs are not good. I ask if we should switch on the TV. She says no, we've got to talk.

'I can't pretend I've had a good day, Victor. As you know, I spoke to Joanna. She rang me again after I'd spoken to you. Turns out she's gay or lesbian or whatever as well. Probably thinks of other women while she's having sex with Brian. It's a funny old world when people having sex with someone aren't really having sex with that person, just with some bloke or girl up the road.'

'Look Marie, you didn't give me a chance to tell you last night. I do really love you. I loved having sex with you. I ….'

'Yes, I'm sure it was really, really pleasurable for you. Able to have sex with whichever man you happened to fancy that time.'

'That's not fair. It wasn't like that.'

'Well, if it wasn't like that, I don't know what it was like. Anyway, we're not having sex anymore, so I suppose it doesn't matter. What happened? Weren't there any more men you fancied? And now there are. So, Henry, if there's some man you fancy, you'd better get on with it. You're not getting any younger.'

I don't like the way this is going. She's so angry she won't listen to anything I say. I decide I'd better just shut up.

'Anyway,' she says, 'I can't go on living with you if you stay as irritable as you've been over the last month or so. So, you'd better go to the Coach and Horses, that's the nearest gay pub, isn't it? Or go onto one of those Men Seeking Men web sites. Find a man wherever and sleep with him. If he wants to sleep with you, that is. You'd better get on with it or it will be too late. Your charms, such as they remain, will soon have completely disappeared. Then I'll think about what happens next. Just now I'm going up to the bedroom to read. Feel free to stay here. But when you want to go to sleep, you know where to go. Maybe we'll need to get a more comfortable sofa.'

I don't know what to do. I feel I've been given a licence to have sex with a man and I want to use it. But if I do, Marie and I will probably split up. And I don't want that. I *really* don't want it. In fact, I've already made a tentative go at putting in an entry in *The Guardian* soulmates web site. I lost courage and didn't get as far as putting any details in, so I haven't got what they call a profile. But it's a start.

The next couple of days I manage to get into work and, with Alison, start to work out the best way to circulate our regular donors with the new web site images. The evenings, Marie and I eat dinner together in silence and then I go to my study. I watch the BBC news at ten, but she doesn't join me. I suppose she's watching it on her iPad in the bedroom.

A couple of evenings later I drift over to The Coach and Horses to find out what it's like. It's terrible. The place is bare of decoration except for a poster saying there is a piano bar on Thursdays. Tonight is Thursday but there is no piano bar.

'What can I do for *you*, darling?' says the man at the bar in a mincing, suggestive tone of voice. He's bald and unattractive, at least to me. I've noticed how men like to flirt with the women who serve in pubs and wonder if the people who run gay pubs think about how the looks of the man behind the bar really matter. I ask for a pint of bitter.

'We don't do beer, dear. You can have a lager.'

'I thought there might be live music.'

'No, dear, no live music tonight. We do a drag queen.'

So, I order a half of lager and sit in a corner to watch. Five balding, middle-aged men and one young man, lip-sticked and face-creamed, are talking at the bar. Two men are sitting separately, reading newspapers. After a few minutes, the young man disappears only to return in full drag about ten minutes later. The place begins to fill up so that now there are a dozen or so customers, including a lesbian couple. Our man begins to sing. Not a bad imitation of Judy Garland, but halfway through 'Over the Rainbow' I decide I've had enough and exit.

A google search for gay pubs for older men produces a more promising result. Clearly all the action is in Soho or thereabouts. Sunday evening seems a good time to explore. It's a part of London I haven't visited since I was in my twenties. It's certainly changed. As I remember, it used to be a bit coy about its sex. Now, it's really come out. Once you turn off Shaftesbury Avenue, it's immediately in your face. If it's not shop fronts advertising Girls, Girls, Girls, it's Sauna and Massage parlours, exotic looking girls in doorways inviting you in to peep shows and adult videos. Nothing obviously gay, but I know where I'm going.

Now however I'm a bit anxious. Could I be a target for queer-bashing? However, at the door to The Yard in Rupert Street the black bouncer looks me over, decides I'm no threat and welcomes me in. It's a much more congenial place than the Coach and Horses. There are photographs of attractive men on the walls. The music is only moderately loud. I discover that upstairs in the so-called Loft, there is a young gay scene with dancing and a drag queen on the stage, but downstairs there are a number of obviously straight couples as well as a preponderance of older gay men. The atmosphere is friendly. And there are some promising-looking men more or less my age on their own.

Suddenly, I catch sight of one of the gays I see on the neighbouring tennis court. He's talking with three men. The one I've recognised isn't the man to whom I feel so attracted but I stare at him a bit all the same. Not surprisingly, he's the only familiar face. After a few minutes, he notices me and comes over.

'Hi, what are you doing here? Aren't you the guy I see every Sunday playing a foursome?'

'Yes, that's me.'

'Well, I can't quite see what you're doing here but you must know what sort of a place this is. All alone?'

I admit I am.

'I'm Alan. Come over and meet these friends of mine.'

We start talking about tennis. We have a laugh about the vagaries of the man at the Council who takes the booking for the courts. I ask him about how the four of them got to know each other and play together.

'Well, as I'm sure you realised, Hector and Simon, the two who go off together, are an item. They're in a civil partnership and hope to get married soon if the law changes. Have been living together for about five years now. I used to live with Simon, but we split up. We've remained good friends though. I don't live with anybody now but Jim (he points to one of the other three men) and I get together once or twice a week.'

I tell him a bit about myself. Not much, but enough for him to understand I'm looking for a man to have sex with.

'You should come and talk to Terry (he indicates one of the other men he's been talking to). He's a bit of a sad sack but I think he's freelance at the moment. He might be interested in you if you're interested in him.'

So, I go over to Terry, a shortish bloke perhaps fifteen to twenty years younger than me and with a lot more hair both on top and on his stubbled cheeks and chin. We detach ourselves from the others. I offer to buy him a drink. We both take pints of draft Buds to a side table that has just become free. With great originality, I begin:

'Is this a place you come to often? It's my first time.'

'I'm here pretty regularly Tuesdays and Saturdays. I'd like to come more often but I can't afford to.'

He's wearing jeans and a none-too-clean sweater with a hole in one sleeve.

'Life's very expensive these days,' I say, though with both Marie and me on decent salaries, we hardly notice what we spend. I clearly can't tell him that.

'No. You're telling me. I retired as a teacher about five years ago. I worked for about thirty years, but even so, my pension doesn't amount to much.'

It turns out he was married for a few years, but it didn't last. He's a retired History teacher who has spent some time in Kampala, a city I know quite well. We talk about how dangerous it is even to be thought gay in Uganda, never mind actually getting involved in gay sex. We buy each other a few drinks, or rather I buy us a few drinks.

I notice the place has filled up. There is now nowhere to sit down. It's getting noisier and I begin to feel restless. But Terry and I get along pretty well. He seems a bit depressed but he's definitely good-looking. I begin to feel I'm attracted to him. Maybe he is to me too for he asks me if I'd like to come around to his flat sometime. He gives me his address, we exchange mobile numbers and arrange an evening the following week.

Meanwhile, Marie and I are leading semi-detached lives. I don't tell her what I'm up to. She's very cool with me though we do eat together and play tennis as usual on Sundays. I'm sure Hettie and Leonard have realised all is not well between us. Maybe she's talked to them, I don't know.

Before I go around to Terry's I start to build up what is going to happen. I watch a fair amount of gay porn, imagining how it's going to play out between us. He might begin by stroking my thigh as we sit close together. This might lead to our turning our faces to each other and kissing, our tongues licking and caressing. At this point I have an erection and I imagine my cock bursting against my fly until he realises what is happening and opens my zip. He gropes for my cock and I for his. I strain not to come too quickly now, thinking of anything that comes to mind that will prolong my pleasure.

But after I arrive at Tony's flat, it isn't like that at all. It's clear from the start all he wants to do is talk. He's living in two rooms in a flat off the Holloway Road. His living room is lined with books and I notice two shelves devoted entirely to nineteenth century American history.

'It looks as if you are really into history,' I remark.

'Yes, I'm supposed to be writing a book on Martin Van Buren. He's an American president hardly anyone has heard of. But he did a great job getting the American economy under control when it was in a complete mess.'

This sounded quite interesting. 'Tell me more,' I said.

But it turns out all Terry wants to talk about is how, when he and his wife split up, he got virtually nothing and much of his smallish income goes to her.

'You see Victor, I'm bi. A bit AC/DC. I had one or two flings with men at teacher training college but then I got hooked to this Sylvia who turned out to be a real bitch. She was quite wild, got pregnant and said I was the father which indeed, I might have been. I think she just thought I had the best financial prospects of all the men she'd slept with. The others can't have been up to much.'

'Was Sylvia the woman you married?'

'She wasn't just the woman I married; she was the only woman I ever had sex with. She discovered I was having sex with one or two men and just kicked me out. Just like that. That was when I got the first of my downers. Really depressed, I became. That's what led to my going to Kampala. Just to get away really. But being gay in Kampala is no fun, you have to be incredibly careful. I came back. That led to my second downer.'

'Hmm,' I said, though he could keep going without any encouragement.

'By this time, I couldn't really get a regular job. I had to keep taking too much time off work. So, I started doing supply teaching. It was hand to mouth. She'd taken the house and car. All I can do is live in rented accommodation. And I don't see much of Michael, my son. He's twenty now.'

All this time, I'm only half listening. I can't take my eyes off his face. I want to stroke his stubbled chin and go further, much further. But when I make a move, he pushes my hand away.

'I'm sorry, Victor. I'm not up to any of that right now.'

I tell him a bit about myself, but I can tell he's not really interested. All the same, I continue to find him extremely attractive and I want to see him again. Maybe something physical will happen next time. Anyway, he's certainly keen to continue to see me. When we part after a couple of hours, he shakes my hand, looks me in the eye and tells me he would really *love* it if I came again.

I resist remarking I haven't come once yet, but clearly our relationship hasn't reached this level of familiarity, so we fix another meeting in a few days. I have a feeling I ought to confirm the arrangement beforehand, so I ring his mobile the day before. An unfamiliar, younger voice answers.

'Yes, is that Victor? My dad said you might phone. I'm afraid he's been admitted to hospital.'

There is a pause. 'I suppose there's no reason why I shouldn't tell you. You probably know about his so-called attempts to end his life. It's twenty tablets this time. Just enough to get himself admitted but nowhere near enough to put him in danger. That's my dad.'

I thank Michael and realise I haven't offered to go and see Terry in hospital. I don't really want to. There's no prospect of having sex with him there and I admit to myself that's the only reason I would like to see him. I consider my other options. Maybe I should pick up again on *The Guardian* Soulmates website. I probably should have persisted with that anyway.

Meanwhile, life goes on, partly the same, partly very different. At work, I've recovered my grip. Indeed, the new campaign is going well. Henry's web design has turned out to be really successful and the donations are rolling in, with one or two major companies chipping in with hundreds of thousands. Alison is impressed.

At home, in contrast, life is very different. All that is left of my existence with Marie, because that is all it really is, are our meals, eaten in virtual silence, and one or two regular arrangements, one of which is our Sunday game of tennis.

It's a month after the match in which I lost my cool and the four of us are playing again. After six games, the score is three-all. Marie serves well. Hettie puts a weak lob high over my head. I think about trying to reach the ball to smash but decide against. 'Yours,' I shout. Marie runs for the ball but hasn't a hope of getting it. She stops, loses balance and falls rather gracefully, onto her bottom. She looks both ludicrous and lovable. We both laugh. I go to her and pull her upright. We are facing each other and immediately it seems the right thing to do is to pull her towards me and give her a hug. She smiles up at me; the first smile I've had for a month. We embrace. Then over her shoulder I see Alan on the next court looking at us. He's supposed to be waiting to receive service but instead he has turned towards me, gives me a puzzled look and shrugs his shoulders. My arms drop from around Marie's waist.

'We'd better get on with the game.' I say.

PLUS CA CHANGE

'You don't seem to have put on any weight, George,' said Pierre. His English is perfect grammatically, but his accent is appalling. He sounds like a Frenchman imitating Maurice Chevalier. I'm very fond of the man, although sometimes the temptation to imitate him is overwhelming, I manage to resist as I know how hurt he would be.

'It's only a week since you last saw me, Pierre. You can't expect me to put on weight in a week.'

'Of course, I don't. But you're thin as a rake.' In fact, he says 'teen as a reek' but I know what he means. He goes on: 'It's a year now, George. You've got to start living again.'

We are having our weekly Wednesday lunch in the Brasserie Magnan. It is a warm September day. The tables on the pavement outside, opposite the light terracotta stone Palais de l'Agriculture, are empty. Inside, apart from ourselves, there is just a Dutch family, father, mother and two very well-behaved young children. It is an ideal place for quiet conversation.

Pierre is not only my closest friend, but my family doctor. His 'cabinet' is on the ground floor on the same staircase as my own third floor surgery. We both work in the apartment block, L'Oceanique, on the Promenade des Anglais. I live there too. He sees his first patient at 7.30 am and works until well into the evening, but he always takes Wednesday afternoons off, as I do.

'Living again, Pierre, as you put it, can't be done to order. Anyway, I'm not sure I want to 'live again'. I miss Eloise, miss her dreadfully. Most of me doesn't want to stop missing her.'

'That's OK. You don't have to stop missing her. To begin with, you just need to eat properly. By the way, this *truite aux amandes* is pretty good. I've nearly finished mine. You're still pushing yours around the plate. You're not a picky three year-old. You're a grown 75-year-old man.'

'Seventy-four, as a matter of fact. No need to exaggerate how grown-up I am.'

The Brasserie Magnan isn't the greatest restaurant in Nice, far from it. But it's convenient and it serves perfectly acceptable food. As Pierre says, I should indeed be eating more. I know I won't bother to cook anything for myself this evening. Pierre isn't the only person to tell me I should put on some weight. Margaret, the Canadian woman I chat with on the beach a couple of times a week when I go for a swim before breakfast, has told me if I had a bit more fat on me, I wouldn't shiver so much when I got out of the sea.

In contrast, Pierre could do with eating and drinking less. Over the last twelve months since we've been coming here his paunch has swelled alarmingly. He's only about fifty and is eating himself into an early grave.

'You do put it away, Pierre. And I know Chantal will give you vast quantities for dinner this evening.'

'I shall carry on eating just as much as I want. What I tell my patients about their weight has absolutely no relevance to me. By the way, George, Santé. Just drink your share of this not too horrible bottle of Sauvignon or I shall have to drink too much. Then I won't be fit to drive home.'

It's amazing how doctors treat their own bodies so differently from the way they treat their patients. There are still quite a few French doctors who smoke. At least the French dentists I know do look after their own teeth properly, even if too many of them are nicotine-stained.

Pierre lives in a large house with a decent-sized pool in Aspremont, a village on the outskirts of Nice. About once a month I go up there for lunch with him and his family, Chantal and his two nearly grown-up kids. Chantal is a fabulous cook, as well as being a chic, very attractive lady, warm and generous. She gets really upset when I don't do justice to the meals she serves up. Pierre always seems very happy at home. He's obviously proud of Chantal, of the way she looks and of her considerable culinary talents. I do wonder if she feels quite as positively about him.

After our lunch at the Brasserie, I go back to my apartment where I sleep it off. I'm expecting Joao, the 16-year-old son of our Portuguese concierge, Angela, who comes to see me at 5-o-clock on Wednesdays after he gets back from his lycée. I've been helping him with his English for many years. Now that he's beginning his baccalauréat course I know that Angela thinks this session with me has become quite important for him. To my surprise, on this occasion, he pitches up with his mother. She is obviously a bit embarrassed. As she speaks very little English, he has to translate for her.

'Ah, *both* of you. Hi. Come along in. I'm afraid I've only got two patisseries, the millefeuille for you, Joao, as usual, and the éclair for me. But Angela, you must have half my éclair.'

Joao translates. His English is now really quite good. He should have no trouble getting a high mention in his exam, but he's got to keep it up.

I make coffee for the three of us. Angela declines her share of my éclair, pointing to her invisible stomach and shaking her head. She tells Joao what to say.

'My mother is telling you that I don't really want to come to see you anymore. I have other things to do after school.'

My understanding of French is pretty good, so I know that Angela has put things a lot more politely than this, but there you go.

Angela continues, and Joao translates:

'My mother is saying that she wants me to continue. She thinks it is good for me. She thinks I am missing a big occasion, no, a big opportunity.'

Joao then talks angrily and at length to his mother in French. She replies and tells him he must translate for me.

While they are talking between themselves, I look out of the window. Along the Promenade there is the usual procession of walkers and cyclists. A mother on roller-skates is pushing a pram, while trailing a tiny dog on a lead behind her. It's a lovely, sunny afternoon, and there are half a dozen people in the sea and quite a few on the beach. Along the cycle lane two Velcro-clad athletes crouched over their handlebars seem to be engaged in their own stage of the Tour de France. The road traffic is heavy. A sudden roar of noise from a motor scooter brings me back to my senses. Joao is saying:

'She says that she knows you have always been a very big people in my life. Me, without a papa from a baby, you have always done papa things with me. Even before I went to the *école maternelle*, when I was four years old you used to walk with me to the park near the museum and play football with me.'

'Well, that's true, Joao. But I got a lot of fun out of it.'

'Yes, but she says you taught me how to swim in the sea and look, now I swim for the school. But you know all this.'

'Yes. But tell your mama that I know you've been getting bored in the time you spend here. Perhaps I should have told you not to bring your phone. I can see that when we are talking you always have half an eye on it to see if anyone is calling you.'

'Well, it's natural, Monsieur Gould.'

'Of course, it is, Joao. And you must tell your mama that I know that since Madame Gould passed away, I haven't been very lively. You have been too polite to say anything about it, but I know I have nodded off, you know, had a little sleep in front of you, when you are here. Go on, tell your mama. She needs to know that it's not all your fault.'

Joao does so. Looking at him while he's talking, I register that he's grown into a good-looking teenager. When he first came to me for English lessons, he was just a kid. Now he's got a mind of his own, however much his mum wants to carry on making all his decisions for him. I go on:

'I just haven't had much energy recently. When Madame Gould was here, she used to ask you questions and find out about your life. I know you liked that. I don't do that so much. Well, what shall we do? You want to stop coming altogether, or maybe come once a fortnight? Why don't you ask your mama to go back to your place now and we'll discuss what to do, just the two of us. It's getting a bit tiring, all this translation.'

Angela is a bit reluctant to leave. As she's going out, she looks back as if she can't trust her son to make a good decision on his own. After she's finally gone, I ask Joao a bit about how his life is going now. He is uncommunicative. But then I hit the bull's eye.

'I just wondered if you had a girlfriend now, Joao? After all, you're sixteen. It would be natural.'

That really sets him off. It's clear he wants to talk about this with someone and he can't talk to his mother.

'Yes, I do. Her name is Odette. She's in my class at school. She is wonderful. She is so attractive. And she is easy to talk to. Every day we go to the park, you know, the one where you and I used to play football and we just talk. She is not very happy that I can't go with her on Wednesday afternoons.'

'Well, I quite understand that, Joao. No normal 16-year-old would want to talk to an old dentist, when this means he is missing talking to his girlfriend. What do you say to the idea that you stop coming now for a few weeks and maybe, when the exam is a bit nearer, you start again? I don't want you to miss the patisseries for the whole of the rest of your life!'

Joao shows no inclination to leave. He digs into his millefeuille with enthusiasm, while asking:

'Monsieur Gould, when you were sixteen years, did you have a girlfriend?'

'No, as a matter of fact, I didn't. But things were different in those days. And perhaps in England, things were different then from how they are in France today.'

Joao looks disappointed. He doesn't seem happy with this reply, but it is agreed that we will take a break from the lessons. I'm really quite relieved. His visits remind me of the time when Eloise used to make a fuss of him. 'Her little boy,' she used to call him, even though he's nearly six foot tall now. Added to that, I just don't have the energy to go through practice papers with him anymore. Finding English books that are interesting for him has become almost impossible. So, we part with mutual relief.

After Joao leaves, I read *Nice Matin*. Not much news there apart from the fact that the completion of the tramway that is to run at the back of our block has been delayed a few more months. There's only a tiny bit of national news and this time it's about how unpopular Macron is getting. Frankly if he wasn't unpopular, he wouldn't be doing his job. The French employment laws are just crazy. They've got to change. I do the sudoku and then watch a DVD of *Top Hat* with Fred Astaire and Ginger Rogers. Eloise used to love American musicals and we built up quite a collection. It's hard I can't share this pleasure with Eloise any more. I still feel it.

She and I used to go out to the cinema, to restaurants and to visit friends three or four evenings a week. Now, apart from Pierre and Margaret, my twice a week early morning swim friend, I hardly see anyone these days.

Next morning, Annette arrives at half past eight to get the instruments ready for my first patient at nine. She replaced my wife as receptionist doubling up as dental nurse a few months before Eloise died, when she was too ill to work anymore.

Annette is Australian and speaks good French. She's blonde, mid-thirties, attractive. More important for me, she has a very warm manner with my patients. It's still difficult for me to remember that coming to see a dentist makes most people feel anxious, but Annette never forgets. Her reasonably fluent French is a great advantage. Indeed, she sometimes has to help me out translating with the small number of locals I see. It's thirty years since we came to live in Nice but I'm still hopeless at expressing myself even though I do understand everything.

Annette can see I'm struggling a bit with the work.

'You've only got five to see this morning, George,' she says, 'And three of those are check-ups. One's a filling that you put off last week because you couldn't face doing it at the time. And then there's Mrs. Lowther for her crown fitting. It's arrived, so there's no problem there.'

'Yes, that doesn't sound too bad. By the way, I didn't put the filling off because I couldn't face it. I just thought it was going to take me over my next appointment.'

'Well, George, that's how it seemed to me. You know best.'

Annette clearly isn't convinced but is too polite to push the point. I concede:

'No, you're right. I ought to be giving up. I'm really too old to carry on. Most dentists give up in their late fifties, let alone carry on as long as I have. I just feel I can do the job and there really is a need in Nice for an English-speaking dentist.'

'There certainly is. It isn't just the English and the Americans and the Canadians and the Australians. Even the Germans and the Scandinavians seem to prefer English when it comes to talking to a dentist.'

'You don't think, Annette, it might just be they like coming here because I've got a reputation for my dentistry?'

'Yes, of course. Not very tactful of me. Sorry. Anyway, you really should retire when you feel it's right for you.'

Annette busies herself getting the instruments ready. I know that she isn't worried about losing her job when I stop. She'll easily find another. In any case, her husband is a computer nerd who works at the Nice silicon valley place in Sophia Antipolis just up the road. He's on a very good salary.

'Annette, just make sure to stay in the room when I'm seeing Harriet Lowther. You know what she's like. Last time she was here, and you were just out for three minutes, when I leant over her to check the crown fit, her knee was on my thigh in no time. These American widows ...'

'Trouble is, George, you're so attractive. And now you're available as well. You can't blame the poor lonely souls.'

'Just stop teasing.'

Annette obviously doesn't suspect anything, but at least she must realise that it's only a year now. I'm not as shattered as I was but any idea of another relationship just makes me feel nauseated.

The morning goes well enough. Harriet Lowther behaves herself though, even with Annette in the room, she can't resist a bit of innuendo.

'Rumour has it, George, that you're thinking of retiring. What *are* you going to do with your afternoons, let alone your evenings? You'll have loads of spare time. You really ought to think of getting out a bit. What about it now?'

I can't muster up the energy to think of a reply, so I just grunt.

That afternoon at five, there is a meeting of the Conseil Syndic, a small, elected group that meets every three months or so to deal with issues that affect the block. There are around fifty apartments. The owners meet altogether once a year and the members of the Conseil keep an eye on things in the meantime.

I count seven people at the meeting, which is held in the concierge's office, though she isn't there. It's chaired by the President or Chairman, a no-nonsense man in his sixties, stocky, ex-Army, sports a large moustache. There is an ENT surgeon, Henri, who speaks, with great authority but little knowledge, for all the health professionals. There are about a dozen of these in the block. Two psychiatrists, a podiatrist, three nurses and I can't remember what else. An elderly, deaf French lady, Sandrine, who is a self-appointed spokeswoman for all the dissatisfied owners, constantly chatters away partly to herself and partly, in a confidential manner, to the President who sits next to her. He ignores her.

There are a couple of Italian ladies, one of whom, Andrea, is rather sensible, while the other, Maria, is completely mad as well as deaf. They sit together. Maria's French is non-existent, so she has to get Andrea to translate for her. They talk to each other in Italian throughout the meeting regardless of whether anyone else is speaking. I'm there but, as English and a dentist, regarded as of little significance on both counts. A man from the agency which manages the block is available to advise, take notes and record any decisions. Rather him than me.

The main problem is the security of the block. Once there is a brief moment of relative silence, the President opens up on the topic.

'Welcome to everybody,' he begins. 'I've had three reports of problems relating to security since our last meeting. Two weeks ago, there was a man found at seven in the morning on one of the staircases, asleep and with used syringes beside him. Angela found him there when she arrived in the morning.'

Sandrine interrupts.

'It wasn't Angela, it was me. I woke him up by hitting him with my shoe. I took my shoe off because I didn't have anything else to hit him with. He was disgusting. Smelt of … I don't want to say. I called Angela and she called the Police. But he ran off before the Police came.'

The President carries on as if she hadn't spoken.

'Then there is the lady on the sixth floor. She's bringing men in, as we all know. I've had a complaint about her.'

Andrea explains this to Maria to whom she has to repeat the story.

'Si, si, prostituta. Prostituta. PROS TIT U TA.' In the end she is shouting the word so that even Sandrine can hear. A couple passing the window of the concierge's office hear the noise, stop and look in with interest. Henri makes an irritated, shooing away gesture.

We all know about this lady. The man who rents her the tiny apartment in which she plies her trade has been written to half a dozen times to no effect.

'Then,' the President goes on, 'There was the frightful attack on Mme. Drouot, last week. The attack reported in *Nice Matin.*'

'How did he get in?' asks Andrea.

'He seems to have climbed over the outer fence, then got onto the bicycle shed and pulled himself up onto her first floor terrace. The window was open,' explains the President. 'He's been arrested. Had a record.' Our President does not waste words.

There then ensues a wrangle over the security of the doctors' consulting rooms. The problem is that all the residents know that if you push the entryphone button for any of the doctors' consulting rooms the outside gate opens automatically. None of them enquires who wants to come in. I'm the same. It clearly isn't right, but I've been doing it for years. All the other residents object to this system. Andrea is particularly angry.

'I can't understand why the doctors can't pull themselves together. I thought doctors were supposed to be concerned for everybody's benefit, not just their own convenience.'

Henri explains:

'We don't all have receptionists. And, if we are seeing a patient, we can't just stop everything to answer the bell. If I'm looking into someone's ears or down their throats, I'm just not going to do it.'

Thinking of Pierre, I add:

'That's true. And remember some of us depend on drop-ins, passing trade, people who see the name on the plate and decide they want to see a doctor. Pierre Gaspard is one of those. He asked me to make this point.'

The discussion goes on for another half an hour. People talking over each other. Nobody listening to anyone else. At one point, Henri's wife appears at the window and makes gestures letting him know that it's dinnertime and she wants him to come home.

In the meeting, I hear the same old arguments that have been going on for at least five years. I used to find this funny, but now it's just boring and depressing. In the end I raise my hand, asking to speak. Because of the chaos, the President is unable to bring me in for nearly five minutes. Finally, he does and asks me what I want to say. I don't express myself well in French, but I try.

'One thing is important to understand. Whatever the doctors do isn't going to stop unwelcome intruders entering the building. Think of the three things that have happened since we last met. Probably all those would have happened anyway.'

There is a general murmur of agreement. I go on:

'But let's agree, it would be better if those doctors who only see people by appointment and who do have receptionists agreed only to let people in if they identify themselves. At least that would be a start. And that's what I agree to do. If, from now on, anyone gets in by pushing my bell when they haven't got an appointment, I'll buy you all a bottle of champagne.'

There is laughter at this. Shortly afterwards, the meeting breaks up. No decisions have been taken; they never are. Henri comes over to me.

'Ah, you English. So reasonable and pragmatic. And you have a sense of humour too. Wonderful.'

His praise merely depresses me more. All I've done is what anyone could have done. What a stupid, hopeless world this is.

I make my way back to my apartment, where I try to think about supper. I used to enjoy telling Eloise about these meetings, making her laugh. She always produced a particularly sumptuous dinner to follow them. In the end I boil myself some eggs and toast a baguette to go with them.

That evening, when I have my just before going to bed pee, I notice some blood in the pan. It's clearly nothing to do with my urine. It must come from my vagina. I'm alarmed and spend part of the night awake thinking what this might mean. The next morning the same thing happens. I touch my vulva and there is blood on it. At nine I ring Pierre on his mobile. He's the only person in Nice who knows that I'm trans. I suspect he's not even told Chantal, because she's often quite flirtatious with me. I doubt if she would be if she knew.

'Pierre, sorry to trouble you this early. I've had some bleeding from my vagina. I'm not sure the best way to handle this. It's going to mean some thinking about.'

'Yes, it certainly will. Let me think a bit. (There is a pause). You had better come up to Aspremont this evening after supper. I'll have a look at you there and then we can discuss what's best to do.'

I don't have a car. The public transport is so good here it would be a total waste of money. I take an Uber up to his place and arrive at about half past eight. He has a small consulting room up there and takes me straight inside. He's clearly told Chantal and his kids I'm not there for a social visit and they are not in evidence. After I've repeated what has happened and he's felt my abdomen, he tells me he must feel inside my vagina. 'Is that OK by me?'

'Yes, go ahead. It's going to feel very strange, but probably even stranger for you.'

To have a man feel inside the part of my anatomy I wish I didn't have is disconcerting, to say the least. But Pierre takes my mind off the procedure by talking me through it. He tells me there is certainly a good deal of blood around. He thinks he can detect a lot of irregular tissue on one side. Then he has a look with what I suppose must be some sort of scope. Then he tells me to dress while he washes his hands, very thoroughly and thoughtfully.

'Right. Let's go out onto the terrace. I'll fetch some Scotch. We're both going to need it. Me as well as you.'

So, we sit by his pool. It's a lovely evening. The water in the pool makes a gentle plashing noise and glints in the light from the living room. Way down below us the street lights of Nice twinkle brightly in the distance. On the sea, moving out of the Baie des Anges a cruise ship, probably on its way to Corsica, has its three decks clearly illuminated.

When we're settled, Pierre asks me what I think the bleeding might be. I say obviously I'm worried this might be a cancer of some sort. I can see he's relieved he doesn't have to be the first to mention the word.

'Well, George, I think you know what I'm going to say. You definitely need further investigation and you'll need to see a gynaecologist. Whoever it is will probably start off with an ultrasound. Then they'll do a biopsy, followed by either a CT scan or an MRI. You know about those'

'And the chances?'

'From what I've felt and seen, I would say there is a pretty high chance this is some form of cancer. The question is, if it's there, how much it's spread. And on that score, I really have no idea. These days, if it's not spread, or even if it's spread a bit, the chances of full recovery are very good. But it's just too early to say.'

'Who do you suggest I go to see? I've been thinking all day whether I should go and see someone outside Nice. But apart from the inconvenience and so on, I've begun to think there's not much point in trying to keep this secret any more.

There's so much stuff in the papers about trans. It's not like it used to be.'

'No. You're right,' Pierre says. 'You know I'd never met a trans patient up to five years ago, but now I'm seeing two.' He goes on, 'Would you rather see a man or a woman?'

'I've thought about that too. It really doesn't matter. For some reason, I thought a woman but just the best person.'

'I'll fix for you to see someone in the next week or two. You know, George, although we're friends and you're my patient I don't really know anything very much about this part of your life. Can you tell me a bit about how you came to Nice? But first I've got a confession to make.'

'A confession?'

'Yes. I've looked it up. Trans people who are on long-term high levels of testosterone are at risk of developing the sort of cancer I think you've got. Some people think it's a good idea for men like you to have regular screening tests.'

'Don't worry, Pierre. I think you're a great doctor. Forget it.'

I think about what Pierre has just said. In fact, I'm quite pleased I've not had regular tests. I've been spared a lot of unnecessary anxiety. It's really very relaxing to be sitting on the terrace by the pool up here. I'm in a mood to confide and go on talking:

'You want to know how I came to Nice? I've been your patient for about fifteen years, but I've been in Nice for much longer than that, about thirty-five. Eloise and I came here in the early eighties when we were in our mid-thirties.'

'But how come you wanted to settle in France in the first place?'

'Before we came to Nice, we lived in a place called Chichester in the south of England where I worked first as an assistant to a dentist and then had my own practice. It's a rather smart, conservative place. I was a woman then and Eloise and I were a couple, living together. I think people knew we were gay, but we didn't make it obvious. No physical affection in public and so on. Remember, this was the seventies.'

'So, what made you want to change?'

'Everything was fine for us, except one thing. I had always known, from quite a young child, I was really male. Just had the wrong body. I got more and more unhappy about the fact that I was, as I saw it, just pretending to be a woman. I had no doubt I was a man.'

'What did Eloise think about this wish of yours?'

'She understood it. She was very happy as a woman and extremely happy with our relationship, as indeed, I was.'

'But if you changed sex, she would be sleeping with a man. As a lesbian, how would she feel about that?'

'Yes, but luckily for us both, she just wanted to be with me. She was really bi. She had slept with one or two men as well as a lot of women before she met me. So that would work out OK.'

'How did you go about it?'

'We decided I would have a sex change but also we would move to France. Eloise was half French anyway. I found out I could have both my breasts removed in Bordeaux and start on testosterone at a clinic there.'

'You didn't want to go further? Have your ovaries and womb removed. Have some sort of penis fashioned for you? I suppose that wasn't possible then?'

I thought about our time in Bordeaux. It was a worrying time. We didn't know how Eloise would react to a woman without boobs. She thought it was going to be OK, but she couldn't be sure. Neither of us wanted me to take risks with more drastic surgery. I answered Pierre:

'No, it certainly wasn't easy at that time. Now I guess you could get all that on the National Health Service. But not then. I could have gone to Morocco where they were doing that sort of surgery. I just wasn't brave enough, I suppose, and neither was Eloise.

'Anyway, it must have been almost like a resurrection?'

'Yes, we really did start completely new lives. We spent six months in Bordeaux while I had the operation and began the injections. I was lucky. After about five months, my face had changed, my voice had deepened. I needed to shave and was beginning to have some hair on my chest.'

'So, how come Nice?'

'We'd always lived near the sea. I used to sail. We'd made a lot of money selling our house in Chichester. Property in England is much, much more expensive than here.

We saw advertised this practice in Nice where the dentist had suddenly died of a heart attack and his widow wanted to sell the lot, equipment included. We couldn't believe it when we saw the view from our front rooms. And, of course, with the EU, I could practice over here with very little additional paper work.'

I looked again out at the view. It was certainly attractive, but I'd never been able to understand why the Nicois didn't prefer to live on the sea front rather than miles away, up here. They said it was too noisy, the traffic and all that. But to be able just to cross the road and swim off the beach was, in our view, in Eloise's and mine, certainly worth putting up with a bit of noise. Pierre was asking about our arrival in Nice:

'Did his patients stay with you?'

'To be honest, not many. The French assume anyone trained abroad must be useless or worse, dangerous. But there is a large expat community in and around Nice – Cannes, Antibes, Monaco, Menton. A lot of them were quite keen to see someone who spoke English. With word of mouth, within a year we were doing pretty well.'

'So, it was all really easy?'

'Look, Pierre, being trans is never easy. We were very, very lucky. We were lucky enough to be in love. And we stayed in love after I had had my change. Of course, we had our ups and downs. We certainly had arguments. At first, when I began the injections, there were some little mechanical problems with the sex. But we had money and I had an occupation I could practice most places. All the same, I can't say it's been all that easy. We were worried we would be recognised in Nice by someone from home, visiting.'

'Were you ever recognised?'

'I never was. I really have changed in appearance. Once or twice I've seen people I knew from Chichester in the flower market, but they just passed me by. Eloise was recognised. People asked her about me and she just said that her life had changed, giving the impression that she was no longer with me. And I suppose, in a sense, that was true. She was no longer with the old me. She'd moved on to the new me. It just happened the new me had a lot in common with the old me.'

Pierre refers me to Agnès Dupont. He asks her to arrange to see me in a way that my trans wouldn't be revealed, but it doesn't work out that way. I have to wait in a reception area with three or four women. There is another man, but he is clearly there with his partner. I sit apart from the others in the waiting room and, the French being the French, no one asks me any questions.

Mme. Dupont is very matter of fact with me, as if she sees trans patients the whole time. I'm sure she is not, but she is confident in the way she goes about the examination and I can see she knows what she's doing.

As Pierre has predicted I have to have an ultrasound, then a biopsy, and finally an MRI. It is indeed a cancer, but it hasn't spread outside the womb. This means I can have surgery followed by radiotherapy with a good chance of success. I have to close the practice earlier than I have envisaged, but that's no bad thing. I've got quite enough to live on.

While I was waiting to see Mme. Dupont, I thought I recognised one of the nurses in the Clinic who has been a patient of mine. I suspect this and the fact that our concierge took delivery of a letter from the gynae clinic addressed to Mme. Gould, meant that my being trans was no longer a secret; it was all over the place.

The day after I get the letter, giving my date of operation two weeks ahead, I see Joao in the street walking towards me with three of his friends, including what I assume is his girlfriend. I expect to say hallo, but he doesn't acknowledge me. He and his friends just walk straight past me. I stop and look round, hardly believing he cannot have recognised me.

I see they have stopped. Joao is pointing at me and laughing. No difficulty guessing what he and his friends are laughing at.

The morning after this distressing event, I decide to come clean to Margaret. I've been meeting her on the beach at eight-o-clock, every Tuesday and Friday for years. She's a Canadian widow, about my age, who came to Nice many years ago with her husband. We usually have a chat before and after we swim. The French don't get up in the morning; we usually have this part of the beach entirely to ourselves.

'Margaret, after we swim, would you have time to have a coffee? There's something I would like to talk to you about.'

She looks startled. We've never met each other except on the beach, mostly chatting while up to our waists in water. I used to tell Eloise, who hated swimming and hardly ever went on the beach, about what we'd talked about. Nice gossip, the corrupt administration, the awful evening bus service, that sort of thing.

I swim faster than Margaret, so I'm ahead of her after a few strokes. When I'm well clear I look out to sea. It crosses my mind that I could just turn towards Corsica and swim until I'm too tired to go further. Then I could just give up. After all, what is there to live for? No Eloise any more. No real friends. No possibility of finding another partner even if I wanted one, which I don't. No interests beyond my work which I'm soon going to have to give up. No nothing, really.

Then I remember I've made an arrangement to have a coffee with Margaret. I'm not the sort of man who breaks arrangements. It's ridiculous I should think this way, but I do. So, I turn back when I'm parallel to the Radisson and swim back to where I've left my things.

We go together to a café on the Avenue de la Californie, just behind my apartment block. I start to tell her my story, but she interrupts.

'If you're going to tell me you're trans, George, of course, I knew that the day we first met. I'm an ex-nurse, remember. Your mastectomies were beautifully done, but there are very fine scars. The hair on your chest isn't all that thick that it covers them completely.'

I'm completely taken aback by this reaction.

'That's amazing. We've been meeting all this time and I never had the slightest inkling you knew.'

'It wasn't just the scars, George. You always wear floppy swimming trunks, but when you come out of the water, they stick to your crotch and it's obvious there's nothing under there.'

'You know, when I've been talking to you, I've not thought about being trans, not once. It's just not been part of how I've thought of myself while I've been with you.'

'How *do* you think about yourself then, George?'

I think hard about this before I reply.

'Well, as a man, of course. As a dentist. As a pretty good dentist. As an Englishman. Definitely not as a Frenchman. I suppose I have about ten identities. Let me carry on. As a Nicois. I've been here quite long enough to feel part of the city. As a widower. As an old man, I suppose.'

'But you're not an old man, George. At least, if you're an old man then I must be an old woman. Can't accept that.'

'No, you're quite right. You're not an old woman. So, I can't be an old man. Except that I feel one. Not just an old man but a sad sack of an old man. There you go.'

I suddenly feel cold. Usually I have a hot shower after I've been in the sea but this time I've come straight to this café. I look round. The place is nearly empty, but there is a German couple having their breakfast at a nearby table. They are probably refugees from the breakfast in the hotel next door, which is notoriously mean. Not even croissants. Margaret is talking:

'It's interesting you haven't felt trans while we've talked. After I realised it, I never thought of you as trans either.'

'No. But now I do. Being trans was about tenth in the list of ways I thought about myself. That is, until about a week ago. Now it's pretty well top. You see, I've had this vaginal bleeding.'

I tell her about my visit to the gynaecologist. I go on:

'All this has taken me back to when I was in my twenties. Being trans was very much part of who I felt I was then. I thought about it all the time. I hated having to pretend to be a woman. And in those days, in the nineteen sixties and nineteen seventies, being found out to be trans was a disaster. I would certainly not have been able to find work as a dentist.'

'Well, I'm really sorry to hear about your bleeding. But I have to tell you, I don't think of you as a trans man. You're just a man I enjoy chatting to you on Tuesday and Friday mornings. In fact, George, I think you're lonely. I've told you about these evenings once a week when I invite people over for drinks. They're on Sundays. Why don't you come over next Sunday?'

'It's very good of you to ask me. I just couldn't face a whole group of people.'

So, we part. I go back to my apartment, musing about what Margaret has told me. A few days later, I have my operation. Agnès thinks she got all the cancer out, but I have to have a course of radiotherapy. They're now much more sensitive at the Clinic and I'm seen apart from all the women.

* * *

Three months later. I still think about Eloise pretty well all the time, but good things are happening. I've started to attend a sculpture course. I was always interested in the modelling aspect of dentistry. Now I've begun to move beyond the mouth to whole faces. I've been to one of Margaret's salons. Not sure about it, but I might go again.

Yesterday, Joao called me on his mobile. He asked if he could come and see me.

'M. Gould, I wonder if I could start my lessons again. I'm not getting good marks in my English. I've broken up with Odette now so that isn't a problem.'

'Yes, of course. It would be a pleasure. Shall we start next Wednesday? Millefeuilles still your favourite?'

'There's something else I want to ask you, M. Gould. There's a boy in my class who thinks he's a girl. There's big problems about his changing his name. It's not a big change. Just Francoise from Francois. But nobody likes the idea. Not the students, not the teachers. And there's which toilets he should use. That seems quite a headache. Can we talk about that?'

We start to talk about it. Then I realise he's very, very interested. It will be a good topic for our conversations in the future. I doubt the vocabulary will be all that much use to him in his Bac, but at least we'll be talking more freely than before. And I shall certainly stay awake.

After a break for my hospitalisation, I've started my lunches with Pierre again. Today, he's obviously preoccupied. When we're onto coffee, he breaks the sad news.

'George, I have to tell you. Chantal has left me. She has another man. A really rich bastard. Banker. Worse, he's in Aspremont. She wants to live with him.'

I can't say I'm terribly surprised. Pierre has always been the infatuated one. He has been immensely proud of Chantal, of having such a good-looking, elegant wife. I always thought she had her eyes open for other opportunities. He goes on and I can see he is becoming tearful:

'It's a disaster. We'll have to sell the house. We'll share the boys, so I'll need to find a place big enough for them to sleep over.'

'I'm really sorry, Pierre.'

'Yes. You know, you and Eloise had such a wonderful relationship. I just wish Chantal and I … Ah, well.'

And I begin to weep. We look round. A waiter at the counter is looking at us. This is not the sort of behaviour expected of men lunching together in the Brasserie Magnan.

IN THE PUBLIC INTEREST

For the last fifty years, except for really special occasions, I've always had chicken noodles for lunch accompanied by a glass of Tsingtao beer. It's the beer my dad always drank for lunch back home in Hong Kong. This *is* indeed a special occasion, so I'm lunching off lobster thermidor with a half bottle of Chablis. This is followed by fresh strawberries and cream. As I savour the lobster, I go over yesterday's events. It certainly was a helluva day!

It began quietly enough. I always rise at around 5.30 and, after shaving, showering and dressing, move to my office next to the bedroom usually arriving at around six. There, on my desk, I find all the main broadsheet and red top UK newspapers in a pile ready for me to read. Sam has left them there. He brings in my breakfast, noodles in broth. Naturally, as I sip, I turn first to the papers that I own.

My broadsheet, *The National,* is usually pretty dull but I read it carefully to make sure it's toeing the line on issues that interest me such as Brexit and the latest Trump gaffe. I also have a quick look at how the markets are doing. My red top *The Moon*, is a lot more compelling. I turn first to page 3 to scrutinise the girl who is baring her bum or her boobs or both. Then I look at the editorial to check the line we're taking on the main news stories of the day. I skim over the others; it's always a good idea to keep an eye on the competition, though usually, like yesterday, there's not much to worry about. The others never really seem to have a new idea between the lot of them.

Just before 7 am, I click on *Hyena News* to catch the latest. When I bought this news channel I couldn't have imagined how profitable it was going to be. Shortly after I got it, I made my older brat the chairman of the company running it. He's done a pretty good job. It's now appealing to the millions who think Trump is the most wonderful leader the US has ever had. As a result, after only five years, it's making us a fortune. Terence is a good lad. I sometimes feel the name of Terence Wang is better known than my own, but most people know it's me, Lewis, who started and still really runs the show.

By 7 am, I'm ready to call my editors to tell them what I think about today's papers. An owner is supposed to be hands off as far as his editors are concerned. That's all very well if you can trust the bleeders to keep turning out papers that people will buy. In my experience, you can't. In my view, I've got every right to make sure the ship's sailing in the right direction. Yesterday, I had good cause for complaint. My editors know I can sack them. I don't need to remind them; they know it very well. So first I ring Carol.

'Look, Carol, Lewis here. Not a bad issue, today. But I really don't like the way *The National* will keep referring to every improvement in the UK financial position as occurring 'in spite of Brexit'. Why can't you see that much of this improvement is occurring because of Brexit? We all knew the pound was going to fall. Look at me. I'm getting much more sterling for my news channels now the dollar is doing so well. And, by the way, you're allowing far too much negative stuff about the Tories to get into the paper.'

Carol listens to what I have to say; she's got no option. But then she argues a bit.

'Lewis, the whole of our financial section, from Charles, our Finance Editor, down to the girl we've taken on as an intern, think that Brexit is a disaster that's already started to happen. I'm going to lose them if we start pushing any other line.'

'There's always others, Carol. There's always others. I can't let you get away with this for much fucking longer.'

'We've got a really high-quality team of writers here, Lewis. There's not one I would want to lose.'

That's as may be. I know that Carol will change her tune on Brexit very soon.

Then I ring Gerald.

'Congratulations, Gerald, on the piece in *The Moon* mocking the Chinese for trying to break into the cable news business. Quite a funny article about what the fellow who wrote the article calls junk journalism. I must say though, I'm less happy about the way the paper continues to report on Trump's tweets. They may not sound like Confucius but they're a lot more sensible than CNN's stuff.'

'Well,' Gerald says, 'I'll publish something positive about Trump when the opportunity arises; the problem is Trump doesn't say much it's possible to be positive about without looking off one's rocker.'

I let that one go. Facts are: Brexit is good for my businesses. Trump is good for my businesses. That's it. Period. And businesses have to expand to stay alive. I'm always on the lookout for papers worth buying, even if only to put them out of business.

One rag I would like to see disappear down the fucking plughole is *Private Eye*. When I was 18, I changed my name from Wang Loo to Lewis Wang. *Private Eye* got to know that and now the great wits there call my papers *The Lavatory Press* and my company Toilet Corp. I've spent a fortune on lawyers advising me that *Private Eye* has nearly but not quite libelled me and that I probably wouldn't win a case if I brought one. Well, the wankers who write in *Private Eye* can carry on laughing. I'll get the bastards in the end.

My motto has always been – 'give people what they want' and they'll buy it. People who call my red tops the gutter press or the popular press or the lavatory press or whatever they want, think I view the public as rolling in dirt and wanting more dirt. That's not so. The fact that the public likes dirt doesn't mean it's living in dirt. The great majority of my readers live good, clean lives. But they need some fun and they're not looking to Marcel Proust or James Joyce to provide it. *Private Eye* gives a few eggheads in Hampstead what they want and much good may it do them.

I've always won the circulation wars because I really believe in the free market. Those sanctimonious prigs who ran the British press up to the 1970s said the same things, but they behaved as if they knew better than the public what the public wanted. They let their ideals get in the way of their greed. Like it or not, it's greed that matters. Greed not only makes the world go round, it actually improves living standards everywhere. If this means journalists digging up the dirt about well-known people who ought to know how to behave better, then so be it.

So-called celebrities are much more interesting with their trousers down than with them where they ought to be. My editors and the chief executives of our companies know my trousers down approach (the Wang TD approach) to news stories. That's what they're there to achieve and I don't need to know how they do it. The fact that a few people who ought to have behaved better have been destroyed frankly doesn't worry me. And I'm certainly not worried about ending the careers of a few fucking useless newspaper editors and journalists who've failed to keep up with the competition.

They call me ruthless. Very true, and I'm not ashamed of it. I first learned about the need to be ruthless at Charlington, the school my Dad sent me to so that I could learn British values. Making it to head boy as a rather under-sized Chinese upstart meant destroying one or two reputations of other boys, competitors who thought they were my friends. Just the odd insinuation they might be gay seemed to do the trick. Head boys at Charlington always went on to Trinity, Cambridge. I didn't need to be ruthless at Cambridge. Becoming editor of *Varsity* was an easy promotion after my father bought it for peanuts.

At 8 am the faithful Tessa arrives. She likes getting in early as it means she misses the worst of the rush hour. I let her leave at 3 pm so she has it easy on her way home too. She is really the centre of my life now. Wives are for status, decoration and sex. My PA is for what really matters in my life – the business. I have quite a small group around me. As well as Tessa, there is Sam, who can't sleep and is happy to bring in the papers at 5 am. He doubles up as my chauffeur. There are Delroy and Doug, my heavies. Delroy doubles up as my personal trainer. And there are Petra and Paula, my secretaries, who really don't have enough to do, but I like having two secretaries around.

When Tessa arrives, I get her to send off a tweet approving Donald's latest crazy. The old narcissist ought to be happy with that when he wakes up. Now there's a man whose trousers are hardly ever up but no one would never dream of pointing it out. Any of my editors who made a mistake on that score would soon be on fucking welfare.

At 8.30 I start on the serious side of the day. Although my papers don't make much money, they're very helpful promoting other sides of the business. At the moment our main headache is the attempt being made to censor the content of Wangoo, our search engine. We know that IS terrorists, paedophiles and all sorts of other nasties are posting messages on it, sometimes in code, anyway with piss poor attempts to disguise what they're doing.

Problem is once we start editing out stuff we have to take on vast numbers of new staff. That's expensive. Then there are all sorts of issues about what sort of stuff we should be stopping. It's complicated, unnecessarily so. If we let the public decide what they want to read and what they don't, they do the work for us. Trust the people to judge content, I say. It's cheaper and it bloody works.

Trouble is there's this Secretary of State for Communications or whatever she's called woman who takes a different view. I draft a paper on the subject to send to Terence, but there are other ways of getting at the opposition. I ring Gerald.

'Look, mate, it's time to get serious about Stephanie at Communications. She'll be stopped in her tracks on the Wangoo business once she knows you've got all that stuff about her having fun and frolicking with that woman at her college. Just get one of your clever Charlies to draft something and let her know you're thinking of publishing. OK, you say she's got no worries about being outed, But apparently, she doesn't want the other woman brought into it. Incidentally, how do you know about that?'

'I don't think you need to know all the details there, Lewis,' Gerald says. He sounds cagey. I know he's trying to protect me, but he doesn't need to.

'Anyway,' he goes on, 'However we know, and however we got to know it, Fran whatever, the girl she bedded at college, is also married but it isn't going too well. Fran's worried that if her husband gets to know about her past, he'll ditch her. I don't want to do it. We've tried to get Fran to talk. Offered her 100k for her story, but she won't do it.'

'Well, looks as if she's going to lose her hubby and finish up poor then, doesn't it? Just do it, Gerald. Do it.'

'Lewis, I really don't want to. Give me a week and I'll find something else on Stephanie.'

'OK, mate, you've got a week, but no longer.'

At 9.30 am I go down the corridor to my gym. Delroy is already there. He's been one of my two heavies for the past three years. After he joined the staff, I realised he was into fitness and body building but didn't have the remotest clue how to go about it. I paid for him to go on a course so that he could double up and work as my trainer. No point in paying two salaries where one will do.

Basically, I'm in pretty good nick for my age. The arthritis in my right hip means I have to use a stick. It's difficult to use the treadmill without giving myself too much gyp. Working on the rest of me, building up the muscles in my arms and shoulders, doing balance and stretching exercises takes up a good hour. Delroy is not the greatest brain and, when he tries to get me to do something way beyond my capacity, I tell him so. He's obviously put out but what the hell, he's paid to do his job.

After I've finished in the gym I'm knackered and need a kip. I lie down and sleep for about an hour. Ten years ago, I would have laughed at anyone needing sleep during the day, but, at 84, I can't get through the day without it. I just don't talk about it so only my close staff know.

At 11 am I start dictating to Petra and Paula. I send memos to Terence who chairs the television, broadband, internet and mobile phone companies. I check through their accounts in preparation for my meeting with Harold, my accountant, at 11.30. When he arrives, I give him hell on the amount of tax I'm paying to the UK government.

'Why can't I cut down the amount I'm paying the Treasury? All they spend it on are these vast welfare bills?'

'Lewis, I've been working for you now for nearly twenty years cutting down on your tax. You've got companies in the Virgin Islands, Bermuda and Jersey. I reckon you're paying around 3% on your gross income now. I know that's a lot. Maybe £30 million. But I can't get it down any more without risking having the law on us.'

I have to accept that he's right, but it hurts.

At noon, Tessa comes in.

'You do remember, Lewis, you're getting married at 2. Then there's the Reception at 4.30.'

'It hadn't slipped my mind. It's just there's so much else to catch up on. Could you ring Dara on her mobile, to check she will be at the church at 1.45? Just because she's a so-called celebrity, she thinks she can turn up whenever she wants. No idea of punctuality. She thinks the world will wait for Dara Kashin, no matter how late she is. Well, let me tell you, Tessa, life for Dara is going to change.'

I get Tessa to check through the guest list for the reception and give it me so that I can be sure to get at least most of the important names right. Over my usual chicken noodle lunch, I pore over the list and try to memorise the names. I seem to have coming at least the present and all the former Prime Ministers (except, of course, the one who fucked my last wife). Two former American Presidents is not a bad score.

Donald says he's too busy to make it over the pond. That's quite a relief. I can just imagine his tweet from the reception. Doubtless something about the Brits who've got all the time in the world to party but no idea how to sort their economy out without American help. If they think he's going to let even one American job go just to buy a visit to H M the Queen, they've got another think coming.

The guest list looks all right, so I go on to check the details of the pre-nuptial to make sure it's watertight. It says if we break up we both take what we brought to the marriage. Basically, as all she owns is a pad in Mayfair she got when she broke up with her last, this means she will have to walk away with less than five million. Her lawyer insisted she ought to do better than this, so I agreed to give her a million for every year she stayed with me. She can keep any gifts I make to her. As I'm not intending to give her anything apart from the fucking expensive engagement ring she's flashing around everywhere, this shouldn't create any problems.

Any increase or reduction in my assets are my responsibility. None of her brats has any rights to my assets. She's not entitled to any financial support if we break up. Her lawyer thought she was out of her little mind (a considerable contrast to her great face and body) to accept all this but I know she thinks she can do a great deal better than this once we're spliced. Well, we shall see!

I buzz for Tessa and over the green tea that always follows the noodles I talk to her about why I'm getting married. I know she thinks I'm out of my mind to marry for the fourth time when I can have any woman I want for the asking. I'm sure I could have Tessa but no way. That would leave me without anyone to talk to and I can't afford that.

'I suspect, Tessa, you're asking yourself why I should want to marry an airhead like Dara. Well, it's clearly not for intelligent conversation. Fact is, I need to show I've still got balls. It's the business that keeps me going. I love it; I need it. If I've got a woman like Dara in tow, then people will carry on thinking about me as a serious player. And, you must admit she's gorgeous.'

Tessa doesn't say anything. She probably doesn't like my talking to her in this open way about the sexual attraction of another woman. Too bad.

'You know, it's not mainly about sex. It's the way I'm built. I can't help it. It's what I'm like. For some reason, I need to have won, to possess, to own a woman every man from fifty upwards would like to have as their own. That's what Dara is. A glittering prize I've awarded to myself. Thank you, Lewis.'

After I've changed into my new lounge suit, I realise at once that the jacket buttons only just meet, It makes me look paunchy. Bugger. Sam drives me in the Merc to St. Joseph's in the Strand. Smart place. Where all the English gentry get spliced, I'm told. Dara turns up, to do her credit, only a minute or so after me and we go into the church together.

When I look at Dara, I think once again how stunning she is. She's slim, tall, at five feet eight a good three inches taller than me. She's wearing the Erdem dress she wanted because this is a designer both Kate and Pippa have used. She really does look a woman any man would desire to wed. I feel that, despite what my brats might think, indeed what they've said in a pretty forthright fashion, I'm doing the right thing both for myself and for the business.

I've invited no one to the wedding ceremony itself except my children, their other halves and my grandchildren. So, Terence acts as best man and hands me the ring. Dara has several friends, as well as her four children and her one granddaughter, seven-year-old Charlie who acts as bridesmaid. This wedding ceremony is all Dara's idea. I would have been happy to go to a Registry Office and get the whole thing over in half an hour, but Dara wanted the Church, followed by a grand reception and then a family supper before we turned in.

After we've entered the church together we walk past our respective families, hers to the left and mine to the right, up to the front, where it turns out we've got a woman to officiate. Grey hair, very prim-looking. She takes us through the ritual with an air of great seriousness I find quite inappropriate. What the hell! We're only getting married.

I never went through this caper before with my earlier three marriages but apparently it involves making marriage vows which Dara has proposed we write ourselves. I couldn't think of anything I wanted to say, but Tessa found something on the Internet for me that was neither too sickly sentimental nor too religious. It went:

'I offer myself to you as a partner in life. I vow to love you in sickness and in health. I commit myself to encourage you in good times and in bad. I will cherish and respect you all the days of our life together. Starting anew once again, I give thanks that I have found you. May our marriage be a gift to the world and our families, as your love is a gift to me.' Ugh!

Dara's vow surprises me because it's obviously original and something she wrote herself. It goes:

'I vow that I shall be true to you, Lewis, in sickness and in health. I shall love you to the maximum that I am able. I shall give you whatever I can, so that you will feel properly appreciated according to what you have done for the world.'

First I knew I might be a great benefactor to the world, and I'm not sure I like it. But there's a bit of me that feels touched. After the vows, we exchange rings. I've already given Dara this diamond-studded engagement ring. Now I give her a simple gold band Tessa found for me. She gives me something similar.

The affair goes off pretty well, except that one of Susan's children, the three-year-old, called Florence Venetia, if you believe, completely loses it and bellows throughout both our vows, making them inaudible to all but ourselves and the lady bishop, if that's what she is. Dara mutters to me why doesn't she just take the little monster out and I can see she's pleased it's one of mine and not one of hers that's making all the fuss.

Service over, Sam then drives Dara and me in the Merc to Hertford House to get ready for the reception. I'm pleased to see there are photographers outside already even though it's half an hour before it begins. I know that Tessa will have tipped off the *National* and the *Moon* so that they can get their people in front of the others to get the best pics. It's a big deal to get Hertford House to shut the Wallace Collection to the public three hours early. This is where Dara wanted our party to be.

I've never been to the Wallace Collection before. The staircase at the top of which Dara and I will receive guests is amazing. I go into the Great Gallery where the reception is to be held. We have half an hour before the guests come so I wander round with a nice young girl employed as a guide by the Collection, looking at the paintings. I recognise 'The Laughing Cavalier', but the painting that makes me sit up is called 'Dance to the Music of Time'. It's by Nicolas Poussin.

The nice girl tells me the story of the painting.

'On the right is an old man,' she tells me. 'He is meant to be Bacchus. He is playing a lyre. It's to his tune the four girls are dancing in a circle. The girls are supposed to represent Poverty, Labour, Riches and Pleasure.'

The old chap on the left, while playing his harp, or whatever it is, is starkers. He's gazing, his eyes full of lust, on the four women. I wouldn't mind being in his place! They're all good-lookers. They make me think of my four marriages. They could be the women who danced or, like Dara, will dance to my tune. Of course, there have been others, quite a few others now I come to think of it.

The girl interrupts my train of thought.

'When Poussin painted this ...' she starts to say. I put my hand up to stop her talking.

Yes, they could be my four wives beginning with Poverty (Laura) when I was well, fairly, hard up. Then there was Labour, when I fought like crazy to get beyond just one or two Hong Kong papers and hit the big money in the UK; that could be Samantha. Then Riches, no problem, that's Denise, all right. Then there is Pleasure. I think of Dara and feel a tiny flicker down below. My cock will be a lot harder tonight with the little yellow tablets. I wonder if the painting is ever put up for sale.

'Of course,' the girl says, 'They're dancing in a circle. That's supposed to mean that Poverty follows Pleasure and the whole thing starts again.'

'Well,' I say to myself, 'There's no way Dara is going to leave me poverty-stricken. I think I've taken care of that all right.'

The nice girl tells me our guests are going to start arriving in five minutes, so I move to my position with Dara at the top of the staircase. Our families come first, and I'm pleased that, at least, I can remember the names of Dara's four children, even if the names of their partners are quite beyond me.

Then comes a vast concourse, something like a hundred and fifty in all, of politicians, actors, musicians, composers, newspaper editors, and God knows what else. They're followed by a gaggle of Dara's friends, most of them dressed outrageously so as to maximise their chances of being photographed on the way in. This lot all arrive a bit flushed at the fact they've really been noticed.

When mostly everyone has arrived and been welcomed, and they're all tucking into canapés and bubbly, Dara and I are released to join the party. She immediately goes over to her girlfriends and, within minutes, there are shrieks of laughter from their corner of the room. The groups all stick to their own kind. The politicians get into a huddle with Tories and the Labour lot all joining in together.

I feel like an outsider at my own party. I sidle up to the Prime Minister to see if I can get her to see a way out of our Wangoo problem. I've already greeted her when she arrived, so she knows who I am. She smiles at me.

'Congratulations, Lewis. A great party. Sorry I can't stay longer.'

'It's really good of you to come at all, Prime Minister.' I wonder if I might have a few words with you about this problem over the content of Wangoo.'

'Ah yes,' she says. 'I haven't really been kept up to speed on that. Something to do with copyright? Is that right?'

She clearly doesn't have the faintest idea what I'm on about. She wanders off to talk to the politicians.

I find myself standing alone. My editors come over, but conversation is not easy. Small talk is just not my forte. I'm beginning to think I'm not going to last out until bedtime. We hang around for a bit and then are told that supper is ready in the Dining Room.

Dara has said we have to have this dinner so that our two broods can get to know each other. We sit at two tables with me at one and Dara at the other, the members of our families all mixed up with this in mind. After about fifteen minutes I can see that the mixing seems to be going rather too well. Susan, my younger brat, is clearly making a pass at one of

Dara's sons, name now forgotten. He looks as though he's really interested and, although I'm too far away to be sure, it seems to me likely there is already some footsie going on under the table. Their two spouses seem to be aware of what's going on and don't like it.

It's not long fortunately before Susan's attention is drawn elsewhere. Her three-year old, the said Florence Venetia, is protesting about the food. Apparently, she doesn't like the avocado mousse and is asking for chicken nuggets or crisps or pizza or a burger and cheese. Hertford House doesn't seem able to come up with the goods under any of these headings. I can predict with a fair amount of confidence that she's not going to like the lemon sole goujons that are to follow or the filet de mignon cordon bleu that is to follow that.

Florence Venetia's hollering threatens to drown out the discreet sounds of the music played by the harpsichordist Tessa has thoughtfully arranged to accompany the dinner. I had suggested to Susan that she didn't bring her brat to the meal, but that hadn't seemed possible. Anyway, in the end, bloody Florence Venetia has to be removed from the room. Susan has to go home with her. At least that means we are saved from a family scandal on the same day that Dara and I get married.

At last, Sam drives us to the Beaumont where Tessa has booked the Roosevelt Suite. We are rapidly flunkied up to our room. It's vast. Totally over the top. It's laid out as just one bedroom but it's big enough for five. I can see the curtains are silk and the rugs hand-made. There are expensive-looking sculptures and paintings all over the place. There's a kitchen and two, if you can believe it, fucking bathrooms. Talk about a king-size bed. This one's big enough to sleep an emperor and his fair-sized harem, both. Whose idea was this? Dara's, I'm sure. This is the last time I let her book any hotels we stay in.

I waste no time, go into the bathroom and take the little yellow pill my doctor has sworn is the latest and most powerful successor to Viagra. Dara arranges her clothes, while talking to me about who she's spoken to at the Reception.

'I thought the party went really, really well. It was great talking to Antony Gormley. Did you know he's designed one of the rooms in this hotel? What a man! How clever can you get? Sculptures all over the place and designing rooms. It's just amazing. I don't think I like Elton John though. When I suggested he come and sing at one of our parties (I've got one in my mind for next month), he didn't seem to think that was the greatest idea. Quite rude, I thought.'

I sort of listen, but mostly I'm waiting to see if I can feel the tablet working. It does after about half an hour. And ten minutes later, I've got a quite respectable hard-on. We undress each other but I insist Dara keeps her knickers on and poses à la page 3 while I take a photo of her.

Dara gets me going a bit and lies on her back. I put my stick beside the bed in case I need it during the night. I usually have to get up at least twice for a pee. After I've sorted out my teeth, feeling completely whacked and ready to sleep for ever, I get into the bed and begin to move on top of her. Suddenly Dara freezes.

'Lewis, just wait a minute. I think there's a camera or something just above us. Look, just up there.' And she points up behind my head. Well, I'm not that flexible. I can't turn around to see what she's pointing at.

'I think there's another in the corner of the room, over there.' This time she points to the ceiling just above the bedroom door. I can see this one all right. My God, the room's been bugged. Dara gets out of bed and walks all around the room, experimenting to see which parts of the room seem like they are out of the cameras' fields.

'I think it's OK over here,' she says. As well as above the bed, she has also noticed what look like the lens of surveillance cameras in two corners of the room. She gets out of bed and experiments standing in different parts of the room.

In the end she reckons there's only one part of the room she thinks the cameras don't cover. She puts a chair over in this corner as there's no way of moving the bed there. You'd need four strong men to do that. Using my stick, I make my way over to the chair and sit on it. Dara goes into the bathroom. She's a few minutes there and when she comes out, for reasons I don't understand she's got dressed again. I'm naked and suffering from a painful hard-on, not easily managed when you're sitting down.

She brings a chair over to the corner where I'm sitting, places herself on it and sits down in front of me. I realise I can't move. My stick is only a couple of feet away, but I can't reach it. Without my stick I can't haul myself up.

A few moments later and I realise I've been tricked. Dara has a look I've never seen before. I can see she's really pleased with herself. I don't have to wait long to find out what's been going on.

'Right, Lewis,' she begins. 'You're going to have to listen to me. Not just for a few seconds like you usually do, but until I've finished. I've a lot to say.'

'You've probably guessed, because you're not stupid, that it was me that arranged for those cameras. I've locked the door to the living area and I'm not letting you have the key. You can shout for your heavies if you like, but I've paid them off. They're not outside the door as you think. It was them that fixed the cameras. The hotel allowed them into the room once they'd made clear they were your security people.

'Believe it or not, for just ten thousand apiece, Delroy and Doug were happy to go AWOL this evening. They know they're going to lose their jobs but for a mere ten thousand smackers on the nail they thought it was worth it. I don't know what you pay them, but it can't be much. And they don't exactly love you. In fact, they seemed delighted to oblige once they realised I was going to make a fool out of you.'

'Just fucking get on with it, Dara. I can't tell you how painful this hard-on is.'

'You want to know why I'm here, Lewis? I want you to know just how much I hate, yes, really hate you so much. Let me tell you why. I had a best friend in school. Diana. We were close, really very close. It was a smart, private school so only rich people could afford to send their kids there.'

'I've got no idea what you're talking about.'

'Just listen, Lewis, for a change. And you'll know soon enough. This girl's Dad was a highly paid British Airways pilot. He was a really nice man. I met him a lot because he was often at home between long haul flights. I knew her family life was miserable. Her Mum and Dad didn't get on.'

'Dara, why are you telling me all this? I'm cold. It's not the right moment for me to be listening to the troubles of your schoolfriends what must be thirty years ago.'

'Just you listen, Lew. Anyway, this dad of hers had an affair with one of the flight stewards. One of the other stewards who probably had the hots for him too, got in touch with *The Moon*. Your people really got onto him. Headlines like 'BA Lothario cocks it up' and 'Top BA pilot and his dishy crew' began to appear with pictures of both of them. *The Moon* helped the girl who shopped them get some tiny cameras into their hotel bedroom, so there were even pictures of them half-naked. A bit like you are now, Lewis. To cut a long story short, BA sacked both of them.'

'Well,' I said. 'Maybe they ought to have thought about what might happen when they started the affair.'

'You know perfectly well, Lew, that affairs like that must be going on all the time. He was just doing what I'm sure loads of pilots do. No, it was *The Moon* that ruined his life. And not just his life. My friend had to leave the school because there was no money to pay the fees. I kept in touch with her. She went to another perfectly good state school, but she began to hate her dad for what he'd done. She developed anorexia. He left home, couldn't find another job, began to drink heavily. The last I heard he'd gone into some sort of mental place. The whole family went to pieces.'

'You can't blame me, Dara, for a family breakdown that might have occurred anyway.'

'Don't try and wriggle out of it, Lew. Of course, it might have happened anyway, but it was *The Moon* that caused all the public shame and humiliation and probably made BA sack him.'

At this point I become aware of some knocking on the door. It sounds as if there are men out there, paparazzi it sounds like. They shout through the door.

'Hey, Lewis,' I hear. 'Dara told us we could have some pics of you both. Would it be convenient for us to come in now?'

Dara takes no notice but goes on:

'And, of course, it's not just you, Lew. And it's not just my friend and her Dad whose lives have been shattered. There were three hundred people whose phones were hacked by Rupert Murdoch's *News of the* World. Why do you think Richard Desmond's *Express* paid out £550,000 to Kate and Gerry McCann for messing up their lives even more than they had already been messed up by Madeleine's disappearance? Why do you think the *News of the World* paid out two million to the Dowler family and Rupert gave another million to charity? They were all guilty as hell.'

'Look, Dara. I've never been found guilty of any criminal offence. I just own a couple of newspapers. If journalists, off their own bat, choose to use what you might call unorthodox methods, that's not my fault. Just let me get to bed and bugger off if that's what you want to do.'

'I shall do no such thing. You're right about journalists. It's their call. But when they've got editors who are desperate for what I know you call 'trousers down' news, and when those editors have got owners who don't care how the circulation figures are improved so long as they go up, what can you expect?'

'Let me tell you, it's lucky there are some good journalists out there with principles that stop them getting involved in all this shit. They're our only hope against bastards like you who believe, and I think you really do believe, that it's greed and nothing but greed that makes the world go around.'

'I'm just a business man, Dara. Not just a business man, but a bloody good one, too. I keep tens of thousands of people in work. Most of them would be on the streets if it wasn't for my businesses.'

'You think you're a great business man. Let me tell you, Lewis, that the only reason Terence allows you to keep on looking after *The National* and *The Moon*, making big losses as they are, is to keep you so busy you don't have time to mess about with the serious stuff, the telecommunications. Both your papers lose money; it's just that Terence is coining it, so he doesn't need to worry. And, by the way, Lewis, don't think it's your age that repels me and makes you so disgusting that I wouldn't dream of ever having sex with you. I've had plenty of fun with a couple of quite frisky men your age. It's you I can't stand.'

'You bitch. You fucking, fucking bitch.'

At last my erection fades. I can move from the chair far enough to grab my walking stick. I pick it up and with all the strength in my arms that Delroy's training has given me, I hit Dara a massive blow on the head. She may be three inches taller than me, but she's sitting down and I'm able to stand over her.

'You fucking bitch. You and all the other fucking bitches who've been in my life.'

She wasn't expecting this and doesn't attempt to protect herself. She falls off the chair, her face bleeding. I stand over her and hit her again just where I had struck before. I look at her on the floor, moaning and bleeding, for a few moments. She's conscious, but only just. I don't want her to lose consciousness. I want her to feel all the hurt I'm feeling. All the hurt she's inflicted on me.

Blood is coming from her nose and mouth. It's trickling on to the dress she wore for the wedding and is wearing now. Grasping my stick, I hobble over to the door and open it to the paparazzi. 'Here's your story, lads. The best you'll ever get. And what about this for a picture? Now this really is in the public interest.'

As four or five men, cameras at the ready, enter the room. I go over to where Dara is lying, I stand over her, my stick raised. The paparazzi take their pictures, making not the slightest attempt to go to Dara's assistance.

Apart from being taken on a magistrate's order to the remand cells in Wandsworth prison, that was the end of yesterday. As I tuck into the lobster that the faithful Tessa has, against all the rules but doubtless with a bit of help from higher authority, sent in for me, I go over what has happened.

There have probably been better wedding nights, I reflect, sipping the Chablis, But perhaps none where the outcome has given the groom greater satisfaction.

Assisted Dying

It's four-o-clock in the morning. I'm alone. Totally alone, except for the pain, that is. When I woke half an hour ago, there was almost complete silence. Just the sound of one of the night staff walking in the corridor past my room every few minutes on her way to another resident. Pain, an unwelcome intruder, has woken me. It's colic – a sharp stabbing sensation in my belly that lasts a few seconds. It gradually dies away and then returns in anything up to a few minutes but never longer.

I knew I wouldn't be able to get back to sleep, so, as I usually do, I put on the World Service. The news is full of the Brexit referendum, due in a month. Journalists, as always, turning it into a drama. It's obvious that the vote will be for Remain, thank God, but they have to make it sound as if the result is uncertain.

I've removed the blankets. The weight of them seems to make the pain worse. It means the room is a bit chilly, but I like this. The feeling of being cold takes my mind off the colic. Doreen says the colic is caused by spasms in my gut which is refusing to give up on the idea it is still pushing food through even though the crap is coming out of my ileostomy higher up.

I mainly sleep on my left side, but every fifteen minutes or so, my back feels sore, so I have to turn on my right. This brings on the other pain, the sciatica, which shoots down my left leg. After a little time, this subsides. I'm left accompanied only by the colic until I have to turn over again. It will be just the two of us (three when we're joined by the sciatica), until Hortense comes in at seven.

I know some people turn to God for spiritual comfort when they are experiencing terrible pain. Not me. I'm proud to remember that I was only about fourteen when I realised that there can't be a God, or at any rate, if he or she has created a world in which such awful pain exists, a God who cares tuppence about any of the human race.

Goodness knows, I'm as aware as anyone of the arguments that claim the existence of a caring deity is quite compatible with human suffering. Some of these arguments even suggest that the experience of pain is further proof of God's existence. Well, tell that to the terminally ill. If this was the only world God could create, he wasn't much good at his job. And if he's deliberately created a world of pain then he's a bastard who, if he ever decided to take a stroll out of heaven, should never be let back in by St. Peter.

The care staff, especially Doreen, who manages this place, think I'm out of my mind not to increase the stuff they give me to control my pain. At the moment, I'm just on paracetamol. I know this can only have a trivial effect. But I'm not going to take more powerful medication precisely because my main fear is of being out of my mind. I took morphine for a couple of days a month or so ago. It made me feel as out of my mind as I could imagine. Drowsy, muddled, incapable of putting two thoughts together. And putting thoughts together is what I live for. What I've always lived for. Perhaps the only thing I've really ever lived for.

On morphine, I could remember very little of what I wanted to remember and certainly I couldn't think clearly. My memory and my reason are my most precious possessions. I'm just not going to lose them until the last possible moment whatever it costs me. Aside from which, though I don't want to tell the staff as I know it would upset them, even their precious morphine doesn't make the pain go away completely. The stabbing of the colic and the shooting pain down my leg are still very much there, just slightly less fierce, that's all.

When eventually Hortense comes in at 7, I'm relieved. I know it's supposed to be her, but sometimes, because another member of staff can't come in and she replaces them, I get someone else. She gives me her usual greeting,

'How you doing, Dr. L?'

Resisting the temptation to tell her I have been awake since half past three, trying to think clearly, occasionally stroking my cock hopefully but unsuccessfully, mercifully dropping off for a few minutes at a time, I reply, also as usual,

'I'm doing fine, Hortense.' I really want to say 'I doing fine.' But I must resist the temptation to tease Hortense on account of her accent. She would rightly be upset and offended. It's taken me many years to stop teasing but I think I'm beginning to manage it. At 94, you might think 'not before time'.

'You really OK, Dr. L?' persists Hortense. 'You don't look too good.'

'I fine, Hortense.' Oh dear, it slipped out. 'Sorry, Hortense, I'm really fine.'

'Right. I'm just going to fix your breakfast. You stay still.'

During my first month here, I was able to make my own breakfast, but that's quite beyond me now. I can't get out of bed; it's too painful and, although my arms remain strong and I can feed myself, my legs are too weak. At least I'm able to have all the things I like for breakfast because the staff buy them for me – orange juice, bran flakes with a little milk and a lot of sugar, biscottes spread thickly with butter, cherry jam and coffee. Up to a week ago I had two soft-boiled eggs for breakfast as I have since they came off the ration. But for some reason, I can't stomach them now.

While Hortense is preparing breakfast, I look round my room. It's pretty bare of decoration. A photograph of Stephen with his partner, Vince. I wince when I look at this, but Steve tells me he's my son and he wants to see it there. Another of Jenny, now dead fifteen years. I wince when I look at this too. This time it's not distaste, it's guilt but also, if I'm honest with myself, sadness that she is no longer around.

But there is one big problem with these photographs. There are none of the faces I would love to see on the mantelpiece or cupboard. Above all, faces of the women with whom I've had what are stupidly called 'affairs'. There isn't a word that accurately describes that heady mixture of love, lust, conspiracy, deceit and anticipation, so that will have to do. I don't have photographs of any of these women and it would raise eyebrows if I did.

'Here you are, Dr. L. Exactly what the doctor ordered.' Hortense is making her little joke. She's mystified that one can be a doctor without having qualified in medicine. She asked me about it shortly after I arrived here but when I explained, she wasn't really convinced. I know she's equally puzzled that one of the other residents, who is called 'Professor', is indeed a medical doctor. Hortense has told me this is clearly the wrong way round. She stays while I eat my breakfast. I tend to dribble, and she kindly wipes my lips and chin after each mouthful.

Before she leaves me, Hortense asks me if I would like my mini-massage, as she calls it. This involves her gently stroking my back several times, then rubbing my scalp very vigorously until it's warm and tingles pleasantly. I never turn this offer down.

I should really like to talk to Hortense about the thoughts I had between 4 and 6 this morning. Jack Richards, now long dead but once an old chum with whom I used to drink the occasional sherry before Hall, was an anthropologist. Most of his early work had been done in Africa, studying primitive tribes, though one probably isn't allowed to call them that now. As a young man, he had been on safaris in those far-off and more exciting days when game were shot with bullets rather than with digital cameras.

Jack told me this story about a dying female elephant. The elephant had been fired at but had only been wounded and had managed to move away into a clearing with other members of her herd. The hunters caught up with her there and saw what happened next. As she became weaker, presumably from loss of blood, one of the adult males entered her and continued to copulate with her until she fell over and died. Was the male satisfying his lust on a vulnerable partner who could not refuse him? Or was he making sure that her last moments were as pleasurable as he could make them? No one knew. But Jack and I agreed that if it were possible to arrange for sex to be part of one's last moments that would be a pretty good way to go.

I remember, as a young man myself, crying with laughter about men who had suddenly expired while deeply inserted usually into women to whom they were not married. Such stories were usually extended with graphic details about how they had to be prised away before rigor mortis set in. They don't seem so funny now. I haven't had sex with a partner for twenty years or an erection for ten, so, perhaps fortunately, that fate is not going to be possible for me. All the same I've not lost the desire for sexual pleasure.

It's odd the way my inability to have an erection has not been accompanied by any loss of interest in sex. I still find some women sexually attractive and desirable and others not. I would still quite like, no, come on, be honest, Kenneth, it's not just that I would quite like, I passionately yearn to have my body, especially my cock, stroked by a woman I find desirable. And not just at the moment of death but now, now, now. And yes, to the end of life.

I'm not in the most promising situation to make this happen. But at least there are women around. When I was living by myself in north Oxford with only the brisk, repellent twice a week cleaning lady (right, I've done my job, thank you for the thirty quid and I'm off now) for company the possibility of sexual stimulation was even further off than it is now. Even though I'm told this place is very reasonably priced, it seems to me that I'm paying a vast sum to be here. Of course, I know that sexual services are not provided as part of the deal. But one way or other I need to persuade one of the staff to oblige.

The only candidate at all a possibility to give me what I desire at the time of my death, is Hortense. With her dark chocolate skin, full lips and well-shaped, deliciously curved breasts she has a face and a figure fit to satisfy any man's lust, let alone that of someone in my desperate situation. She seems to like giving me my morning mini-massage, so she clearly doesn't find my body all that repulsive. She likes pleasing me. I can make her laugh, which, in my experience, is the key to all sexual success. So just maybe, just maybe, she would agree. It's not an unreasonable last wish, after all.

Doreen, the manager, only puts her head round the door once a day. She isn't bad looking but she seems so busy I can see she would never have the time even to engage in a conversation, let alone indulge my wishes. Then there is 15-year-old Kerry, here for work experience from the local comp. She's a pretty little thing, long dark hair and an engaging giggle. It's strange this business of age and sexual attraction. When I was a teenager I used to find girls attractive who were my own age and maybe up to two or three years older. As I moved into my twenties I regarded women more than three or four years older than myself as old hags, even if they were in their early thirties. As I moved through my forties, fifties and beyond, I found that my tastes extended upwards in age at the same rate, but I never lost interest in those younger than me.

So, the age range of women I found desirable gradually extended eventually to include even those of immensely advanced years. I'm not alone in this. When André Gorz, a French journalist, was in his mid-eighties, he wrote a love letter to his wife. It started: 'You're 82 years old. You've shrunk six centimetres, you only weigh 45 kilos yet you're still beautiful, graceful and desirable. We've lived together for 58 years and I love you more than ever. I once more feel a gnawing emptiness in the hollow of my chest that is only filled when your body is pressed next to mine.' I think Gorz would have found 15-year-old Kerry attractive too, but, like me, he probably couldn't have contemplated her as a sexual partner.

Then there is Eileen, my other 'named' person. She may be my 'named', but I can't bear her. She's tall, bony, and has a strong Ulster accent I can't abide. When she gives me a bed bath, she's rough and, on one occasion nearly tipped me over the side of the bed when she was turning me over. 'Forgot' to put the bed sides up. The thought of her being sexually obliging to anyone, let alone me is laughable. She'd probably dig her nails into my most sensitive organ. Then, of course, there is Frank, who is in his mid-fifties and obviously gay. He's a nice enough man, indeed thoughtful and pleasant, but, even though I might be the right sex for him, he's the wrong sex for me.

I do have the occasional visitor. Steve visits very dutifully once a week and we talk about nothing very much. We can't talk about him and his partner because I can't bear to think about them in bed and, in my mind, that colours everything about their relationship. We can't talk about Brexit because he has been militantly in favour. He seems to think that his piddling little advertising agency will do better if freed from the control of Brussels. He's wrong, of course. Perhaps we wouldn't have fallen out over that, but I suppose I went over the top when I told him I was ashamed to have a son whose political views were shared by a bunch of racist xenophobes. We do talk about Trump.

Today passes quietly enough. In the morning, Simon, the Prof who is *really* a doctor, pops in for a chat. He's in much better nick than me. But then, in the early afternoon, I have a very unexpected visitor, Barbara Knott. When the staff told me in the morning that someone of that name was coming to see me, I found it difficult to remember who she was, a bit surprising in the circumstances.

Anyway, she arrives at about three and sits herself down by my bed. She must be 70 now but she's still not bad looking. Tall, unlined face, slim figure. Only a wrinkled neck and those ghastly brown spots on the hands give away her age. She still has a lovely smile though I didn't see much of that during our conversation. Just once or twice when she forgot how angry she was.

'It wasn't easy to find you,' she begins. 'You do remember me, don't you?' I nod. 'Good. I had the awful thought that you might have lost most of your considerable quantity of marbles. That would rather have destroyed the point of my visit. It took quite a bit of courage for me even to begin to find out where you were. Caxton wouldn't tell me at first, so I had to pretend I was your sister and had just heard you were unwell. It really would have been too bad if I had made it here only to discover you had no idea who I was or what had happened.'

I remember now alright, even though it was a long, long time ago. 'Ah, yes.' I said, 'it must be thirty-five years, though.'

'Forty-five, to be more precise'.

'Good God! As long ago as that?'

'Yes, I was in my prime of looks and you were in your prime of achievement. A dangerous combination, as it turned out. I bet you thought you would never see me again.'

Her mention of betting brings me back with a rush to the reason why we met in the first place. She had come to me for supervision of her thesis which was on Pascal's Wager. It was a vogue topic both for philosophers and for mathematicians at the time. Pascal's idea that you should base your life on what you thought the odds were that a God existed came to life in the 1960s with the invention of what was called, if I recollect correctly, game theory. Assuming you were certain that God existed and that you would suffer eternal damnation if you behaved badly and eternal celestial bliss if you were good, then the arguments for behaving well were compelling. The advantages of behaving well were infinite, lasting for eternity, while the pleasures of behaving badly were finite, only extending until one's death.

But there were complications depending on the odds that God existed at all. If you thought it was highly improbable that God existed, then opting for the pleasures of today became a more attractive choice. That was where game theory came in. From a knowledge of the odds not only of God's existence but of God having the power to consign you to paradise or the other place, you could mathematically calculate the chances of behaving one way or another. That was more or less the theory. If only life and, indeed death, were so simple.

Barbara's still attractive voice brings me back to where I was and with whom I was talking.

'Yes. I can see you do remember. Just to remind you further. It was me that had the idea of bringing Pascal's Wager and game theory together. I had done a Maths 'A' level and got a first in philosophy. St. Hilda's offered me a scholarship to do a doctorate. I had joint supervisors. Felicity Prynne at St. Hilda's was my Maths supervisor. They didn't have a suitable moral philosopher to hand, so they had to look outside. You were approached to be my philosophy supervisor. You said you would have to meet me before deciding. I can still see the gleam in your eyes when you opened the door and caught the first sight of your new supervisee.'

They were indeed delicious intellectual and romantic meetings between us that Michaelmas Term. Some of the best, if not the best I had. In those days, and I'm not sure much has changed, the one to one meetings between supervisor and pupil at Oxbridge colleges and possibly elsewhere (I really don't know) were virtually an invitation to seduction. One shut the outer door, 'sported one's oak' as it was called, and had an hour of uninterrupted opportunity.

'You weren't at all good-looking,' she went on. 'In fact, you were on the small side and a bit pudgy. Not much pudge on you now, I see. And I was an inch or so taller than you. Not what I had imagined for the love of my life. But you had this aura of celebrity, even at that time. My goodness, you had actually been on television. Felicity Prynne kept on suggesting we have some joint supervisions. It's only looking back I realise what was on *her* mind. And by the time you took me on, you had all the skills of a successful seducer. You had a special name for me. No one had called me 'Baba' before. I loved it, even though even the name you called me turned me into your little lamb. You took my ideas seriously, listened to me, praised the drafts I wrote for you so that I felt appreciated for my mind. But at the same time, you complimented me on my clothes, made me feel a woman.'

There's a knock on the door. Kerry comes in and asks:

'Hello, Dr. L. would you and your visitor like tea now?'

I tell her that this will come with delicious cakes and biscuits, but Barbara just wants to pursue her agenda. She declines, not all that politely, completely ignoring Kerry who leaves, banging the door behind her.

Then she continues:

'Why was all this so important to me? I can't imagine. I had been married only two years, for goodness sake. I had no idea whether Chris took me seriously intellectually. I didn't understand the biochemistry he was so involved in. Certainly, he showed no interest in how I dressed. Anyway, when you told me at the end of the third supervision that your next pupil had cancelled and suggested we go into your bedroom, I was neither surprised nor unwilling. Indeed, I couldn't wait.'

Baba's account of our meetings was clearly making her angry. She flushed when she talked about the way it had all gone.

'Come on, Baba,' I said. 'All this must have been around the early 1970s. I wasn't as glamorous as all that.' But perhaps I had been. It was a rather pleasant thought.

She went on. 'Those four-o-clock supervisions rapidly became the highlight of my week. It was a ritual. One hour discussing my thesis. The problems with John Locke's view of Pascal. Whether Leibniz had effectively demolished Locke's argument. Doubtless most people would have found all this less than fascinating. But I loved it. And all through the first hour there was the titillating expectation that became a certainty that when the hour was up you were going to invite me into your bedroom for a second hour of very different pleasure. Amazing how the writings of a seventeenth century philosopher should be responsible for such fun three centuries later, I thought. And then, after we had put our clothes back on, you would offer me sherry and I would say I had to run because Chris was expecting me.'

It did indeed sound pretty perfect. Going into Hall those evenings I remember I felt rather uplifted and pleased with myself. Indeed, I couldn't quite remember why it had ended. I did recollect that Barbara had some reservations when I made it clear she and her husband would have to come and have dinner one evening with Jenny and me. I had told Jenny about my new supervisee and she would have smelled a rat if I hadn't invited her back as I did all my doctoral students. The same thought seemed to have struck Baba.

'And then you had the nerve to ask Chris and me home to meet your wife. One of the most dreadful evenings of my life. You didn't look at me once. I didn't look at you. Chris had no idea what was going on. Once he had met you I know he couldn't have imagined us sleeping together. He just thought you were an odd bloke.'

'An odd bloke? Why should he think I was an odd bloke?'

'Well, it might have had something to do with you not being able to get through two sentences without having to check a fact in your Encyclopedia Britannica. It made for a very disjointed dinner, which was awkward enough anyway.'

'I can't remember why it all stopped. It sounds from what you say and indeed from what I can now remember myself, as if it should have gone on for ever.'

'You've obviously forgotten I got pregnant.'

That was it. 'That's right.' I said. 'You gave up when you were expecting. I do remember wondering if it could be mine. In a way, hoping it might be, but realising things might not be so easy for you if it turned out to be obvious it was. So, remind me what happened?'

'Well, I had the baby. Luckily, when she was born, it was clear Emma was Chris's. Blue eyes, blonde. Everything you weren't. Not that Chris would have suspected anything if she'd been born dark and brown-eyed. He didn't have that sort of imagination. Full of ideas about DNA, but not a clue about people.'

'Yes. But why didn't you continue with the doctorate after the baby was born? I don't remember.'

'Oh, Chris got a permanent lectureship in Leicester. Little woman had to go when big man needed her to. I couldn't travel from Leicester to Oxford for two supervisions, one with you and another with Felicity P. Not with a baby and no money for child care. In any case, I was beginning to realise that academic life was all a bit of a game. What was it Voltaire said of Pascal's big idea? He thought it 'a little indecent and puerile'. The idea of a game and of loss and gain seemed childish to him and did not befit the gravity of the subject. Voltaire was right on the button.'

'So that was the end of it?'

'No, it certainly wasn't the end of it for me. Not at all. My sex life with Chris never got back to normal. I couldn't talk about what had happened to anyone. When I had psychotherapy for my depressions I never let on about my feelings of loss. Emma suffered, of course, when I wasn't fully with her during some of her childhood. But she survived. She has two of her own now.'

I looked round the room, my eyes lighting on the photograph of Steve. He's forty-six now, so he would have been just a baby then. I tried to think of him at that age. Fact is, I probably spent more time thinking of Barbara than him. Never used to get home before he was in his cot and asleep. Barbara went on:

'After a time, I did a bit of supply teaching in Leicester. I did, of course, notice when your book came out. I got it out of the local library. I must say I think I deserved a bit more than just to be listed as one of thirty-two people in your Acknowledgements section. I suppose I was lucky to be mentioned at all.'

'Oh, come on,' I thought. 'By the time the book came out you'd been gone something like four years. There had been plenty of others with whom I'd discussed the ideas.'

I looked at Baba. How was this going to end? My pain suddenly seemed to be returning with full force. I soon knew.

'Well, I came here to tell you that, after forty-five years I'd plucked up the courage to come to tell you that you were an utter bastard. Doubtless you were the same with other students. Trouble is, now I'm here, I've got that ghastly sense of loss coming over me again.'

With that Baba looked at me, began to sob and rushed out of the room. She left the door open and I heard what happened next. She sat on the bench outside my room, still weeping noisily. A member of the staff, it must have been Frank, saw her and sat down next to her.

'It's alright,' He said. 'I know Kenneth looks terrible and he doesn't have long to go. But we are not going to let him suffer. He'll have all the medication he needs.'

'Oh, I'm not crying for him. It's myself I'm crying about.' And she was off.

Seeing Baba immediately brought back a flood of memories. Also, I have to admit, some emotional tremors, though none as extreme as hers. 'The Moral Fallacy in Pascal's Wager' was easily my best-regarded academic book. Ridiculous to suggest she deserved more than the mention I gave to others. But there you go. That's academic life. Rivalry over who thought what first, when, nearly always, it wasn't someone a year ago, but some obscure Greek well over two thousand years earlier.

She was right. She wasn't by any means the only supervisee I had made a pass at. There was that equally glamorous, but stroppier Somerville girl. She very nearly made a complaint to the Master. Ridiculous. I never even touched her. Of course, I made it plain that I found her very attractive. It would have been silly not to. What was wrong with that? I also made it plain on more than one occasion that I wanted to sleep with her. In the end, she decided not to complain but asked for another supervisor for her thesis, refusing to give any reasons. That wasn't the end of the matter. It isn't easy to change supervisors in the middle of writing a thesis and I wasn't going to make it easier for her. Bitch!

Later, I got quite a reputation for having a sane voice over complaints of these sorts of alleged misdemeanours. I agreed with the general view that having sex with women without their consent was wrong. The problem comes with defining both sex and consent. What, after all, is sex? A question Bill Clinton was made to consider. Men have always made passes at women to find out if their attentions are welcome or not.

Indeed, I used to say that by the time she got to her mid-twenties any woman who claimed she had never been touched on the leg or had a hand put on her knee by a stranger in a cinema merely had a bad memory. Caxton started to admit women as undergraduates in 1979. After that complaints by women that they had been what came to be called 'sexually harassed' began to increase. The College appointed me to a Panel, to be one of three dons considering such complaints. I was in my mid-fifties. It was probably the fact I was a moral philosopher that made them think I was made for the job. I probably wasn't the most suitable person. But I could hardly tell them that. I would have had to explain why.

I think we must have upheld two of the thirty or so complaints made during my time over the next roughly twenty years. Mostly the complaints were trivial or strongly and convincingly denied or both. The two men involved in the ones we took seriously were indeed spoken to, but they were both outstanding scholars and bringing great kudos to the College. We were able to make sure they stayed on without any other repercussions other than a gentle talking to.

It's late afternoon by now. As my mind wanders, Kerry, the work experience girl, knocks on the door and comes in. She's obviously been told she should talk to all the residents about their lives before they came in to the home. It's got to be my turn and obligingly, I tell Kerry some of my story when I was her age. I was fifteen when World War Two started and the young are always eager to know what happened to us then. In fact, like all children, I just took the war years for granted. If this was what life was like, this was what life was like. It was as simple as that. I hardly noticed the fact that we were at war. Instead I was revelling in being top of the class winning all the form prizes. Doing well in examinations came easily to me as it did later. The prize was a life at Caxton, though looking back, I'm not sure this was the best way I could have spent my life.

At that time, even more important than success at school was my 15-year-old infatuation with Sylvia, the girl about two years older than me on the bus I took every morning to school. I never even spoke to her, nor she to me. I only know her name because this is what her friends called to her when they shouted from elsewhere on the bus. I can't really remember what she looked like. All I know is that it was she and the thrilling hard-on that came with just seeing her that made the fifteen-minute bus ride to school the high point of the day. Sometimes it was topped by the scent of her as she brushed past me to get off the bus at the girl's school, the stop before mine.

To make Kerry laugh, I tell her about the school dances.

'Sylvia was at the sister school to ours. The only contact we had with these girls was a school dance held for the sixth formers. All I can remember is the ghastly embarrassment of having to hold a girl's left hand with one's right while one's own left was round her waist.' I put my hands up to demonstrate the required position. Kerry giggles.

'There had to be pretty well exactly two inches between chests. More than that and the awful woman teacher supervising would press our backs to push both bodies closer together; less than two inches and a hand would be put between boy and girl prising them apart.'

Kerry thinks this is a bit of a laugh but really wants to hear about the war. So, I tell her about listening to the radio and rationing and the bomb that fell half a mile away but didn't kill anyone and, to her disappointment, how little difference the war made to my life when I was her age.

She then tells me about herself. I had hoped for some lurid revelations about teenage sex. Not a bit of it. She has loads of girlfriends, but no boys at all in her life. I ask about that.

'That's for later', she tells me. 'Probably much later. After I've got a decent job.' Impressive but also a little disappointing. It's a relief when this prissy girl leaves and Hortense comes in with my supper.

Hortense doesn't have to ask. She already knows quite a bit about me, though not about the special service I should like her to provide. When I first came here about three months ago, able to walk and do everything for myself, the puzzle about me being a doctor but not a medical doctor came up. Now, sitting on the end of my bed, she pursues this matter further. Hortense came over from Jamaica when she was about sixteen years old. She hasn't lost her sexy, lilted accent.

'You must be very clever. Everyone say so. You written books? I thought so. What sort books you write?'

I've sometimes been asked to step out of my ivory tower and give talks to Oxford comprehensive school fifth formers on moral philosophy. So it's not hard for me to explain about the way my work involves studying how we decide what is right and what is wrong. How for some people this is a very straightforward matter but it's really much more complicated than it seems. I tell them it's these complications I think about and write about. When I'm talking to fifth formers I try to use examples not too far from their own experience. Is it OK to steal from the supermarket if you're a mother with no money and you can't feed your children? Would it be wrong to lie to the police if you were protecting your own brother or sister? Does family loyalty cap telling the truth?

I use different examples with Hortense.

'Suppose, Hortense, a man has a wife with dementia. He hasn't had sex with her for years, but he still wants it. His wife hardly recognises him. He has a woman friend he finds attractive. She tells him she won't have sex with him until his wife dies. Is that wrong of her? Or is he wrong to put pressure on her to sleep with him? After all, his wife couldn't possibly know about it.' In fact, I know there is a woman in the home here whose husband is in exactly this position. There are few secrets here.

Hortense sees no problem in this at all.

'If you talking about Gus, he just got keep control of hisself. He made his promises when he married. Now he got stick with them. It's all in the Bible. If he stray, God will know and he will be punished, God rest his soul. Take my Donovan. Now he nineteen. He only thirteen when he think he like to have sex with other boys. School tell me so and tell me I got to like it; it's his choice. That rubbish. My pastor, my good man, tell me so. That's what's in the Bible. An abomination, my pastor say. I don't rightly know what abomination is but I do know it's very, very bad'.

'I didn't know you had a gay son, Hortense. Thirteen does seem very young to start. But you know, my son, Steve, who comes to see me, he's gay. He was about thirteen when he began to show signs he was gay.'

'I didn't know your Stephen was gay,' says Hortense. He seems a very nice man. Are you sure he's gay?'

'Oh yes, he's gay alright. He's been living with a man for years. When we first realised, it was about thirty-five years ago, in the mid-1960s. It was all very permissive in those days. But Jenny, that was what my wife was called, and I were very, very worried. Being gay had only just stopped being a crime. We took him out of the grammar school he was in and sent him to a mixed-sex school with much lower standards. He got depressed. Took no interest in having relationships with anyone at all. It took him ten years to come out of it and when he emerged he was as gay as when he had been at the start. So, you see, Hortense, it may be better to let your Donovan be. Just let him get on with his own life. Make his own decisions.'

Hortense sniffs and doesn't seem at all convinced.

Neither is her attitude to Gus at all promising for my hopes she will cooperate with what I have in mind for her. But then there's a break. She has a think and comes out with:

'Course, I know it's hard for men. They got these urges. Women don't have them like that, but we got to do our bit.'

I have no idea what Hortense means by 'doing our bit', but it sounds much more promising. She gets up from where she's been sitting and tells me she's got to go and give a bed bath to the woman in the next room. I start to think about my own bed bath, due in an hour's time. I just hope it's not going to be Eileen giving it me. This time she might actually succeed in tipping me over the side of the bed.

Luckily, half an hour later, it's Hortense who returns from giving a bed bath to the woman next door. She gives me a grin and with a 'Well, Dr. L. it's your turn for a good wash now. Let's see if we can't make it a good, fun time on this occasion,' she raises my hopes that serious pleasure is indeed on the way. This is more like it.

She flannels my face and then, taking one arm after the other, soaps them gently before wiping and then briskly drying them. Then she starts on my chest and belly. I watch as her sensuous hands move the flannel through my now scanty, chest hair before descending onto my belly, carefully wiping around my ileostomy bag. Previously she has just lifted my cock and very quickly wiped around my balls before moving me onto my side so that she can do my back.

This time it's going to be different. As she moves down my belly I grasp her hand and start to move it down towards my cock with a slow sliding movement back and forward, up and down. My memory of how I used to play this game with Barbara, encourages me to think it might be possible with Hortense. But I only manage to keep her hand in mine for three or four strokes of my lower belly before she realises what is happening. Immediately she pulls away.

'What you think you doing, Dr. Lockwood? None of those tricks with me, please.' And I realise at once this is not going to happen. It is a dreadful, dreadful disappointment. I know very well it is ridiculous that a 94-year-old man should be so attached to the idea he is going to be sexually pleasured that he is seriously upset when he finds this is not going to happen. But I can't help how I feel. As Hortense herself put it only an hour ago, 'It's hard for men. We've got these urges.' And they don't go away.

Later that evening, round about eight-o-clock, I ring my bell to call a member of staff. Frank arrives, and I tell him that my pain is now too bad. The time has come when I want to start morphine. I realise for the very first time in my life that there is something more important than clarity of thought in my life, something that is now beyond me. Frank tells me he can give me some stronger tablets now, but I can't have an injection of morphine until the nurse comes in tomorrow morning.

Sure enough, at ten next morning the nurse arrives, syringe at the ready. She tells me that, if I would like this, she'll fix me up with a syringe driver that will inject morphine under my skin. I can control it myself. I ask if Hortense can be present when I have my first morphine injection. The nurse doesn't understand why Hortense has to be present, but she is fetched.

As the needle goes in I stare at Hortense. She understands. I gaze steadily into her eyes. I hope she feels accused, though whether or not this is the case I cannot tell. Unaccountably, she does not drop her gaze either. It is as if, for some reason I don't understand, she feels she has some reason to be angry with me. I certainly have reason to be angry with her. Yet, is it really the fault of women that they are all, in the end, so disappointing? As the pain gradually subsides, I have a moment of doubt. Then my mind slowly goes blank as I give up.

EPILOGUE

George Bernard Shaw had strong socialist and feminist beliefs, combined with a mission to convert the public to his views. In the 1880s he wrote Fabian pamphlets and novels as vehicles for his ideas. Hardly anyone paid them any attention. Then he began to write plays. Between 1893 and 1914 he wrote fourteen plays, conveying his political views. In case anyone missed the point, he wrote prefaces to put his arguments more explicitly. Not many read the prefaces, but thousands upon thousands went to see his plays because they were amusing and entertaining. In passing they were exposed to political perspectives that would never otherwise have struck them as credible. Shaw had achieved his goal, even if politicians took much longer to translate his ideas into reality. They are indeed still, well over a hundred years later, struggling to decide whether to do so.

At a much more modest level, this collection of stories represents an attempt to interest a wide readership to published ideas, in this case about male sexuality, that might otherwise escape notice. My book, *Men and Sex: A Sexual Script Approach* was published in 2017. At the price the academic publishers set, it was immediately apparent to me that hardly anybody would read it. If their marketing strategy was successful, about a hundred libraries would buy it and a few postgraduate students and lecturers in gender studies might look at it. Perhaps arrogantly, I felt the ideas in the book deserved wider attention. So, I immediately set about writing these short stories.

I knew that this collection would only attract sales if the stories gripped readers' interests, were entertaining and, at least to some degree, amusing. Unless I have been successful in this aim, you will not be reading this. The point of this epilogue is to link the content of the stories to themes in my textbook. Thus, it is equivalent to, though, sadly, it does not reach the same polemical heights, as one of Shaw's prefaces.

First, a brief word of explanation about the sexual script theory that informs my previous book. I was not responsible for developing this theory. It was originally proposed by two sociologists, John Gagnon and William Simon, in 1974. Basically, the theory claims that when people are in a situation that may result in sexual behaviour, what they do is determined by their sexual 'scripts' – a set of ideas covering relevant values, attitudes and, above all, rules about what constitutes acceptable behaviour.

These scripts are formed from a range of influences: the culture of the society in which individuals are living, their personalities and previous experiences; and their interactions with other people with whom they might engage in sexual behaviour. This means that biology, (hormones and brain mechanisms), explains remarkably little. It is true that if men were not driven by hormonally driven desire, they would not show any sexual behaviour at all. It is also the case that there is evidence that both gender identity and sexual preference are influenced to some degree by our genes. But if one wants to know who men have sex with; how often; where; how they feel about sex, (in fact all the interesting things about male sexuality), one can forget biology. Instead one needs to think about the *scripts* that men are reading from and following when they engage or think about engaging in sexual behaviour. One also needs to think about the way these scripts are formed.

Culture is a massive influence on the way men behave sexually. An 18-year-old male in Riyadh in Saudi Arabia will lead a very different sexual life from a young man of the same age in New York or London. Same hormonal levels, a similarly constituted brain, but very, very different sexual behaviour. Men brought up in very similar societies may also develop very different sexual scripts. This variation is explained by their genetic makeup, their personalities and their earlier experiences. Finally, when two people with different sexual scripts meet for a potentially sexual encounter, in the negotiation that follows, one or both of their scripts (often both) is likely to undergo modification.

Thus culture, individual psychology and interpersonal effects account, in varying proportions, for all that follows.

Each of the protagonists in these ten stories has a unique script. There are few common themes, but perhaps one is that they all have some degree of vulnerability, a feeling that they might be hurt in some aspect of their sexual lives or identities. Four-year-old Tom in the first story illustrates how the enjoyment of physical pleasure is learned in the very first years of life. This is the time when the elements of sexual scripts are formed. Of course, they will always change in later life, but the changes will build on what has come before. Freud was right to emphasise the significance of infancy and early childhood in later sexual development. He was wrong to imply infants are sexual beings though a few of them are. All babies and young children are profoundly open to sensual experience.

Tom is sexually abused by his uncle. Many more children suffer abuse from family members than from strangers. The abuse is traumatic for him, but perhaps less harmful than all the events that surround it - the parental separation, the breaks of the emotional ties between his little girlfriend, Amy, and then from his uncle, as well as his mother's depression are all formative in the way he develops into an adult incapable of developing a mature sexual relationship.

Most boys become aware of their sexual orientation or sexual preference round about the age of ten or eleven years. Fourteen-year-old Jamie has been aware of his preference for boys of his own sex for a year or two. Then, when he has a sudden surge of secretion of his sex hormones, his desire to engage in sex or, at second best, to masturbate with images of boys or men becomes imperative. He is inexperienced in the making and breaking of relationships which leads to the misunderstanding with Don, the boy whom he adores but who does not reciprocate. The mixed, north-east London culture in which he lives, so that he has friends who are more streetwise than he is, affects the way he behaves and contributes to his confusion.

Max, the twenty-four-year-old pizza delivery man, is living in a laissez-faire sexual culture. A chance encounter with a sexually inexperienced woman out of his social milieu results in a change in his sexual script and consequently, in his sexual behaviour. A weak personality, perhaps as a result of his childhood experiences, he is coerced by a woman whose financial resources are far in excess of his, to accept a position of dependency. His sexual script has to change to match her needs. When the high-powered surgeon, Fiona, finds herself in trouble at work, she begins to lose interest in sex. Max's sexual script once more has to adapt. As he sees his days with Fiona are numbered, he rapidly attaches himself to another woman, his sexual script adapting accordingly.

The importance of cultural factors is perhaps most obvious in the story featuring thirty-four-year-old Aditya. His Hindu parents have come together in an arranged marriage and his family still lives in a milieu with heavily prescribed mating practices. But Aditya has been exposed to western culture. His sexual script is dominated not by sexual urges, but by his wish to meet a woman looking as much as possible like the Hollywood actress, Goldie Hawn, not a desire likely to be fulfilled if his social contacts are limited to visits to the local temple. Both he and the Jewish woman he meets articulate their scripts in their entries on a dating site. Fortunately, even though his sexual drive is much weaker than hers, their scripts are sufficiently congruent and flexible for them to make a successful match. Naomi's wish to have a baby means that Aditya's sexual script has to change once again in order to make his behaviour fit for procreative purpose.

Henry, the forty-four-year-old real estate Manhattan lawyer, has a sexual script shared with many other power-hungry male philanderers. He is encouraged by a culture in which sexual success is measured by the number of women a man can get into bed. Driven by his emotionally impoverished childhood into greater promiscuity than some of his peers who inhabit the same culture, he continues to crave for constant physical affection. Because of his obsessional personality, it is unlikely that his sexual script, clearly not only self-destructive but destructive to the members of his family, will change.

Men who are violent to their wives or domestic partners, like fifty-four-year-old Ken, have been the subject of much psychological study. Like Ken, they are highly likely to have been involved in other types of violently aggressive behaviour. Ken's sexual script means that he feels he is entitled to have sexual intercourse with his wife whenever he wants to regardless of her wishes. She is his possession so any infidelity on her part is a rock-solid reason to assault her. Any man who sleeps with her has stolen his property and his script tells him not only that retribution is justified but that it is required.

Like most men who prefer sex with men, sixty-four-year old Victor has known he was gay since he was in his very early teens or even a little before. Born in around 1953, he reached puberty at a time when overtly homosexual behaviour was illegal; it only ceased to become so in the United Kingdom in 1967. So, Victor's sexual script told him that the sexual preference in his sexual script was completely unacceptable. Like many gay men, he married without telling his partner about his sexual orientation. He was only able to perform sexually by visualising male partners. For gay men, as for most men, fatherhood is an aspiration, and Victor's ability to perform under the guise of a heterosexual man, enabled him to achieve this.

It was only when he watched gay pornography that the content of Victor's sexual script changed to a degree that he could no longer contain the object of his sexual desires. He then became tortured by the conflict between his wish to fulfil what he thought of as his 'true' sexual nature, and his affection for his wife.

Seeing oneself as a boy or a girl (gender identity) is the very first type of identity to emerge. It arises between two and three years and, in childhood, it trumps all other types of identity. Five-year-old boys would rather play with ten-year-old or three-year-old boys than with five-year-old girls. White boys would rather play with black or mixed-race boys than with white girls. Gender identity also trumps social class identity.

So, seventy-four-year old George has known that, although anatomically he was born male, he is *really* female. His sexual script allowed him to pretend to be a woman until he was in his mid-thirties but then, knowing his partner was bisexual and would stay with him, his desire to come out as a man was so great he was prepared to face the massive social upheaval a gender change required. He was sustained by his love for Eloise and by her love for him. When she died, he suffered the same feelings of bereavement as if their relationship had been a conventional one.

The unattractive eighty-four-year old Lewis Wong has a sexual script that has only tenuous connections with feelings of love and affection. For him, sexual relationships form just one pathway to power and control over the lives of other people. Why his personality developed in this way is unclear, but one might surmise that his father, on whom he modelled himself, had a similar personality and his English boarding school experience reinforced this pattern of behaviour. Most of the time he can keep under control the massive anger that is aroused when his need for control, (central to his sexual script), is frustrated. The end of the story tells what happens when such suppression is beyond him.

Finally, Kenneth Lockwood, the ninety-four-year-old moral philosopher reveals very clearly the contents of his sexual script while he was a don at the University of Oxford. One might wonder whether his sexual script led to his moral relativism or the other way around. In any event, it is clear that the patriarchal university culture of his time opened the way and indeed encouraged his sexually predatory behaviour. There are disquieting reports that, despite the introduction of codes of conduct, such behaviour, especially of male university lecturers towards postgraduate students, persists to the present day.

Some might be surprised that Lockwood has retained a sexual script into his nineties but, while in the past this might have been unusual, this is no longer the case. A significant number of men who live into their nineties, provided they are in good health and their partner has also survived, continue to have active sexual lives, even if, as is often the case, they are no longer capable of full sexual intercourse.

Writing this collection of short stories has been an educational experience for me. In particular, it has brought home to me that explanations of behaviour derived from social science can only provide very partial answers to the questions we ask ourselves about why people behave the way they do. Attempts to explain men's sexual behaviour wholly by reference to their sexual scripts, or indeed to their hormones or to the functioning of their brains involves the neglect of an essential component of knowledge required to complete our understanding.

Scientific explanations are inevitably deterministic. They provide evidence of the factors that make it probable, but only probable that people will behave in particular ways. They remove the sense of agency, the experience of choosing one particular course of action rather than another. Yet this subjective experience that we are free to choose what we do is at the core of human existence. The scientific theory of sexual scripts may illuminate our understanding of sexual behaviour, and indeed I believe it does, but it only takes us a part of the journey.

These stories are told in the first person. My characters are all, I hope, drawn in a way that conveys the idea that they could have chosen to behave differently, even if their scripts point them in a particular direction. I am not quite sure why I made the decision that all these stories would be told in the first person. Perhaps, as a psychiatrist, I felt that exploring what life was like from the inside, was something I had been doing for all my professional life. So, first person narratives would be easier for me.

Whatever my original motivation might have been, I soon realised that I might be able to provide in these stories not only an idea how sexual scripts 'work', but also convey a vivid sense of the possibilities of many different aspects of male sexual experience. I hope readers of all genders will feel I have achieved these aims at least to some degree.

Acknowledgements

In 'Learning to be a Man', Tom's objection to being treated as a girl is drawn from Judith Harris (1998) *The Nurture Assumption*. New York, The Free Press, p.218

Local colour relating to a top Manhattan firm of lawyers in 'If You've Got Lemons' was provided by John Grisham, (2010) *The Street Lawyer*. New York, Arrow

The limerick in 'Nothing Like Family' was written by Arnold Bennett. It is quoted in WS Baring-Gould (1967) *The Lure of the Limerick*. London, Hart-Davis, p. 58.

The quotation in 'Assisted Dying' is from André Gorz (2009). *Letter to D*. London, Polity Press, p.1

The idea of a doctoral thesis on Pascal's wager in 'Assisted Dying' came from Ian Hacking (1972). The Logic of Pascal's Wager. *American Philosophical Quarterly*, 9, (2), 186-92.

* * *

Thank you to Robert Cassen, Anna Graham, Nori Graham, Sara Graham, John and Janet Murphy, Mary Shurman, Nicholas Thompsell and David Troxel for reading drafts and for their advice. Thank you also to Leila Dewji for editing input.

I am immensely grateful to Jonathan Barnes, my brilliant mentor, for his skilled help and encouragement during our discussions in the London City Lit cafeteria.

About the Author

Philip Graham is Emeritus Professor of Child Psychiatry at the Institute of Child Health, University College, London. He has written a number of academic books, but this is his first work of fiction. His last academic book *Men and Sex: A Sexual Script Approach* is published by Cambridge University Press.